BOMBSHELL (AVA BUTLER #1)

A WHAT DOESN'T KILL YOU CARIBBEAN MYSTERY

PAMELA FAGAN HUTCHINS

SKIPJACK PUBLISHING

CONTENTS

FREE PFH EBOOKS

ONE

I'M GETTING TOO old for this shit.

The Outlook Calendar warns me it's Monday, June 22, exactly one month away from my thirty-second birthday. I can't make ends meet as a singer without this crap temp-agency job, still only getting by with my parents' help and an occasional boost from public assistance. My nearly-toddler's sperm-donor father is long gone, along with any hope he'll ever help out financially. For once I agree with my mom: I need a real job, a grown-up job, and those are few and far between on the island of St. Marcos.

I open a browser and pull up the *St. Marcos Source* news site, thinking I'll scan the classifieds for something better. The lead story stops me: LAND PIRATES WAYLAY TOURISTS IN WEST END RAINFOREST. Not again.

How many times do these low-life road thieves have to hijack a carful of day-trippers before the Department of Tourism passes out flyers at airport baggage claim? Rule One: no bathing suits except where there's water. Rule Two: keep your fancy-ass cars on the east end of the island.

I click on my horoscope instead of the classifieds, my talon-like nails forcing my fingers flat against the mouse. Before I can process today's guidance, I hear the unmistakable sound of support-hose-clad thighs rubbing together, feet padding along toward me in closed-toe ballet flats. That's McKenna. She runs ABC Temps for her parents, even though she's way overqualified.

I want to tell her she's better without the hose and little-girl shoes, but I don't.

I close my browser. My phone vibrates and I glance down, quick. It's a text from Collin, the Santa Fe cop, muscle-bound and too *Top Gun* cute for his own good: *Why aren't you answering me?*

Collin is my best friend Katie's brother. A notorious player whose clothes I seem to rip off every time we're in the same zip code. He can't take the hint to let me go. Maybe because we burned up the sheets every weekend for two months, pretending the thing between us was going somewhere. I'd told him then I couldn't make any promises. He told me he didn't need any. He should have believed me. I shouldn't have believed him. Now he thinks he knows me, but he doesn't. And that's for the best. Keeping our relationship a secret from Katie is the hardest thing I've ever done, and if I break up with him now, she'll never know.

A shudder runs through me, a terrifying flashback to three officers killed in the line of duty in the last few weeks. Collin's safe, but I can't stand worrying some fool is going to shoot him down. I'm black, and I hate cops killing so many black people for no good reason or not enough of one—but Collin's life matters, too. Yeah, he's got serious potential to break my heart in more ways than one.

I think what I don't type: *It was a fling. I'm not who you think I am. Get over me.*

Instead, I run a finger over my ring, a gift from my parents when I turned sixteen, gold inset with chips of ruby. It's supposed to give me courage. My mom hoped that would be the courage to remain chaste and pure (she'd already missed that boat) and possibly, someday, fulfill her dream that I become a true "bride of Christ" (she was sorely disappointed on that one, too).

I don't know why I still wear it, but I do. I give it a few seconds, but no burst of courage overtakes me, so I ignore Collin's text, again. Like I have the other four. Honestly, I've never understood why people treat receiving messages like they're obligated to respond immediately. Free will, baby. Or, as I like to call it, RNO: response not obligated.

Who am I kidding? Ignoring him is harder than I make it sound. I turn my phone facedown to help me stay strong. I wipe sweat from my brow. It's stuffy and musty and just plain summer hot. ABC can't afford AC.

McKenna brushes past me, escorting a woman to the front door. "We don't keep plants here. Sorry."

The woman is small and Asian and smells fresh, like lemongrass and lavender. She's wearing a white T-shirt that says GREEN THUMB across the front. "I understand." She hands McKenna a card. "In case you change your mind."

The door opens and closes. McKenna slips the card into her skirt pocket.

She comes back my way, plants herself in front of my desk, her arms crossed over her ample bosom. "Ava girl." Her calypso accent is thick, and she's smiling at me like she's reggae Santa Claus or something. "I sending you to the West End today. Pack up."

St. Marcos is only twenty-six miles long and seven miles across at its widest point. You can drive from the eastern tip all the way to the west coast in less than an hour, and most of us locals live mid-island. I've lived in the States. I've commuted half an hour, even an hour to jobs. But it's different here. Here, we moan and groan if we have to drive ten minutes. On-island—that's how we describe the state of being present on St. Marcos, with *off-island* meaning we're anywhere but here—the West End is half an hour and a different time zone from here.

I chuptz, long and loud, sucking a generous amount of spit through my teeth. I make a show of loading my purse with office supplies.

The thought of the drive almost makes me long to return to the cheesy "bar tour" that my fly-by-night manager booked for me last spring—which is how I came to be gigging in New Mexico and reacquainting myself with Collin, after meeting him at Katie's wedding a few years back. The tour turned out to be an endless series of swingers' parties. I got a lot of propositions for threesomes, but no recording-studio producer appeared out of the woodwork offering me a deal. I canned the manager and came home.

Because, yes, this slice of heaven in the Caribbean is my home and the place of my birth. This haven for the brilliant-green iguana, the churring mongoose, the bright-winged macaw, and flowers of every color and description. Of rum, endless coconuts, fragrant mangos, and passion fruit.

It's also an inbred cesspool of politricks as usual, dog fighting, domestic abuse, and desperation. A refuge for drunkards, layabouts, and fugitives.

I feel a sudden temptation to call the manager and beg him to rebook me, even as a glorified lounge lizard. I won't, though. The saving grace of being home is that I'm not spending time away from my too-rapidly aging parents and my one-year-old daughter. I have a few on-island gigs lined up this summer, but they're just the same ole, same ole. Tourists drinking themselves blind on cheap rum while no-count men with more baby mamas than sense make plays for me.

McKenna cuts her eyes at me slow, getting the meaning of my chuptz. "Girl, I mean it. And you're welcome. I hook you up with one of them EDC companies."

I brighten. If she just tells me it's a job as an assistant to a music producer or even a fashion designer, my day is made, even though I know it won't be. My phone vibrates with another text. Collin again. I feel a tug at my heart. I could be in love with him if I let myself, but I'm not the love type. I'd thrown my *I Ching* coins that morning and asked only one question: "Will this man lead to pain?" Well, they gave me my answer, and the coins don't lie.

I'm going to have to talk to him sooner or later, though, since his hint-taking skills are less than optimal. I opt for later.

"Thank you." I blow McKenna a kiss. "What they do, and what I doing for them?" I sling my bag over my shoulder, already moving, my pulse thrumming with renewed hope.

The office phone rings. I ignore it, but when no one else picks it up after four rings, McKenna's stare finally breaks me. I pick it up. "ABC Temps."

A nasally female voice assaults my eardrum. "We're down from the

City for the summer. I must have an assistant. Transfer me to someone who can make this happen ASAP."

Well, la-di-da. "No problem. Right away, ma'am." I switch over to my yank speech style without even thinking about it, dropping my island accent and talking with a stuffed-up nose like a continental, which is one of the nicer things we call people from the fifty United States. It's like breathing to talk local with locals and to yank with yanks. Like how my friend Katie picks up a slow drawl when her Texas friend Emily comes around. Whatever my outer speak, it's always just me inside my head, a black woman with a white father who's spent most of her life repressing her island roots like the good little chameleon she is.

I transfer the call to McKenna's voicemail.

McKenna *is* doing me a solid with this EDC assignment. EDC stands for Economic Development Commission, a business-incentivizing program offered by our local government in cooperation with the Feds. Translation: the US Virgin Islands are allowed to lure in people who have enough money to start a business here. It's attractive, with generous tax incentives. It comes with a price, though, more than just the assumption propagated from popular media that rich people only move to the islands to engage in criminal activities and scurrilous tax schemes.

To gain the benefits, the off-islander must establish full residency (difficult), be subject to our Water and Power Authority (notoriously unreliable and gallingly expensive), and hire local (slim pickings). McKenna, knowing this well, is offering me up to them, because I'm local and NYU educated. Even if it is just a theater degree with a minor in classical studies. Lead roles in community theater productions are good for the ego but don't fatten the purse, and I haven't discovered how to make money yet from Greek and Roman mythology.

"General office work for a company with it own virtual currency. One that own a lot of other companies." McKenna says this in a tone of awe.

To me *that* sounds like Greek. "Virtual current, what?" I say it like "wah." We have a tendency to drop our ending consonants when we talk in local island accents.

"Virtual *currency*. It digital money, using blockchain technology. Fast, anonymous, and no regulations. People say it the future."

"Oh yeah, sure. Blockparty. Technology of the future. And how you know all this, Miss Virgin Island Bill Gates?"

She sniffs. "Stanford MBA. I intern for a company into cryptocurrency." And I just thought she was overqualified before. "You got no idea what blockchain is, do you?"

"None."

She pushes gold wire-rimmed spectacles up her nose. "Blockchain a digital ledger of linked virtual currency transactions, like in a chain. It protect against fraud and the like, because it all encrypted and one link build on another."

"That clear it right up for me."

"You a smart girl. You figure it out."

"Yah mon."

"Show up on time and you be fine. And pull you top up," she adds.

She's the one who booked me last time for a seven a.m. job after the night I'd gigged until three in the morning. What does she expect? I glance down at more brown cleavage than I expected to see. I roll my eyes and hoist the girls. Lime green fabric slips up and over them. Next time I date a rich man, I'm getting a lift. "Jealous much?"

McKenna, wearing a charcoal circle skirt and round-neck white top that covers all her business, hands me a slip of paper with a name, address, and phone number on it. "You gonna find yourself on the wrong end of attention you don't want, girl, and I'ma remind you 'bout this conversation."

"You blaming women dem for bad behavior of men?" I play it cool, like I'm joking. But I learned about sexual attention as a plaid-clad innocent in grade school. Just because a Catholic school hires a man doesn't make him holy, and the same goes for women. Since then, I've seen no evidence to change my mind. And I may not be loaded with money, but I have a whole lot of something with very real value. Yeah, it's currency, and there's nothing virtual about it.

A chill comes over me, and I freeze for a moment. A memory of Father Jerome and the unspeakable things he did to me during my school days bubbles to the surface, but I bury it deep again, fast, with all the other bad things in my life, like too many pills and too much booze, like finding my lover Guy with his throat slit and a bad man trying to frame me as a Jezebel who murdered Guy for not leaving his wife. Guy—Guy Edwards—was a Virgin Islands senator, and if it weren't for my friend Katie, I might have spent the rest of my life in jail for a murder I didn't commit, with too much time to fight off ugly recollections of Father Jerome and his ilk. As it was, my already-not-sterling reputation took a permanent hit. Repression is my friend.

And, no, I don't let anyone blame women for the bad things men do.

McKenna, not one for lingering, rolls her eyes at me and walks off. Support hose grind together again. I shiver. *Save the planet—say no to synthetic undergarments*, I think.

But I don't say it. I'm in a hurry. I have to drive all the way to the West End to meet some blockchain heads.

I VEER LEFT, driving my dad's gas-guzzling beater truck—sorry, Mother Earth, it's my only option—faster than I should. There's a maze of potholes (more like field of landmines) on Centerline Road. It's hard to see them through the lightning storm of windshield cracks that appeared magically a few days after a shoddy island replacement Dad had done recently. Mom's rosary beads are swinging from the rearview mirror, and I'm feeling more hopeful than I have in donkey years. The reason the EDCs are so attractive here to locals is that they're the only decent jobs outside of working in tourism, for the government, or at the oil refinery. No, thank you, no, thank you, no, thank you. The refinery has all but closed up now, too, making everything on-island direr, and it was close to desperate before. Temping at a new EDC is usually temp-to-hire, and they *always* have air conditioning.

I have to land this assignment. I'll treat it like an audition, which means I should run through my lines. I've already found plenty of motivation for my character.

"I Ava, from ABC Temps. Anything you need, we here to help."

Or I could yank. I try it, watching myself in the rearview mirror. "I'm Ava, from ABC Temps. Anything you need, we're here to help."

BAM! My forehead slams into the steering wheel, and all the air is knocked out of me in a whoosh. Sometime later—seconds? minutes?— I realize the truck isn't moving. *What the hell?* I put a hand to my face. Warm. Sticky. I look at my fingers. There are more of them than I remember. My hand is like an octopus. A red octopus. I waggle my fingers, and they're red octopus arms, undulating underwater. I say it aloud. "Undulating underwater." I like how that sounds and try a few more, making up my own alliteration exercises and mouthing them with exaggerated motions like we had in my theater classes. Sipping cider by the seashore. Taking tea in Tipperary. Gah, I'm tired. I close my eyes and drop my head back.

"You dead?" a dry, quivery voice says from just outside the driver's-side window. I glance at it. It's coming from a man with a white afro—*now that's a look, meh son*—over wizened skin, his sharp, black eyes fixed on me. "You bleeding."

Something's wrong. There's no window between us. Aha, it's broken. I peek around the interior. It's covered in shards of glass. The front windshield is gone, too. And I'd hit the steering wheel—air bags weren't standard when this truck was built.

"I know you?" the old man says, drawing my attention to his face, which reminds me there's an electrified cotton ball atop his head.

I squint at him. "Yah," I say, but then pain clouds my thoughts. "My head hurt, I sorry."

He nods. "You Gill Butler's girl. I work with he, years ago. Chappy Nelson."

"Mr. Nelson. Of course." Roger "Chappy" Nelson. A down-islander. Barbados? He'd been old even then when Dad brought him on his regular construction crew. Most island men have nicknames, and my mind floats, trying to place the reason for his. Chapped lips. Getting chapped over things. Being chaps with everyone. I'm feeling woozy, a little baziddy.

"This he truck you mash up?"

"Uh-huh." I mashed up my dad's truck, and I have no idea how or why. This isn't good. "What happen?"

"You crash in a pothole."

Only on St. Marcos. Our potholes are epic. Like vehicle-swallowing sinkholes in the States, except here they're the result of greed and graft instead of natural disasters. Money changing hands for inferior materials and shoddy workmanship. I should have been watching better where I was going.

I move my head and glass falls in my lap. I know I'm supposed to be somewhere. Directive thinking is painful, but I give it a try, and it works. West End. ABC Temps. A job I can't bomb. I rest my forehead on the steering wheel, ignoring the immediate sharp pain.

"Ava?" A familiar voice. Also male, but younger, with a Texas accent.

"Huh?" I groan without looking up.

The door opens beside me. Nelson says, "I call the police?"

"No." My voice cracks. Police mean a job-costing delay, a hassle, an insurance claim, rates going up. Hands grasp me, and I look up. Katie's husband, Nick, scoops me off the seat and out of the truck.

Nick says, "Thank you, sir. I'll get her taken care of."

"You know he?" Nelson asks me.

"Yes. It all good."

He leaves without further comment, disappearing into a dilapidated building on the side of the road. Trumpet vines grow out of a cracked HEINEKEN sign over its doorway.

Nick sets me down in his own old truck, newer by at least a decade than the one I'd planted nose-first in the pothole.

"You okay for a minute?"

"Yes. Thank you, Nick."

He returns to my dad's truck. Nick is all long legs with a lanky but muscular frame, and he's a fast mover. Cars pass, heads rubbernecking at my misery, and I pretend I don't see them. He comes back with my canvas shoulder bag and phone. He places them on the floorboard and begins picking glass off of me. I hold very still and let him, even when he pulls a chunk out of my forehead.

After a few minutes working on me, he says, "Want me to take you to the hospital?"

I shake my head, regretting the motion instantly. "No, no. I have to get to my new assignment."

"What?"

"For my job. I'm supposed to be on the West End. Now."

Nick cocks his head, pondering me. I'm sure I look dreadful scary. He, on the other hand, is sexy as ever, something I'm not supposed to notice. Olive skin, wild dark hair, intense eyes, sharp cheekbones, and a distinctive nose. A strong face. Hard *not* to notice. Hard not to show you appreciate. But Katie's already forgiven me once for flirting with her man, so I follow the rules.

He grunts, a noncommittal sound. "I'll take you up to Annalise. If Katie releases you, you can borrow one of our cars to get to work."

Estate Annalise is the name of the big-ass property he and Katie live on with three kids, six dogs, and his parents. It's also the name of the teenage slave girl who's been stuck there in limbo as a jumbie spirit for most of two hundred years. Don't judge—we buy into voodoo here in the islands. You would, too, if you lived here. It's as plainly true and hard not to notice as Nick's sexiness.

He steps away from me, brow furrowed, and pushes his hair back. It stands up a little. Katie says he's a gypsy by his Hungarian heritage, but his wiry hair isn't so different from mine. "I'll call Rashidi. We'll see what we can do about your truck. Sound okay to you?"

Our mutual friend Rashidi and I are in a good place, so I say, "Irie." Six months ago, I'd have said no—our breakup was too fresh. Rashidi's forgiven me for not loving him, but no man takes that easy.

My phone rings. Before I can stop him, Nick picks it up from the floorboard and hands it to me. I all but hold my breath, but he doesn't look at caller ID. I do. It's Collin, his brother-in-law, my secret. I take the phone, thinking as hard as I can in my condition. Nick climbs into the driver's seat. I put the phone to my ear at the same time as I press the button to decline the call and send it straight to voicemail.

"Hello? Hello?" I pause for a few seconds for effect, then put the phone down. "No one's there."

But Nick doesn't hear me. He's already talking to Rashidi.

TWO

THANKS to an early warning call from Nick, Katie meets us at the side entrance to their big yellow masonry house, Estate Annalise. I smell freshly turned earth and see they've planted some juvenile coconut palms in their front yard.

She gasps. "Did you cut your face?"

There's something old-fashioned about Katie's kind of pretty, like the movie of her life would be shot in black and white. She's tall and slender with alabaster skin and long red hair. Today she's holding it back with a twisted blue bandana. Her nose is smudged, but her blue-jean shorts and T-shirt got the worst of whatever dust devil attacked her.

I push hair off my forehead. "It's in my eyebrow, right?"

"Right." She clucks, leaning in to get a better look at my cut. "I think there's glass sticking to your eye."

"I don't feel it. I have my contacts in, thank goodness."

"You're sure you don't want to go to the hospital?"

"If I don't die waiting to be seen, they'll kill me for sure." Nobody goes to the hospital on St. Marcos unless they plan to leave in a hearse. My looks are important to me, but I can overcome a scar in my eyebrow. "It's okay. I can get my contact out."

We walk into the house together, through the kitchen. Katie's petite mother-in-law sticks her head around the doorway leading into the great room.

"Hi, Julie," I call to her.

She waves, her face contorting at the sight of me. "Oh no, poor you."

I smile at her, which probably makes me look worse.

"Are you okay with the kids while I take care of Ava?" Katie asks her.

"We're fine."

Katie's twin girls are about the same age as my daughter, Ginger. Julie hefts one onto her hip—Liv—and takes Jessie by the hand. They babble to no one in particular and each other and seem so much further along developmentally than Ginger, walking and talking. I push the thought away.

Taylor, the four-year-old, is on his knees, zooming a dump truck along the hallway carpet runner.

"Come on, Taylor, we're going downstairs to Grammy's apartment." Taylor gives no sign he's heard his grandmother and rams the truck into the wall. "Taylor?" He does it again.

"He's killing me. I'll meet you in my bathroom." Katie sighs. "Taylor, didn't you hear Gram?" She takes his arm. "Come *on*."

He looks up, surprised, it seems to me, and squalls as she pulls him behind her. Their feet clomp down the stairs, punctuated by his screams. I can't be sure, but it sounds like he's screaming, "Annalise."

I stay in the kitchen a little longer, stalling on dealing with my contact problem. I grab a glass of water and drink it slowly. Katie finished out this old deserted rainforest house herself, and I love it, the large outdoors-inside kitchen best of all, with its rainforest-green granite countertops and mahogany cabinets. I'd even lived here myself for a time, house-sitting when Katie moved to Texas. But that's a whole 'nother story—one I don't mention around Katie, since when I left for New York her house got vandalized and robbed and its sale fell through. Katie ended up back here anyway, with her inheritance intact and a law degree to fall back on if it all went sour, so it worked out fine for her. I was the one that got knocked up in Venezuela and dumped back on St. Marcos still broke, so I'd say I got the raw treatment. But honestly, I felt terrible about what happened then, and I feel bad about it still.

When I get to Katie's bathroom, I put my purse on the counter and arrange my supplies. I carry spare contacts and a case with solution already in it for emergencies like this, plus a pair of glasses. I'm so myopic I can't see to cross the street without the help.

I wash my hands good then touch the lowest edge of the contact. If there's glass or other grit stuck to the surface of the contact, I don't want to accidentally press it into my eyeball and rip my cornea, so I move slow and gentle. I don't feel any debris, so I ease the contact downward to my white. I watch myself in the mirror, bracing against a scratching pain that doesn't come. I squeeze the contact gently between my thumb and forefinger. When it's off my eye, I squish it around in my fingers. I do feel something sharp. I throw it straight in the trash and repeat the process on the other side, starting with rewashing my hands.

I consider the spares, but what if there really is glass or something stuck to my eye? I decide it's best not to put anything in them and put the spares and case back in my purse. I wash my bloody face, being extra careful but thorough with my eyes, rinsing them four extra times.

I slip my Coke-bottle specs on, and I'm contemplating the spa-like master bathroom and claw-footed jet tub, wishing I could take a dip for old time's sake, when Katie appears. Her face is splotchy.

"What's the matter?" I ask her.

She bites her lip, crouching and digging in the cabinets under the sink, emerging with hydrogen peroxide, cotton balls, Neosporin, and butterfly bandages. Her medicine cabinet is well stocked. On St. Marcos, we don't dial 911. People have to be self-sufficient. Double that up in the rainforest at Estate Annalise. Katie points at the toilet. I drop the lid and sit. She washes and dries her hands, then wets the cotton ball.

As she blots my wounded eyebrows, I wince, but she doesn't stop. "Taylor skipped the terrible twos and threes, but he has the fearsome fours down to a T. He won't listen, he's uncooperative bordering on flat-out oppositional, and he lies. He's destructive and sometimes a little mean, more to me than anyone. I worry it's because I'm not his birth mother, and that he remembers Nick's sister and misses her. Julie tells me not to worry, but it's hard." She tosses the used cotton ball at the trash but misses. She stops, picks it up, and drops it in.

"What was he screaming to Annalise for?"

She continues working on my face. "He talks to her. He says she talks to him. Today, at least she was on my side, telling him to mind his mother. The jumbie doesn't talk to anyone else, so I have no way of knowing if it's real, or if he's just got an active imagination."

"It's possible. You see her. Most people don't. Yet we believe you."

She sighs. "You're right."

"But that's not what's bothering you."

She angles her head, smiles at me. "You know me well. We're working a case that has me rattled." She and Nick are private investigators. I like the name of their company: Stingray.

"I know what would help."

Her mouth hangs open as she concentrates on dabbing the cream into my wound. "What?"

"Sing with me." Katie had reneged on our chance to record a demo in New York after she married Nick and adopted Taylor. It had been the closest I've come to making it big. Holy Mary Mother of Jesus how I want another chance before I have to give this dream up for good in favor of adulthood.

Her mouth twitches, almost a smile. "Those were the days."

I put a hand on her wrist, holding it, but soft. "I'm serious. We're good. You're good."

She shakes her head and scrutinizes the butterfly bandages. "I can't. Not the way you want me to. I'm good for the occasional gig, but I can't throw my whole self into it."

I don't answer. The same sadness as always makes it hard to find words.

She inspects my forehead without meeting my eyes, then blows on my cut. It stings. After a few seconds, she squeezes it together and closes it with three bandages. "There. Short of a plastic surgeon, that should do it."

The atmosphere between us is still awkward. Katie pulls Clorox wipes from under the sink and attacks the countertop sullied by the nursing of my injuries. I assess myself in the mirror. No one's going to notice the scar I'll get, most of the time. And Katie was liberal with the clear butterflies. The cut isn't that long. "Thank you."

Katie's pocket chirps. She pulls out her phone, reads, smiles. "I can't believe it. Emily says Wallace and Ethan set a date, and the Supreme Court only lifted the ban on same-sex marriage a few weeks ago."

Emily had started out as Katie's friend and paralegal, but she's my friend now, too. Through Emily, I'd also gotten to know Wallace, a Child Protective Services investigator in Texas. "That's great."

Nick barges in. "Change of plans. We have a vehicle shortage. I can take you down to the West End now, and Rashidi says he can drive you home whenever you need. He's got a hitch, and he's going to tow your dad's truck in to the shop first."

"That'll work." Except for my clothes. "Can I borrow a top?" I ask Katie.

Nick puts his hands up and backpedals out.

I shuck my blood-spotted shirt. It has a built-in bra, so my girls are free.

Katie stares at my breasts. "Ava, you've got a lump."

I look down. "Yah mon."

"Have you had it tested?"

"Dr. Megahy says it's nothing."

"I'll take that as a no."

I don't like where this is going. My lump is nothing, like a mole. Katie always thinks she knows best, like she's my mommy, but I've already got one of those. "Take it as my doctor's got it covered. Now hand me a top. It's cold in here."

She frowns, then snorts. "I don't think I have anything that will display your assets quite like yours did."

I slip into Virgin Island patois. "We see 'bout that."

NICK DRIVES fast down and around the curves and potholes, out of the rainforest, his hand drumming on the steering wheel as he sings along with Sean Paul about drawing the longest line for his sunshine. You'd hardly know the man is a freshwater West Indian just two years on-island, the way he handles his truck in full song. On St. Marcos, we drive American cars with the driver on the left, but we follow European driving practices, with the car on the left, too. We keep the ass to the grass, so to speak, which makes left-hand curves exciting as you wait to see what's coming around the bend on your side of the road, most often a rum-soaked tourist from Alabama or Mississippi.

Despite Nick's agility, the truck strikes a pothole, and it jars the glove box open. A gun clatters to the floorboard.

I jerk my feet up. "What's that?"

Nick glances at it. "It won't bite you, Ava."

I hate guns. All guns. Yeah, guns are sexy on a cop. Yeah, Emily saved my life with one a few months ago, but they scare me, and they too easily fall into bad hands that do bad things with them. I think about nine dead African Americans in a Charleston church. It's more than sobering.

"It's gonna shoot my foot off."

"The safety's on. Can you put it back up for me?"

"Uh-uh. I'm not touching it."

"Really?"

I cross my arms.

Nick stops in the middle of the road, grumbling. He returns the gun to its place, then floors the truck. We don't speak, and I scroll through the text messages that had come through while I had a signal at Estate Annalise. Service on-island is spotty and mostly nonexistent in the rainforest.

McKenna: *Why aren't you at the client's offices yet?*

Collin: *I won't stop until you answer.*

Another Collin: *If you're not dead, call me.*

Still another: *What the hell have I done to piss you off?*

My heart feels funny, bad funny. The man's a catch. He deserves better than me. Love. Commitment, fidelity. He'd soon figure out I can't give them to him, if I stick around. He'd have options, and he'd exercise them. Less hurt now is better than more hurt later.

I see I have a voicemail from him, too. It takes me a moment, but then I remember him calling right after the tumble into the pothole, when Nick had first shown up. I'll listen to it later, where Nick can't overhear. Where Nick can't see the reaction I'm not sure I can hide.

The road flattens out into the lowest section of the rainforest, the part where the hills empty onto the beach. We hurtle past mahogany and kapok trees. It's pretty, distracting, soothing, and I try to put Collin out of my mind. Greenery and twisting Tarzan-worthy vines, hibiscus blossoms growing wild. The beauty of the island is one of the reasons I moved back a few years ago. I bounced around for years in the States. NYU to study theater, waitressing in Vail, working at a dinner theater in Waco. But my parents were—are—getting older, and I'm an only child. Plus I was sick of following my longtime boyfriend, Zach, from one acting job to another. I finally dumped his cheating ass in Texas and hightailed it home. Then the boy hit it big on one of the *CSI* shows. Lord knows he's gorgeous. Even talented. Here's a tip, though: never date an actor unless you're prepared to try to forget him with his face plastered all over the TV and Internet.

"Where am I taking you?" Nick asks.

I give him the address.

"Huh." He says it surprised-like, not a question.

"What?"

"That's where I'm going."

I raise an eyebrow at him. He doesn't look at me, so I ask, "Why?"

"Meeting a client. Harry Darnell."

I pull the sticky note off the wallet in my purse, the one that McKenna had written on. *Mahogany Management. Harry Darnell.* "Same guy they're sending me to temp for."

Nick shoots me a sideways glance. "What do you know about him?"

I wave the sticky note. "Only what it says here. And that his company owns companies that do some digital money thing."

He doesn't respond. I watch him for a few seconds. He's as sphinxlike as always, so I don't bother.

We're weaving along the beachside road now, and things become more civilized. Danish arches and colorful, peeling paint on masonry buildings signal our entrance into West End. That's the town's name. Literally. It's also the name of the long white-sand beach stretching from the south side of town to the south shore of the island. We St. Marcos folks, keeping it simple.

Nick pulls straight into a parallel parking spot on the main drag.

"This isn't it." The address McKenna gave me is on the waterfront. We're a block off of it.

"We'll take the alley. I want to leave town in this direction."

I huff, but I get out. Walking over cobblestones in platform sandals isn't as easy as I make it look, and I take care. I adjust Katie's top—which fits my figure nice and tight, especially since I pulled it down snug and safety-pinned it to the inside of my pants. It's a risky move, but I don't plan on doing any hip gyrations, so I should be good.

The buildings along the alleyway are seedy. This is where what passes for nightlife in West End goes down. A sign with a buxom woman bent over at the waist, legs spread, looking over her shoulder, reads XXX CLUB, the XXX in the name necessary because the picture isn't explicit enough, I guess.

But the sign isn't what catches my eye.

There's an actual woman sitting with her back to the front door of the club, her chin on her chest. The angle of the sun misses the awning above the door, so the light shines right on her. She must be roasting. I can't see her face, but from her long black legs splayed in front of her and her supple skin, she's younger than me but getting closer to skin cancer every second. Her miniskirt is barely covering her tun tun, and her sparkly tank top hangs off one meager shoulder. If her mother could see her, she would not be a happy woman.

"Cheese and bread." I shake my head. "She's ass-up and no one's even moved her out of the sun." I walk over to her, studying on how I can drag her into the shade.

Nick is right behind me and leans her forward. He hooks his arms under her shoulders and around her chest. She's limp, and her head falls sideways to her shoulder. I recognize her instantly.

"Oh no." I fall to my knees in front of her. "Lailah."

"Who?"

"I used to babysit her. Or, no, she was friends with a girl I used to babysit, but she was always over." I tap her cheek with the tip of a finger, trying to rouse her. How could the innocent girl I knew end up like the woman crumpled in front of me? "Lailah? Lailah?" She doesn't answer. I shudder. I put the back of my wrist under her nose for long seconds. "She's not breathing." I grab her too-cool wrist and feel for a pulse. Nothing. I probe her neck, not sure exactly what I'm searching for but finding nothing. Nothing except a deep red mark in the crease of her skin. I look up at Nick. He sees it, too.

He sets her down gently, exactly where we found her, and I dial 911 on my cell.

THREE

THE POLICE ON ST. Marcos are a joke, including the ones milling around today, too many of them doing too much of nothing. Most of them are crooked, and the rest are incompetent. My longtime friend Darren Jacoby and his brother were the exception, but it turns out the life expectancy for a good cop on St. Marcos is short, and they're long dead and gone.

I text McKenna: *Mashed up truck. Got ride. Found dead girl. Police harassing me. Hurrying!!*

I leave out that I know this girl, that I am rocked, and I brace for her answer. At least I have Nick as an alibi witness to my day of calamity for McKenna if I need one.

Her reply comes in seconds: *That jacked up.* Then: *You okay?*

Me: *Not really.*

McKenna: *Need to go home?*

Yes, I think, but then I consider for a moment all my wonderful job options. Me: *Nah, just stall for me?*

McKenna: *I try.*

I turn back to the scene. Had this alley always smelled like hog piss and rotted Big Macs? I put the back of my hand to my nose.

"Ms. Butler?" a deep voice asks, booming from a narrow chest. The officer is small and dark, his eyes a green as surprising as his voice.

"Speaking." I take a closer look. "Ah, meh son, we go back a way to St. Mary's school." Like I did with Lailah, who was years behind me but also went to St. Mary's. The officer's name comes to me: Woodworth Bachoo. Big name for a round little boy, back then. What had we called him? Woody? No, too obvious, although I'm sure other little boys teased him with that.

He harrumphs, but nods. "You find the dancer's body?"

Because she is one, it appears. There are only two kinds of dancers at the few strip clubs on St. Marcos. Old, dried-up continental women who've drugged and drank away their money for a ticket back home, and young local girls who the life hasn't chewed up and spit out. Yet. "Yes. I with Nick Kovacs."

"You know she?"

"Back in the day. Hadn't seen her in"—I count years in my head —"fifteen or sixteen years."

I expect him to quiz me on Lailah, but he drops it. "What bring you here"—he pronounces it *hyah* in the island style—"to a house of ill repute?"

His nickname comes back to me, and I blurt it out. "I remember we call you Porky. Look at you now, all slim up and grown, working as a—"

He's not amused, and his voice is hostile. "I aks you what bring you here."

I sigh, feeling the hope of a job slipping away. I probably shouldn't have brought up his nickname. Too late now, though. Time to play I'm-more-local-than-you-are, and in that game, the Virgin Islands woman always has the upper hand. I sharpen my voice. "I on my way to work. Just passing. That a crime now, passing by?" I chuptz softly.

A second officer joins us, this one looking like the grown-up version of Bachoo's nickname, round, with a tilted-up nose. Bachoo says, "This Officer Benedict Winslow."

"Good morning," I intone, because it's bad manners if I don't greet him. Oddly enough, I've never seen him before, and I'm not familiar with his family name. Maybe he's from down-island somewhere.

"Good morning," he says, then stands with pen poised over paper.

The interview continues, inane and irritating. I list the witnesses to my earlier whereabouts, and after far too long Winslow writes down my contact information at Bachoo's prompting while Bachoo presents me with a business card.

"Don't leave island," Winslow warns me, finally speaking.

"You think this *Miami Vice* and you Tubbs?" I pivot on my heel and flounce away, putting some attitude in my step.

"Mm-mmm," Winslow says.

"Babyface." Bachoo's tone is a clear order.

Babyface—Winslow—stops his rudeness.

I grumble a few words about his mother, way, way under my breath.

Nick is waiting for me. "You okay?"

"They lend me a little hell, but I'm all right except for being late and finding Lailah dead. You?"

"Same." He sighs. "Listen, there's another problem."

"What's that?"

He opens his mouth to speak as my phone rings. "Collin," he says.

For a moment I think he's reading my caller ID, but he's not. Caller ID announces Anita, a good Catholic Bahamian girl who ran off with Canadian rake Gill Butler when she was only eighteen and he was on-island to race cars and drink Red Stripe. She's the reason I wore plaid skirts and polo shirts my entire childhood and youth, curtsying to the hated nuns, counting on my rosary beads, and reciting the catechism. The woman who gave me angels and demons, confession and secrets.

The last thing I want to talk to Nick about is Collin. I'm saved by the Mom bell. I hold up a finger, my stomach rebelling against Nick's one word, the C-word.

"Mommy," I say.

"You okay?" Her voice is high-pitched, near hysterical. "I hear you stumble on a melee. A dead woman of the night. What?"

Nick raises an eyebrow. Her voice carries.

How did she already know all of this? But this is St. Marcos, and gossip is the predominant means of disseminating news. Her phone must have been ringing nonstop. I consider telling her it's not some woman of the night, that it is Lailah, but I don't relish the conversation that will start, so I hold up.

I motion with one hand for Nick to walk on. I follow him. "Everything irie. Going to a new job, so I can't talk long."

Her voice perks up. "New job? Like you give up the clubs?"

Which is what she calls my music and theater gigs. I ignore question number two. "New assignment. Temp to perm, maybe, if I ever get there. Between the wreck and a dead girl, it a—"

"A mash up? Baby . . ."

I curse my slip. A dead girl is gossip fodder. My wreck, less so. "It nothing. Just a bump in the road. How Daddy?"

Nick turns onto Wharf Street.

"He having a bad day. Tomorrow be better."

And this. This is the secret reason I moved back to St. Marcos from the States: Dad's Parkinson's. He's deteriorating, and people are figuring out he's ill, which I hate for him. He's proud and private. It won't be long before my parents will have to move to the States for better care. Long-term care. Terminal care.

Nick stops in front of an updated masonry building painted a slate blue, the color of the ocean on a cloudy day. He opens the door for me and I slip through, blinded for a moment to my surroundings.

It makes it hard to breathe when I think about Daddy's condition, so I tuck it away deep inside with all the other dark, painful things I hide. "I'm sorry, Mommy. I have to go now. I love you."

"Love you, too."

Nick and I are standing in the entrance to an atrium-style building with office space facing inward onto a staircase and courtyard. My chest feels hollow, and I suck in air to fill it. I pray Nick doesn't bring up the C-word again, and he obliges, heading for the wide staircase. Behind it, an old mahogany tree, very much alive, stretches up toward a glass ceiling. The light through the ceiling is fantastical, moody, and a death ray all at once. Since we're headed to the same place and he's been here before, I don't ask questions, just follow Nick, the thunk of my platforms echoing on the wood treads. We switch back then reach the second floor. The burnished mahogany bannister continues as a railing between the walkway and the atrium.

I slide my hand along the rail. A glass door ten paces down reads MAHOGANY MANAGEMENT.

Nick presses a doorbell. He tilts his head slightly upward, and I see a camera, a red light on under its eye. The door buzzes and clicks. He pulls it open. The cool air seduces me like an old lover, and I am happy to enter.

Inside, several chairs covered in a palm-tree fabric form a U, with a giant vase of brilliant birds-of-paradise on a coffee table in front of them. Behind them is another door—this one solid except for one-way glass inset at eye level—with another doorbell. Accent tables with smaller vases of sunflowers flank the inside door.

Nick takes a seat.

I've spotted an impressionist painting hanging on one of the side walls, a painting I've seen in a book Mommy keeps on her coffee table, about artists in the Virgin Islands. I make my way over to the painting and congratulate myself, because I'm right. It's a Camille Pissarro. Then, as I study it, my hand covers my mouth. It's an *original* Pissarro.

Shaking my head, I struggle to fathom why they'd hang an original painting by the most notable artist ever born in the Virgin Islands in their small lobby. Surely it's expensive. And if this is the lobby art, what do they consider special enough to put on the walls inside—Van Gogh and Matisse?

"You see what this is?" I ask Nick.

Nick puts a finger to his lips, then says, "Good afternoon."

Over a PA system, a women's crisp voice says, "Good afternoon. Yes?"

I make a face. Someone is watching us. I survey the room. No cameras I can see at first, then I spy a little red light. It's in the center of a sunflower in one of the vases by the door. *Tricky.*

Nick smiles, like he would if he was meeting someone in person. "Nick Kovacs of Stingray Investigations for Mr. Darnell." He nods at me.

I don't smile, because it feels too weird, but I straighten my glasses and clear my throat. "Ava Butler of ABC Temps for Mr. Darnell."

"Appointments?" the disembodied voice says.

I answer first. "Uh, ABC Temps sent me here for a temp assignment."

"So, no appointment."

I don't know how to answer her.

Nick comes to my rescue. "Ms. Butler is late for her appointment as she was in a car accident. Mr. Darnell called me in and asked me to come as quickly as possible."

"So, no appointment for you, either?"

Nick's lips stretch thin, but his voice doesn't change. "Uh-huh, thank you."

The interior door flies open. The person who rushes through it doesn't look like the woman I expect from the audio exchange. He stops short, black eyes wide, just as surprised to see us, it appears. His shoulders rise. Big shoulders, straining the seams of his yellow golf shirt, arms bulging against the sleeves. *Welcome to the gun show.*

His voice is surprising, too. Melodic. Smooth. "Pardon me." He steps between us, slow and calm now.

The hair on my arms rises, along with a sudden need to take off my horrible glasses. And then he's out the glass exit door, leaving the scent of leather, sweat, and something dangerous I can't place. A knobby-kneed woman in hot pants with dingy blonde hair is standing in the corridor, hand out toward him. I think back to the ground-level entrance. No security desk. Ah, hence the double door and video cameras. The man doesn't stop and the scrawny woman follows him, messing up my view of his bana. Bana. BAH-nah. Even the sound of the word is sexy. My pulse thrums at the base of my neck. He is gorgeous. I swallow hard. *Down, girl.*

The interior door reopens. A pear-shaped woman with half-glasses perched on the bridge of her nose glares at us. Her cardigan is open, revealing a silver chain with a cross hanging from it. It seems heavy on her oddly sunken chest, like the cross and its weight have caused a cave-in. Her mousy hair is thin at the temples and scraped back in a low bun. Her lips purse and lose color as she studies me, unspeaking.

"Mr. Kovacs, Mr. Darnell will see you now."

Nick stands, looks back at me, shifts on his feet. "Ava?"

The woman shakes her head. "You."

Nick's mouth does a sideways lift, an "I'm sorry."

I shrug and flutter my fingers "goodbye" at him.

The room empties, giving me time to turn away from the sunflower camera and adjust my girls and top, pop a few mints into my mouth, and freshen my lipstick. Normally I'm all about "Earth first" and not abusing my body with chemicals, but I draw the line with bad makeup. Bobbi Brown all the way, baby. My mom's skin is much darker than mine, but I'm black enough, and Bobbi Brown works for me, except for my lips. With them, I'm MAC, usually Ruby Woo. It all balances out; I use aluminum-free deodorant in biodegradable packaging.

I feather some hair over my butterfly bandages. To my dismay, there are brownish-red drops of my own blood dried on my feet and sandal straps. I spit on a finger and rub them. The blood doesn't come off. I take the hem of my harem pants and scrub.

The exterior door opens. I smell him before I see him, and he smells delicious. I whip my glasses off and stuff them in my purse.

"You're still here." Butter would melt in that mouth. He's black but not local, and his accent sounds like he's from the Southeast. Georgia. Tennessee. The Carolinas. No farther north than Virginia.

A shiver runs through me, all the way through me. I turn to look up at him, which is to say I present my face for him to see, because he's now just a blob to me. I tilt my chin down and let my lashes fan slightly. I automatically yank in response to his continental diction. "I'm here. You're here. Seems like that means something."

He smiles, flashing white. His teeth are like ivory. "I like how you think." He steps toward me.

I feel his aura as he comes closer, bumping into mine. "My name is Ava."

He reaches for my hand, takes it, pulls me to within inches of him. "I was guessing Venus." His scent grows stronger. "I'm Samuel."

I take a quick moment to thank the goddess of the moon and stars that my close-in vision is just fine. "Sam-yew-ELL," I draw out, as I ponder the Venus comment.

Venus and I go way back to teenage rebellion against the nuns. Nothing ticks a sister off more than suggesting Mary reverence is really *worship* and a throwback to paganism in Rome and Babylon. Especially if you throw in that not only is Venus the goddess of love and sexuality, but prostitution as well, and that she sexed up about every god she came over, and a goodly number of mortals as well.

His eyes lock on mine. "Correct. The man you're having dinner with tonight."

"Oh, I am, am I?"

"A car will come for you at seven."

"You don't have my address."

His eyes flash, something yellowish-orange deep inside. "Is that a challenge?"

I put both my hands on his chest, and the heat is incredible. "Um, nice." I stand on tiptoe, whispering just to the side of his mouth. "Are you up for it?"

He grabs both my wrists, hard enough that it almost hurts. "I guess you'll find out, Ava."

I swallow. This. This is why I have to convince Collin I'm no good for him. Because I *am* no good. Not for any man for any length of time. I don't have the faithful gene. I have to hurt us—Collin and me—now, before I hurt us more later. Then I realize I'm thinking about Collin while a dark, sexy new guy has his hands on me, which has never, ever happened before. I'll have to ruminate on that wrinkle later.

Nick's voice startles me. "Your turn, Ava." His voice sounds hard.

Samuel releases my wrists, and I put air between us.

I turn and grab my bag. I long for a fan, only it wouldn't be ladylike to fan where I'm needing it right now.

"Great. Thank you."

The oblong woman is standing beside Nick, only her expression has grown even more sour, morphing her into a pale Angel of Death. My top feels askew, and I tug at it, hoping my chest didn't shuck it off of its own accord when Samuel touched me. That wouldn't be the way to make a great impression on her. But no, I had already made a really bad one. *Please don't let her be important.* Once, long ago, my boyfriend

Zach and I were making out—okay, we were a little further along in the process than just making out—backstage at an audition for a regional production of *Rent*. Someone busted us. That someone turned out to be in charge of casting. Zach got the part. I got a lewd proposition.

Not the result I am hoping for today.

"See you tonight, Venus." Samuel's velvety tones stop me midstride. "And expect it to be hot. I'd dress accordingly."

I wave without turning back to him, trying to will my unrestrained nipples to chill out, but it's hopeless. I slam my shoulder bag over my chest and walk behind the Grim Reaper through the door, scrambling in my purse for my glasses, only realizing when it shuts behind me that Nick isn't with us any longer.

HARRY DARNELL DOESN'T LOOK like the kind of man who buys a Pissarro and hangs it in an obscure lobby on the wrong end of an island in the middle of the Caribbean. He looks like Indiana Jones in *Raiders of the Lost Ark*. Prickly, rugged, smart, and safe, all in one handsomely aging package.

He's on the phone, but he raises a hand in greeting from behind a really nice terrarium of succulents. I can't help but check out the art in his office. There aren't any more museum pieces, but he does have a great eye for local talent, and they're all originals. The Pissarro in the lobby is for showing off. The pieces in here are for him to enjoy.

The Angel of Death points to a chair in front of his desk.

I sit, and it rolls backward. I accidentally bump into her.

"Ouch," she says, sucking in a breath.

I smile. "Sorry." I try to sound contrite.

Indiana Jones hangs up the phone.

She glares at me. "Ava Butler, sir."

"Thanks, Paige. Ava and I will talk for a little while, but I'll be done in plenty of time for your party."

She sniffs and leaves.

Party? The only party I can picture her at is a wake.

As if reading my mind, Indy smiles. "She's retiring. We're having a dinner for her. She's been with me since I started my first company in Charlotte thirty years ago." He extends his hand around the terrarium, a laptop, and jumble of papers on his desk. "Harry Darnell."

I stand to reach him, shooting the chair out behind me across the room, where it hits a potted fern. The fern doesn't yield. "Whoops. Ava Butler."

We shake.

He gestures at two armchairs in front of a window on the side of his office. "I'll join you over there. Less dangerous."

The window overlooks the West End harbor and the cruise ship dock stretching out a mile from the wharf. Sparkling turquoise waves leap toward the shore, diving into disappearing curls of foamy white. The sky is a lighter shade than the water, the clouds larger versions of the breaking waves. Brilliant sunlight bathes everything, from the cars parallel parked on the street to the hulls of fishing trawlers and fronds of the mature coconut palms planted every ten feet along the shoreline.

I perch on the edge of one of the striped poplin chair cushions. "Nice view."

"Isn't it? Hard to have a bad day with a view like that." I try to cover my surprise when he comes around from behind his desk without getting up. Instead, he wheels his chair, right past me, in fact, to a mini-fridge. "Want a bottle of water? I'm getting one." He leans at the waist and reaches in.

"Yes." I sound like a strangled cat. I squelch the urge to ask for tap water in a glass, for the sake of our planet. "Yes, please," I repeat, sounding clearer.

He comes out with two waters, straightening, putting them in his lap, then wheeling over to me. I realize he has function from the waist up. I can't remember what that type of paralysis is called. I know it doesn't matter, and it's not what I should be thinking about. I need to hit my marks, to impress upon him that ABC Temps and I can take care of his office needs.

He offers me the water, and I take it, the cold, dewy bottle helping me reground myself in my part.

"Thank you," I manage.

"Football injury," he says, positioning himself so that he's facing me and not the view. "Paraplegic since I was eighteen. No, it doesn't hurt."

"I . . ."

"Everyone is curious. Best to just get it out of the way so it's not a distraction, and we can talk about business."

That's my cue. I stare at my hands, twist my ring, then lift my eyes to his. "Thank you. For that, and for having me here. How can ABC Temps help you?"

The door flies open, and a man of about my age all but leaps into the room.

Behind him, I hear Lady Death screech, "He has someone with him!"

The newcomer is white, maybe Hispanic, which in St. Marcos usually means Puerto Rican. He's a little goofy, like a Labrador puppy, but more substantial. "Boss man, I got the security upgrade rockin' on Amphy—" He catches sight of me, and he stops, literally freezes midstride.

Harry laughs, a joyful sound. "Cat got your tongue, Jarod?" He turns to me. "Ava, this is Jarod Alexis. He's head of our Odd Pod, literally, the geeks whose lives are numbers, binary and otherwise. He's the master of our blockchain system." He bobs his head at Jarod. "Jarod, this is Ava Butler."

I walk over to Jarod, and I see color blooming at the collar of his long-sleeved shirt. Buttons at the cuffs. Quite a contrast to Harry's short-sleeved golf-style shirt. The pheromones are shooting off Jarod like Cupid's arrows, and I wonder what effect I'd have had on him without my glasses. I put my hand out. "Hello."

Jarod rallies, kisses my hand. "Hey. I'm your man if you ever need any hardcore programming, or a guided tour of Amphitrite."

"Amphi-*who*?"

"Amphitrite. That's what we named her. She's our bitchin' blockchain system. She administers the SeaCoins."

I know my face is blank, because Jarod laughs. I turn to Harry.

"We hadn't gotten to that part of the interview yet. Thanks, Jarod."

Jarod salutes and pulls the door shut behind him.

I return to my chair by Harry.

"You're familiar with virtual currency, like bitcoins?"

"Yes," I say, leaving off, "only since today, and at the shallowest possible depth."

"We call ours SeaCoins, a play on C-notes."

"Clever."

"Thanks. We think of them as the treasure of the sea, Poseidon's treasure, if you recall your Greek mythology."

"A little."

"Poseidon, god of the sea, was married to Amphitrite, so we call the technology that keeps the currency in line Amphitrite." He looks like a young boy for a moment, wide open and sheepish. "Silly, I know."

"I like it." SeaCoins makes me think of sand dollars, too. I'm starting to wrap my brain around the idea of this virtual money stuff.

"Jarod is the brains behind the currency operation. Amphy is his baby."

"So you have a computer genius. What do you need someone like me for?"

He tents his hands on his thighs, tapping his forefingers. "Paige's retiring."

I nod.

"We don't really need a Paige." He smiles and lowers his voice, putting a finger to his lips. "The woman is a bell cow, for sure. She decides what she wants to do. If it matches what I need, it's a lucky coincidence."

I laugh, then clap a hand to my mouth. "Sorry."

"It's okay. For a lot of years it worked for me, but it turns out it's not a match for here. For either of us."

My head is bobbing, and I'm chewing my lip, thinking I see where this is going.

"I need help navigating local bureaucracy. A rich white guy from the States, much less one in a chair, can't get much done on St. Marcos."

I nod. "To them, you're a baldhead."

"What?"

"It's a lyric in a Bob Marley song. Baldheads—people without dreadlocks, non-Rastas, outsiders from the white man's Babylon. It's used in a number of ways, none complimentary, I'm afraid. Pronounced 'bal'heads.' They see you coming a mile away. Well, not you exactly, but . . ."

"I get it. I live it. The simplest things—hotels, rental cars, catering in lunch, containers for shipping—are torture. Dealing with the post office, the police, or the government? It can drive you crazy." He shakes his head, circling it just a little.

"I can imagine."

"But can you help?"

I decide my accent will help me sell myself, and switch to creole. "I specialize in getting people dem do what I want."

He purses his lips, lost in thought, not laughing like I'd expected. "Some of the people you'll have to work with. That work with me." He shakes his head. "They can be difficult. They're—"

"Entitled Statesiders expecting everything yesterday and acting ugly American when things not go their way?"

Now he smiles. "You've met them?"

"Baldheads." I snort. "I know the type."

He laughs. "And you can handle them."

"Yah, meh son. No problem."

He swings his chair to the view. "What makes you different than the rest of the women I meet here? Because most can't."

I step around to look out the window, too, standing beside him. "My mom Bahamian. My dad Canadian. I grow up here, until college. NYU Theater School."

"Really?"

I yank for a moment. "I know how to play a part, Mr. Darnell."

"Call me Harry."

"Harry." I become the local girl again. "I work theater in New York, Colorado, Texas, and on-island. Service industry, too, because artists dem make no money. My degree worthless on St. Marcos, so I do a little of everything. Bar singer, temp work, property management. I used to smiling and pretending bad behavior okay. Working for tips and hope of a good review."

He rolls his lips for moment, eyes on the water. "If you don't mind my asking, why'd you move back here?"

"Family," is all I say.

He nods, turns back to me. "I've got about thirty employees here and fifteen partners in Mahogany Management around the world. Ten times that trade on our currency exchange, with more all the time. I own companies. They own companies. We own companies. The only thing we all have in common is Amphitrite, and this island."

I think about Sam-yew-ELL in the reception area and wonder where he fits in. "So, what you need first, Harry?"

He turns brown eyes on me, warm but shrewd. "I need you to pick up a colleague at the airport and help him get settled in." He hands me a folder. "Everything you need to know should be in here. Paige can set you up near her until she vacates her office."

I flip open the folder. A picture of a jowly white guy stares back at me. The label on the tab says MATT FREED.

"Any questions?" Harry asks.

I start to shake my head no, but stop. "You have a car I can use?"

———

I PULL the Range Rover around the side of my white duplex. Relief courses through me when no vehicle swings in behind me.

Matt, the Mahogany Management guy I chauffeured around today, had pointed out a dark sedan behind us more than once. Well, actually, what he'd said was, "I hope that's not some deadbeat you date tailing us." Matt isn't going to win any congeniality contests. Still, I have a few losers in my past, Collin excluded and two thousand miles away, so I'm glad not to drag whoever it was to my sanctuary.

My mom is standing in the doorway, baby on her hip. Ginger is waving and squealing for me. I walk to her, stretching my arms out. Mom hands me my Little Mermaid-pj's-clad girl.

I squeeze her tight and she giggles. "Ginger Thomas flower." I nuzzle her.

"Gggggg," Ginger says. Another day without talking, but I'm trying to stay chill about it instead of going helicopter mom.

"Ginger clean and ready for bed. She eat rice and pigeon peas with some fry fish. There some left on the stove if you peckish."

"Thanks, Mommy." Normally I pick Ginger up at my parents' but tonight I'm running late. Mom brought Ginger home, fixed dinner, and executed the bedtime routine. As a single mom, I can't imagine what I'll do when my parents have to move off-island to get long-term care for Dad.

"Nice wheels," Mom says.

"Company car." I sniff Ginger's dark curls. Johnson's No More Tears formula. She smells even better than her namesake, the national flower of the US Virgin Islands.

"You keep it? As a temp? Overnight?" Her voice goes up an octave, sounding just like it had when I was a young girl and she'd tell me, "Nothing worth keeping comes for free, Ava girl."

"I don't know. At least when I work late."

And had I ever "worked" late. Harry's fussy new partner, Matt, had redefined *ugly American* and probably *racist* and *sexist* as well. His bags didn't arrive with him, and the best attire Kmart had to offer was all I could wrangle after five p.m. His refrigerator wasn't stocked to his liking, so he sent me to Pueblo with a list I'd told him in advance I couldn't fill. On St. Marcos, grocery shopping is best done with a hopeful heart and an open mind. He had neither, but he did have a sharp tongue, which he used on me before sending me home with a promise to report my incompetence to Harry in an email before he put his head on the (too thin) pillow and (worn) sheets.

I dread going in to Mahogany in the morning.

My neighbor's screen door opens. A short woman cranes her head in our direction, the porch light almost reflecting off her crown of white hair. "Good night, all."

"Good night," we respond.

"Ava, your mommy tell me your bed too short and blanket too narrow today."

Even growing up on St. Marcos as the daughter of an islander, it had taken me awhile to grow used to Angel's heavy calypso accent and colloquialisms.

"Oh, Nana, it no big thing." She isn't my real Nana, but she insists I call her that, and she treats me like her real granddaughter. My paternal grandmother lives in Canada. I barely know her. My Bajan grandmother died when I was only nine.

"Peas and rice, it murderation, that what it is." Nana walks over, a plastic baggy zipped tight and clutched in her hand. Her steps are slow and wobbly over the rocks, but I don't help her. She guards her independence with a ferocity that hints at the woman she must have been at my age. She hands the baggy of marijuana to Mom. "For Mister Butler."

Yes, Nana is our octogenarian dealer, which makes me the adopted granddaughter of a Rastafarian pot farmer. Really, though, her prices are quite reasonable, and quality excellent. She grows all her product herself in bathtubs in the bush behind our house.

Mom takes the baggy, her mouth a prim line. "My purse inside. I fetch my wallet." Purchasing marijuana, even for medicinal purposes, doesn't sit well with her.

Nana waves her off. "Next week." To me, she says, "No pie-assin at that new job of yours, now." And with those words of wisdom and encouragement, she begins the trek back to her side of the duplex.

She's one of my favorite people on the planet.

Mom and I enter my Spartan house together. Elvis launches at me, rubbing himself frantically on my ankles. My furniture is mostly rattan and wicker and has seen better days, thanks to the fat black cat. The walls are decorated with sea fans and other natural art forms collected around the island. No Pissarro for this girl. A sisal rug covers the white ceramic tile floor. And that's about it for the living area. It's all clean and functional, though.

My parents own the duplex, and Ginger and I live here rent-free—with Nana a long-term renter in the other unit—in exchange for me letting them spend time with their only grandchild. Theoretically I help them with their property-management business on the weekends, but that slowed down when Ginger was born. Yes, I feel guilty about it. I'd love to help them financially instead of them me, especially since Dad's medical condition drove their business into bankruptcy a few years ago. They've rebounded, but it's been hard. Now Mom's like a pinball bouncing from Dad to Ginger to their business. There are new wrinkles around her eyes from it, but other than those tiny flaws, she's ageless.

I brush my lips across Mom's cheek then strike a match and hold it to some patchouli incense until it catches and glows. "Thanks. Tell Daddy I sorry about he truck." I waft the smoke toward me, inhaling. Ginger burrows further into my shoulder, her breath warm and sweet, her face smearing drool between us on my chest.

Mom eyes the wicker love seat. I know she's thinking of planting herself there until I spill every detail of today's events. I pretend I don't see her do it. I love her, but I can't wait for her to leave so I can pour myself a rum and coke.

"I just gonna lie down with Ginger and go right to sleep." Ginger's head has fallen on my shoulder. She snuffles softly, a sign that she's out.

Mom's brow crinkles.

I blurt out, "It a tough day, Mommy." Which she knows, although she doesn't know my connection to the dead girl, Lailah, and that's fine by me.

Headlights illuminate the whole interior of my house. The duplex is private, and Nana never has visitors. Mom and I look at each other, her eyes reflecting the question in mine. My heart thumps as I recall the dark sedan. The lights pass us and the vehicle stops. A door opens and shuts, and whoever it is leaves the motor running. A large figure fills the doorway, but I can't see who it is. My mom, ever the one in charge, steps between the intruder and her family.

"Who that?" she says, her voice an unwelcoming squawk.

Elvis runs at the front door, yowling like he's some kind of guard dog, but he stops short six inches from the screen.

"Samuel Lewis." The smooth voice rolls out like a red carpet, and I'm not dressed for the occasion. In fact, I'd completely forgotten about it, and Samuel.

"Ava?" he says to Mom. It's an understandable mistake. We look enough alike to be sisters—her the pretty one, me the sexy one—and the twilight masks our age difference.

"It okay, Mommy." I place a hand on her arm then walk around her, making the two short steps to the doorway.

I drop my glasses on the table as I pass it. "Samuel." His chiseled features and broad cheekbones come into focus as I get closer. "I sorry."

"Ah, there you are." His head tilts sideways and back, his eyes on the sleeping girl in my arms. "Daughter?"

I nod. "Ginger. And this is my mother, Anita Butler. Mommy, this is Samuel."

Mom nods.

He does as well. "Pleased to meet you, Mrs. Butler."

"Mmm-hmm."

"Long day. I forgot you were coming."

His teeth gleam white, his most visible feature. "I told you I'd find you."

"Yes, you did."

He holds up a bottle of champagne.

"Another time. I'm very sorry."

"I'll be looking forward to it." He steps back, his eyes holding on mine. "Venus."

Samuel, his white teeth, and his champagne disappear into the darkness. A car door opens and closes again, then the vehicle slips away, tires crunching on gravel. It looks like a dark sedan. Maybe that's how he found where I live—by following me today.

Mom's voice is pious. "It not too late you change your mind and take the vow."

I wheel on her, my temper a flame shooting from my heart and out of my throat. The church. The woman is without a clue. "Do you not see the daughter I holding?" My voice hisses. "Like I become a nun. Not before Ginger. Not after. That your lost dream, not mine."

She chuptzes. She's still not over my recent stint as Mary Magdalene in our community theater production of *Jesus Christ Superstar*. In her view, I seem to always be playing the wrong Mary.

I breathe deeply. "Look, I tell you all about him and everything else tomorrow."

She crosses her arms.

Ginger cries out and flails once against me. "I promise." I back toward Ginger's tiny bedroom, across the hall from my own of the same size.

Mom relents. "I hold you to it."

FOUR

THROUGH THE WHIRL of the first few days of the new job, I've lost count of the calls and emails from Collin. I'm pining for him, and that's not okay. Nick and I haven't talked about "the C-word" yet either, after his pronouncement that we need to. Wednesday night, I pray for guidance to the God of all that is not Catholic, then fall asleep.

When I wake up Thursday morning, there's a text from Collin: *Some numbnuts shot me in the arm yesterday. I'm fine, but pissed.*

I thrash about, shucking off covers. Collin's been shot. I knew it. I knew it was only a matter of time. I run in circles like a chicken, Collin's news almost wringing my head off my neck. This is what I can't take. I fan my face, I curse and rant. I know he's fine. This time. But what about next time?

There can't be a next time. Maybe this is the answer from the God of all that's not Catholic.

I reply to him: *I'm glad you're okay, this time.*

And then, before I can talk myself out of it, I send the break-up text, even though it rips at my heart: *It's over. We're still friends. I'm moving on. You need to, too. Stay safe.*

And I'll call Nick, soon.

I fall backward onto my bed, a dead drop. I do nothing but breathe for ten minutes. *It's going to be okay,* I remind myself. *It's better this way.* I repeat it like I'm hypnotizing myself, like counting sheep. When I finally have myself together enough, I get myself and my daughter ready for the day.

I take Ginger to my parents'. She's spending more time there than I'd like, but it gives me a chance to check in on Dad every day.

I strap Ginger into her high chair. Mom is scrambling eggs.

"You wearing that to work?" she asks me.

Her comments hardly register. Just normal vexing between us. Mom tells me I'll learn it's just a mother-daughter thing someday with Ginger.

"My habit in the wash." I think my stretchy white dress is relatively demure, with cap sleeves and almost no cleavage. Plus it looks tight with my white espadrilles, which are good for all the walking and getting in and out of the Rover that I have to do. "See you tonight. Thank you."

I smooch Ginger, kiss the cheek Mom offers, and exit through the back porch. Dad is in his lawn chair, sparking grass, looking out over the unkempt mess that used to be his garden and home to his prize-winning zucchini year after year at the Ag Fair.

"Love you, Daddy."

He holds in a mouthful of smoke. When he releases it, he smiles. "Love you, too, baby girl."

The marijuana helps his symptoms—the jerky movements, the instability, the freezes—but the disease continues its relentless assault. He never complains.

Heavy thoughts and emotion too early in the morning weigh down the day, so I scatter them as I drive away. Time to be mentally at work. I've learned this week to stack a work errand or two into the morning, so that no one notices whether I'm on time or not. It's not that I'm late. I'm just operating on St. Marcos time, which holds to a flexible view on the subject.

I arrive at the office around eleven to find a potted orchid on my desk. I look around, thinking I have an admirer, but I see that everyone has one, all different kinds. I'm worn to a nub from scrambling all over the island glad-handing and kissing babies like a politician all week.

But I'm getting paid for just being me, knowing everybody, and looking good while making nice, *and* they decorate with orchids. I like this job. Even more, I like Harry. He's smart, fair, and kind. Matt—a whitey continental ballhead if there ever was one—complained about me to Harry, as promised, but it fell on deaf ears, because I'd already told Harry my side of the story.

About the only thing I don't like is Paige, but she's leaving before noon today.

She's already in, of course, and standing five feet from my temporary desk, holding a loud cell-phone conversation. She talks like she's telling a secret, but right out loud. "I thought I'd stay here after I retire, but I can't get back to Charlotte fast enough. The people here are awful. The men are patriarchal and chauvinistic, but it's the women that get me. Tight, skimpy clothes, flaunting themselves all the time, living in tiny houses with six children by six baby daddies, all of them on welfare."

My fuse lit, I begin a slow burn. Partly because some of what she was saying is true. This is a harsh place. People don't have money and they don't have options. Girls learn young how to use their bodies to get something when they have nothing. Some fall victim to the notion that having babies, a lot of them, will mean somewhere along the way one of the daddies will step up and love them. Take care of them. Only it rarely happens, and the cycle starts again. I escaped that mentality. I won't apologize for owning my sexuality, but I do know I got lucky. My parents gave me options.

I walk up behind her, close, and say loud enough for the whole room to hear, "I only have one baby daddy, thank you very much."

I pretend like I'm going for coffee, and I walk slinky and round-hipped to the break room. There are laughs and claps behind me. When I get to the break room, though, I don't make a drink. I just lean against the wall and count to ten, breathing hard, before I return to my desk all smiles and teeth and get to work. She's off the phone but doesn't look at me.

I won't miss her.

Harry says her office is mine the second she leaves. And as she walks around the office making her goodbyes, I'm nearly bouncing up and down in my chair. When the door shuts behind her without a goodbye, I dash into my new office with my box of supplies and the laptop I've been issued. There's no ocean view, but there are walls and a door and a computer all to myself. I place a photo on the desk of Ginger in a pink sun hat, playing in sand.

I spend fifteen minutes setting up my new space, thinking about how it has gone these first few days. Slowly but surely Harry has introduced me around the place. I'm swimming in names, but about the only new one I've memorized is Cora, a local woman about my age who went to public school on-island. She's Harry's personal assistant and does the Human Resources stuff, so I've seen a lot of her. She's the one who handed me my magnetized key card for the door, issued me a laptop, and pressed a fob for the Rover into my eager hand Monday. I've kept eye and ear open for Samuel, but he hasn't shown. I don't know what his role is with Mahogany Management, or M-Squared, as I call it. Or if he even has one. A lot of the employees work from home but are in and out of the office like it's a hive. Jarod has hailed me up a couple of times, and I've caught him cooping me on the sly more than I'm going to allow, going forward. Right now I'm just trying to fit in. His Odd Pod is the real office fixture, super-geeks tied to their megacomputers and talking in a language I don't understand, although even they can run their precious Amphy from offsite, which is pretty cool—the virtual currency can be run virtually. Their area is behind yet another set of locked doors that divides the office space in half, so they keep to themselves. Harry gave me a tour, but not a key or entry code, and he stresses the limited access and security to the area, so I don't press.

At a quarter to noon, I bring out my leftovers. I unwrap the aluminum foil, trying not to fixate on the fact that Collin hasn't answered my big break-up text from this morning. I read the *St. Marcos Source* online, about the woman Nick and I found outside the strip club.

On Monday of this week, St. Marcos residents Ava Butler and Nick Kovacs reported finding the body of Lailah Moore outside the XXX Club in

West End. Ms. Moore was killed with a garrote. Police report that she was sexually assaulted.

Ms. Moore worked as a dancer at the XXX Club. The police have no suspects at this time but have reason to believe Ms. Moore was engaged in prostitution separately from her job at the club. Her co-workers claim Ms. Moore told them she was scared of a customer of the XXX Club and expressed fear for their own lives. They also have reported another co-worker missing, Nevaeh Allen, who was last seen leaving the XXX Club in West End early Saturday morning.

Ms. Moore attended St. Mary's Catholic School in Taino. If you have information about the death of Ms. Moore or whereabouts of Ms. Allen, please contact Detective Woodworth Bachoo at the St. Marcos Police Department.

The article included a picture of Lailah, with a bright smile and haunted eyes, and the other girl, Nevaeh, a gaunt dishwater blonde with long, stringy hair and sunken sockets around washed-out eyes.

I feel sad, but something else, too. Angry. The article called Nick and me out by name, for finding the girl. There's no reason for that. No reason at all.

I pull out the card Porky gave me at the crime scene. It lists a mobile number for him, and I dial before I think it through.

"Bachoo."

"Ava Butler. Why you give my name to the *Source*?"

There's a long silence. "It a matter of public record."

"It got nothing to do with who kill she."

He doesn't answer.

"She go to our alma mater. You see that?"

He grunts.

"You gonna find the animal who do this? To our classmate?"

"That my job."

"That not my question." I flap my hand, even though he can't see me. "Never mind. You got any leads?"

"Just what the paper say."

"That she trickin' and it some bad man who scare the girls dem?"

He grunts again.

I take a bite of cold fungi and fish wrapped in roti, chewing in his ear and peering at the picture of the woman identified as Nevaeh. I know her from somewhere, and my gut tells me that I know her well.

I'm about to ask him about her, when a light flashes on my desk phone. Harry is calling for me over the intercom.

"I gotta go."

Porky hangs up.

I throw a few words at him. That's when I notice *my* phone. I have it on silent, but the caller ID's lighting up. Collin. I'd expected him to text me. Isn't that the etiquette of digital communications, to return a message in the same format it was delivered? I see missed calls, too. Katie. Collin. Katie. Collin. Nick. Katie. Collin. I get a bad, bad feeling, and suddenly the fish and fungi has a funky, off taste.

The intercom light goes away. Harry has hung up.

For now, I've got to ignore the personal. This is the best job I've ever had, and I need to keep it. I dial my boss.

He answers without bothering to say good morning. "Can you come to my office for a moment?" I'll have to work with him on his lack of greeting. It's nonnegotiable in the islands to start every interaction with good morning, good afternoon, good evening, or good night.

I swallow hastily. "Sure."

I repair my lipstick, fold up the aluminum foil, and put it and my fork in my (my!) desk drawer. I grab a pad of paper and a pen. My office is just down the hall from Harry's. I knock.

"Come in," he says, his voice raised loud enough to be heard through the closed door.

I swing the door open, smiling and ready. Samuel is standing by Harry's desk, and I stop so fast the door I'm closing behind me bumps my heels.

Harry says, "Ava, I want you to meet a colleague, Samuel Lewis. Samuel, this is our new Island Liaison, Ava Butler."

Samuel inclines his head, but doesn't move toward me to shake hands. "My pleasure to meet you, Ms. Butler."

I'm flummoxed. Why is he pretending he hasn't met me? I'm a pro, though, and I can play along when someone goes off script. "Nice to meet you, Mr. Lewis."

Harry waves at him. "Samuel has prospects on-island this weekend. He needs help entertaining them tonight. I suggested you."

Harry wants me to go out with Samuel? Sweat slicks my palms and I long to wipe them. Seconds tick by as the men stare at me. My mind draws a blank about my plans for tonight. Then I remember, and I blurt, "I can't. I have a gig."

Samuel grins. Given that he found out my last name and where I live, I suspect he also learned about my other life as a performer. He doesn't look surprised, anyway.

Harry double-takes. "What do you mean?"

"I'm a singer. We talked about it when I interviewed," I remind him.

Harry beams. "That's right. Where's your gig?" He fumbles over the word, and it makes him even more Indy. "We need to tell people, so they can support you."

I give him the details, a little horrified.

Samuel walks over to the window, drawing my eyes with him. "I'll bring my prospects. We can grab dinner there, watch your show, and maybe I can introduce you when you're on—what do you call it, break, intermission?"

Harry nods. "Yes, yes, that's great."

To Harry, maybe. I nod, thinking I want to fall into a crevice in the earth. I don't have a band. It's just me doing cover songs against backing tracks. Just when this job is going good, too, they'll think I'm a delusional karaoke singer.

"Okay," I say, ooching toward the door.

It has to be, since it's happening. I look for the bright side. The Boardwalk Bar & Grill management will love it. And it might mean more tips in the jar.

"One more thing." Harry holds up his index finger like he's testing the wind. "We'd like to make you a regular employee, if it doesn't cause problems with ABC Temps."

A steady day job. Security. My sweaty palms sweat more. I rub them on my skirt, feeling nervous for no clear reason. I hadn't messed this up. There was nothing to be worried about. "I-I think there's a buyout clause with ABC?" I say, stuttering a little.

"No problem. What do you make there?"

The amount is embarrassing. I mumble, "Twelve dollars an hour."

"That's appalling."

I agree, but I don't say so.

"We'll triple that. Full time. Plus benefits, of course. Medical, dental, life insurance. And a 401k. All right?"

I think of all the things I can do for Ginger. Of unburdening my parents. For a brief moment, I think of buying a plane ticket to go see Collin, but I force it away. *Hurt now so we won't hurt more later*, I remind myself. Samuel is standing right in front of me looking fine, anyway. Not two thousand miles away getting himself shot. The apprehension eases and I start to recognize and feel this for what it is. A godsend.

"It's more than all right. It's fantastic. Thank you, Harry."

I close the door to his office behind me, then pump a fist. *Yes.*

ANSWERING my phone was a big mistake.

"Why on God's green earth is my brother calling us to get ahold of you?"

I pull the phone away from my ear. Katie's decibels need a dial-back. I'm walking from the office to "my" Rover. I go with a partial answer, speaking into the microphone of the mobile like it's a walkie-talkie. "I'm sorry. He reached me. We're good."

Which is a complete lie. My mind treads a path worn since my childhood. Bless me, Father Jerome, for I have sinned, it has been seven weeks since my last confession. I did not call Collin back after listening to his multiple voicemails. I lack the courage to face him and the strength to resist him. Mentally, I exit the confessional. Why can't Collin be a normal guy and just never want to speak to me again? Why does he want to *have this conversation face-to-face* and *follow this magic where it leads*? That's just crazy talk. I liked him better when he was talking dirty to me and strutting like the cock of the walk he thinks he is.

"'We're not good. 'We' heard rumors that we ignored because 'we' thought our dear friend Ava would tell us if something is going on between her and *my brother*."

Our reception isn't great, but I get her gist.

"Stop fretting with me and I'll tell you." I bite my lip, pondering how much to spill and thinking not much good comes from full disclosure. "We got together when I was in New Mexico. We kept getting together."

"Why didn't you tell me?"

I wince. "We agreed to keep it quiet." I slip into creole, my voice rising. "He not tell you either and he your blood. Why don't you go yell at him instead of me?"

Collin was the one who'd asked for secrecy, anyway. Not that I blamed him. He was coming off an engagement broken over a pass he'd made at Emily. He didn't want to hear it about trying to hook up with another of his sister's girlfriends, and I didn't want Katie all up in my grill, either. Besides, making it illicit made it sexier.

One night when I'd tied him with red silk scarves to the four-poster bed in his Taos house, Katie called him. I pressed ACCEPT and put it on speaker, forcing him to talk to her while I licked and nipped my way from his toes to his nose. Watching his face contort and turn red, his legs tremble, his tongue dart over his lips while he tried to keep his voice normal and swallow his moans? That was hot.

Secrets could be fun.

Katie was hollering now. "Oh, I will, but not until I'm done with you."

"Well, we gotta be done cuz I have a gig."

"We are so not done."

"We be not done later, then."

Katie growls.

"Katie, I gotta go. Really. I'll talk to you about this tomorrow."

"Tomorrow. Right."

"I promise." I hang up, and I lean over with my hands on my knees, panting.

Collin. Katie. Me. The collision of our three strong personalities has me caged in. I need blue-sky freedom and green-grass softness.

"Ava, you okay?" a man asks.

I don't have to look up to know it's Rashidi, my longtime friend and former lover, and a professor at the University of the Virgin Islands. Something about feeding plants with fish poop—aquaponics, he calls it. I glare at him sidewise without standing up. "I look okay?"

"You always look great, but right now you look a bit puny."

Everything goes black except for little shooting stars. I have a sensation of falling.

"Whoa." Rashidi catches me and holds me upright.

The stars intensify, then the lights come back on and the stars fade away. I'm breathing heavy like I've run to Taino and back, but that slows down, too.

"Thanks." I let my head fall to his shoulder.

"What going on, Ava?"

"Stress."

He studies me. The man knows me like few others do. "Anxiety attack again?"

It had been awhile since my last one. He's the only one in the world who knows I get them. Hard to hide them from him since he'd moved in with me when Ginger was born, thinking he'd save us.

But I don't need a savior. "I think so."

"Trigger?"

I put my hand up in the stop gesture.

"Let we get you in some air conditioning."

"My car. I got a gig."

"You have a car? Since when?"

I point to the Range Rover.

Rashidi's face is grave. "What you do to get that?"

I glower. "It not like that. Company car. I work for Mahogany Management."

His eyebrows shoot sky high, but I ignore him. We get in. I turn the air conditioner on highest air, lowest temperature. I put my face into the stream, even though it's not cold yet. Rashidi stays quiet.

Finally, I speak, turning us away from my panic attack. "How you trip to Texas?" He'd just gotten back the week before. The air starts to get colder. A nanny goat and her kid walk past the Rover, a bell around her neck jingling.

A smile creeps over his face. "They offer me the job."

I lift my hair and turn so the air can cool my neck. "Sweet. More money?"

"Yes, but better than that, it's near Michele."

It takes me a moment, but I realize who Michele is. "That friend of Katie's you met at the wedding?"

We'd all gone to Emily's wedding in Amarillo last spring, me while I was on the swingers' tour from hell. Collin was there, too, and we were busy pretending we hardly knew each other, even though we were already a thing and spent most of our time sneaking off to our hotel rooms. Rashidi had been making the sweet eye at Michele, a petite brunette who I think was Katie's law school roommate.

A dark sedan drives by. I wonder if it's Samuel.

Rashidi's grin is so big now his magnificent cheekbones threaten to rupture his face. "Yah mon."

"You smitten." I jab him in the chest with my finger. "She smitten back?"

His grin fades. "Not yet. But I working on it."

A flattering job offer is one thing. Rashidi in love and moving to the States and never coming back is another. A fist punches me in the gut. "So, you taking it, you moving away?"

He fiddles with the vents, directing the air better toward my face. "I think so."

I stare out the window, unable to find words, my face slowly sinking until I'm contemplating the floor instead of downtown West End.

"Hey, I still visit. You bring Ginger to Texas. She ride a horse. Chase a cow." He lifts my chin with a finger.

I pull away. My voice comes out churlish. "No one in Texas vegan. You have to cut you dreadlocks. Take up hunting. Wear camouflage and cowboy boots." I sound like a shrew. "She worth it?"

"Shh, it okay. I not leave until December. You parents here. Nana, Katie, and Nick here. All you old friends. You new job."

I throw myself across the console into his arms. "But there's only one Rashidi John."

"True dat," he agrees, patting me as he hugs. "True dat."

After long moments, I sit up. I put away the nonsense. He's not going to stay on my account, not when I refused his offer of marriage. Three times, but who was counting? "So, what you doing in West End?"

Rashidi points across the street. A dark car passes going the other direction—the same one from before, maybe?—and I see Nick and Katie walking up the broken, uneven sidewalk toward us. There's no reason for Katie and Nick to recognize the Range Rover, so they don't notice us. Before I can stop him, though, Rashidi opens the passenger door, blocking their path.

Nick throws an arm out to cover Katie as he crouches with the other hand up in a fist.

"Whoa there," Rashidi says, laughing.

"Crap," I whisper. I blot under my eyes with my fingers in case my mascara is smudged. Not because I cried, since I don't. The air conditioner made my eyes water.

Nick throws the non-fisted hand around Rashidi's neck.

Katie leans into the car. "Ava?"

"Hey," I say, my voice weak. I feel tight as a line with a fish on. When we'd hung up a few minutes ago, things were strained, to say the least.

Her voice is cool. "I didn't know you were coming, too."

"I'm not. I've got a gig at the Boardwalk. I just ran into Rashidi as I was leaving. What is it I'm not going to, anyway?"

Her voice grows serious. "We have a meet-up with a client who has big problems."

I forget about tension, sit up straighter. "And Rashidi's going with you?"

Katie hops in the passenger side and lowers her voice. "Yeah, our client wants us working with someone local. He doesn't trust the police."

"With good reason. No-count St. Marcos cops are worthless." I'm still disgruntled from my call with Porky earlier. I glance down the alley, and I remember Lailah as she looked when I found her. A chill passes through me. A killer is out there and I want him to pay. I want justice for her.

"Yeah, and this situation is high stakes . . . international . . . complex."

Intrigued, I start to ask her more about it, but she puts her hand on my arm.

"Enough about me. I've been thinking about—" I bristle, expecting her to say "Collin" but she surprises me with "—your lump."

I roll my eyes.

"I wish you'd get a biopsy."

Arguing with her does no good. Mama Bear Katie, a powerful force. "Thank you. I'll think about it."

"I'm glad." She bites her lip, squeezes my arm. "About Collin—"

Nick sticks his head in. "Hey, Ava."

Katie leaves her hand on my arm, a light tether.

"Hi."

"Did you get the job?"

Hard to believe it was only three days ago that Nick had brought me to interview at M-Squared.

Katie shakes her head, frowns. "I forgot to ask. Am I a horrible friend?"

Sometimes you are, I think. A dream-killer at least. Like when she nixed our demo deal. That was so two years ago, and I need to leave it in the past. "Yah mon." I don't say which question I'm answering.

"Yay!" Katie's smile is Julia Roberts big. So she thinks I mean a job. That's fine. "I can't wait to hear all about it."

Nick shoots her a peculiar look.

"Yah mon," I repeat.

My flat expression gets through to her. "Is it a good thing?"

Nick interrupts. "I'm sorry about how that woman treated you."

"She retired this week. It's all good."

He rakes his hand through his hair. "Still, we should talk."

"Seems like the need for that has passed."

He looks confused. "No, I need to talk to you more than ever."

I'm talking about Collin, but suddenly I don't think he is.

"Right now, though, we have to go." He touches Katie's shoulder. "We're going to be late."

The big hurry amuses me. Their late is earlier than I've ever made it anywhere in my life.

Katie looks at me sideways, like she's doing it with one eye through a magnifying glass, then scoots backward and out of the Rover, finally releasing my arm. "We'll talk soon." Then, softer: "I'm sorry about earlier."

"We'll link up." I put the Rover in gear, my feelings a jumble.

As I drive away, I see the three of them in the rearview. They're watching me go, and there's that sedan two cars behind me *again*. Gotta be Samuel, I think. Maybe he's cruising me because Rashidi was in the car with me.

I keep my eyes straight ahead and start trying to figure out how I'm going to get my game face on for this gig at the Boardwalk.

FIVE

THE BAY IS a mirror reflecting the twinkling lights on the roofline of the covered patio as I set up for my gig. I love performing at the Boardwalk. The boats in the harbor are a backdrop to my stage, with people crossing behind me on the boardwalk itself. The downtown setting energizes everyone in the club, and an ocean breeze drifts across my back and into the bar. Savory smells waft from the restaurant. In daylight, I can look down and see a rainbow of fish swimming below me. At night, I hear the giant tarpon between sets, soft swish-splash-thumps as they do their fishy things, sometimes spraying me gently with seawater.

My stomach is fluttery tonight, though, and I need to get over it before it's time to start. Collin's last message to me was, "You know what? Fuck this." He's stopped calling me, but I can't quit watching my phone. I'm feeling a strange sadness in his silence. Because this is what I want. It's my decision. I shouldn't feel like this.

An image of him floods my mind. Less than a month ago, he'd met me in San Juan. A direct flight for each of us. Easy and inexpensive for me, and just a short weekend that didn't take me away from Ginger for too long. Collin in board shorts, smelling of sun, sweat, and maleness, his six-pack abs sunburned after we'd spent a day deep-sea fishing.

Me, straddling him in my red fringed bikini, aloe vera cool on my fingertips as they slid over the ridges of his stomach, a swig of something sweet and bubbly on my tongue.

"I think I'm falling in love with you," he'd said. Then: "That's not true. I know I have. I love you, Ava."

For a few soul-shattering seconds, I'd clung to those words, almost going there with him.

But I'd recovered. "None of that," I'd said, and snapped the white plastic lid shut on the aloe vera bottle. "But I'll take some of this wood you're hiding in here." I'd pulled his waistband out, grabbed the wood in question, and he'd let me go, let me escape.

I need space, and there's nothing more constraining than those three little words. The fool just had to go and say them and mess everything up. Nothing had been right since.

I refocus by tracing cords to make sure both ends of each plug into the right places. My equipment is really top of the line. Once upon a time I sang with a band. A real drummer, keyboardist, guitarist, and bassist. The drummer moved back to the States, the keyboardist is in rehab, the guitarist is dead, and the bassist works as a scuba instructor. All the sound equipment had belonged to the drummer. I got it for a steal, and Katie and I used it when we gigged as a duo. People didn't think about the lack of musicians backing us. Two hot women singing sexy? That was plenty.

"You setting up for karaoke?" a teenage boy asks. A tourist, or he wouldn't have skipped greeting me.

Teenage boys don't tip, so I chuptz him. I point to my sign on the tripod beside the stage: AVA BUTLER, POP, REGGAE, ROCK, R&B VOCALIST.

"Is that where you sign up? Do you have Drake?"

Apparently he's slow. "Not karaoke," I say through gritted teeth.

But I can't blame the kid. One woman with a sound machine? A mama, no less, the wrong side of thirty with a ho-hum birthday only a month away? It's not like he's the only one who asks. Hell, I'm asking myself.

He wanders off. My eyes check the boardwalk and courtyard entrances and sweep the restaurant and bar area. Samuel isn't here yet.

A jolly couple replaces the kid.

For them, I smile as wide as Katie. "Good evening, Laura, Rob. You coming or going?"

Rob drapes an arm around his wife's shoulders. This always draws stares and tonight is no different. A museum curator and another St. Mary's alum, he looks more like a batty-man than any homosexual on the island, but it just goes to show looks can deceive.

She beams and jiggles. I defy anyone not to adore this woman. She's the librarian at the University of the Virgin Islands. Smart as a whip, too. "Good evening. We coming. Tonight blackened mahi-mahi fettucine alfredo. We never miss."

"And now we get to experience Ms. Ava Butler as well," Rob adds.

Behind them, the bulk of Samuel blocks out my view of the bar. He's with three people as white as he is black. Two men, one woman. The woman has a Janet Reno thing going on. Tall, thick, masculine. The men just look soft, and, beside them, Samuel is virile.

In moments of torment and confusion like these, I turn to the Romans. Roman gods that is, probably because they pissed off the nuns at St. Mary's even more than the Greeks did. So, Diana, goddess of chastity, help me. Because even with my emotions consumed with Collin, Samuel raises goose bumps on my arms. Which confirms I'm right. Collin doesn't deserve this. He doesn't need trouble like me.

"Ava?" Laura prompts.

"Sorry. You saying?"

"I just asking after your parents and Ginger."

Ginger is spending the night with her grandparents, I explain, our usual arrangement when I perform in the evenings. What I don't say: every hour Ginger spends with my dad is precious now. And how Mom sent me off tonight with an admonition that I don't need to work in clubs anymore now that I got a real job, but that I should still leave Ginger to spend the night from time to time.

Rob lowers his voice. "I read about you in the *Source*. You find a dead body. Scary."

I hate his impersonal description of her. "Lailah. Yes. A former schoolmate of ours, younger, though. As is the investigating officer. You remember Porky?"

"Porky? Yah mon. Good guy."

I hadn't yet confirmed that for myself, and I barely knew him back when. I say, "I hope he a good cop. She deserve justice."

"True dat. True dat," Rob says. "You always one for justice. I remember how you call yourself guardian angel for younger girls dem, when the Mother Superior start in. They all love you."

Memory is a funny thing. I hadn't remembered that guardian angel thing, until he said it. But now that I do, it's a great idea. That's who I should be, Lailah's guardian angel, and, if nothing else, haunt Porky until he finds the killer. I can keep calling him, make him put in honest work, motivate him to grease the wheels, to turn them faster. Not entirely unlike the role I'd tried to take for the younger girls in our school days when it was Ava versus the nuns. Something sharp turns in my chest, like a corkscrew to the heart, but I refuse to think about what it means. I focus on my idea, which is quickly turning to resolve: I will be Lailah's unofficial guardian angel.

We exchange a few more pleasantries, and Rob pulls Laura away to order the rich meal that I envy but stay away from these days. After I turned thirty, I had to choose between eating like that or wearing dresses like the one I have on. Time is a cruel beast, and my stomach growls. I didn't have time for a bite before I got here.

I'm due to start at seven, and it's five till. I recite my checklist aloud during my final run-through. Speakers, subwoofer, woofer, microphone, and my crucial wireless-microphone backup (when you play solo mostly for tips, the show must go on, no matter what), but I'm not sure even with the list if I got everything. I do sound checks, but I've played here with this equipment so often, I know the right settings by heart. I adjust my white tube dress—a cousin of the one I'd worn to work today—and smear on some Ruby Woo. I wish I'd gone with real deodorant, damn the aluminum, because this healthy stuff isn't doing the job right now. I rig my wireless mike to a linked-chain belt, and I fasten it. It looks pretty, emphasizes my small waist and the curves above and below it.

"Ava, may I introduce you to my guests?" Samuel's voice over my shoulder is a purr, the kind from a lion rather than a house cat.

My expensive Ruby Woo hits the decking, rolls, and splashes into the water below. *Shit.* I lick my lips and teeth, turn, and my heel catches a nail. I stumble, and Samuel's arm shoots out, his hand cups my elbow, and the goose bumps from earlier go into hyperdrive, pushing my girls through the white stretch fabric toward him. Pushing all of me toward him. *"Remember to leave room for the Holy Ghost"* flashes through my mind. *Screw that.* Collin's face appears next. It has more impact, and I flinch. *Stop thinking of him.*

As Island Liaison for M-Squared, I play up the local bit to Samuel's guests. "I Ava." I smile at them, a little less brightly than I would have seconds before thinking of Collin again.

Samuel introduces everyone. He gives a brief description of what they do, something about entertainment and services, and explains, mostly for their benefit, I suspect, their interest in using SeaCoins to expand their business flexibility. I nod and say appropriate things, but I don't absorb much else except "South Carolina" and "former representative," caught as I was in a web of my unwanted feelings for Collin and the man before me.

Out of the corner of my eye, I see the owner, Richard, tapping his wrist. He's large without being heavy, with long graying hair loose halfway down his back. I nod, and he turns back to the bartender.

"Excuse me. Show must go on." I step onto the stage as they make their goodbyes, trying to keep my eyes from meeting Samuel's, afraid I'll attach myself to his leg or something if any more sexual energy passes between us.

I launch into my first number, an old Sade, "No Ordinary Love." I wish I'd prepared something different, as it amplifies my fragile emotional state. Most of my songs are new since my time with Katie. Even though I'm confident with the direction I've taken, Samuel's presence makes me nervous. My voice is tremulous, not vibrato. I gulp some air before the bridge, turn and gaze over the pier and water toward Marina Cay. I slip into the chorus and feel relief. I'm sounding better.

The audience—patrons—applauds with enthusiasm. The bartender here is a heavy hand with the rum, and it's good for my tips. I return my eyes to them, feed off their energy, and start singing again. Halfway through "Umbrella," I see Richard seating the Bidens. The

Vice President of the United States and his wife are regular visitors to the island, as are their Secret Service detail, but not the Obamas. If Michelle Obama had just walked into my gig, I would need resuscitation. But there would have been triple the Secret Service, and there's already quite a contingent. I spot the muscle in suits at both entrances and at a table next to the second family. Joe smiles and waves across the restaurant, and I boot the next line of the song as Samuel waves back to him.

After the song, I gulp a glass of water. I watch as the Vice President of the United States walks over and pulls up a chair at Samuel's table. I motion for the bartender to make me a drink, over the heads of four men sitting before him. He knows what I like. He salutes an acknowledgment, and three of the four men follow the direction of his wave. Babyface, the detective who works with Porky. The strange virtual-currency guru from M-Squared, Jarod. Plus another Odd Pod guy I'd met this week, Hanif. Jarod and Hanif wave, but Babyface pretends he doesn't recognize me. By the time I've finished the next song, the waiter has dropped off a painkiller. Orange and pineapple juice, coconut cream, rum, and nutmeg over ice. I finish it quickly and hold up a finger for another. The bartender nods. I scan the crowd, noticing that most everyone in the room is watching the Veep talk to Samuel et al., except for a stiff in a garish Hawaiian shirt, with messy brown hair graying at the temples. He's a loud wrong note in the barbershop quartet at the bar. The guy is staring at me. I twist my ring and look away from him.

For a mood reset, I turn to props. I don a huge cross pendant and break into some old schoolgirl pop, belting out "Hit Me, Baby, One More Time." I can almost feel the scratchiness on my thighs of the St. Mary's plaid.

By the time I take my first break, Joe is back with his pretty blonde Mrs. VP. I grab a spare lipstick from my purse and take a moment for touch-ups, adjustments, and a deep breath. I'm on overload today. Harry asking me to go out with Samuel. The full-time job offer. Arguing with Katie. Splitting up with Collin. My panic attack. Rashidi moving. Learning Samuel is a bigger mover and shaker than I'd guessed.

And wants me.

The teenager who wants to do karaoke is still here, sitting with his parents. I put on a Drake CD to cover the break. The kid looks up and grins.

I head for Samuel's table. When I reach it, they've just settled their tab. They're discussing politics, and I hear one of them say, "My money's on Trump."

I stand beside Samuel, and his hand settles on my lower back, too low to be considered truly my back, and just high enough to keep him from getting arrested.

He says, "Ava, you're amazing."

The two men with him stand and move toward me, crowding me, making no bones about ogling me. They're buffoons, even for drunk visitors. They give off a creepy vibe, the kind that makes me pat the mace in my purse. It's nothing I can put my finger on, but I've learned to trust my bad-man instincts.

The taller of the two says, "You're right, Sammy, she's a real Venus de Milo. Will you be joining us for entertainment tonight, Ava?"

I'm confused. Have I not been entertaining them already?

Before I speak, Samuel hurtles to his feet. He gives me a slight push on the back of my waist, digging my wireless microphone into a kidney, and sending me on my way. "No, Ava will be here all evening."

"A shame," he says. "I can make it worth her while . . ."

I'm several steps away now, headed toward the ladies' room, but I hear Samuel chuckle. "No ordering off the menu, Phil. I know you like redheads, so I think you'll be pleased with dessert."

Well, I was right about the tall one being creepy. I walk as slowly as I can, but I don't catch any more. I push through the door, my mind awhirl. I speak my thoughts aloud.

"Entertainment? Ordering off the menu? Do they think I'm a prostitute?" My mind again turns to Lailah. Porky's only lead is a john that's scaring the dancers. Could be a man like Phil. Maybe he's the kind of creep that treats women like something he can order and pay for.

A toilet flushes. One of the waiters exits, washes her hands.

"Sorry," I say. "Talking to myself."

She raises her eyebrows. "I do it all the time. It's the only way you can be sure of an intelligent response."

When she leaves, I lean over and check for feet in the stalls. None. The bathroom is empty, except for me. I peer into the mirror, turn sideways, look over my shoulder. Suddenly, I'm angry, and my voice rises up. "Sexy, yes. Cheap, no."

A horrible thought enters my mind. Harry wanted me to spend the evening with these guys. Was "escorting" part of my Island Liaison job description? And Samuel—he'd agreed with Harry's suggestion earlier today. Just because I was otherwise booked tonight didn't let them off the hook. My blood heats up and by the time I'm finished in there, it's bubbling like Mom's pepper pot soup. I burst through the door, ready to give this Phil a tongue-blistering, and hoping I don't lose my job over what I may say to Samuel.

"Uh, miss?" An older couple is gesticulating to me from the restaurant area, in the wrong direction from where I'm headed.

I don't have time for them. I shake my head.

The old fellow raises his voice: "You left your microphone on in the bathroom."

I feel lightheaded. I check the wireless microphone hooked to my dress. They're right. Somehow the unit had been turned on. I turn it off quickly. My eyes come up and I see everyone staring at me. Remembering what I'd said, I grind my teeth and smile. I execute a quick curtsy to cover my humiliation, and people clap. I resume my mission to find Phil and the gang, with another reason to be pissed off.

I pass the Bidens, notice the stiff in the Hawaiian shirt has left the bar, and come to a quick stop.

A busboy is clearing Samuel's table, the waitress collecting their check. Samuel and his guests are gone.

SIX

HEAD DOWN and enormous black sunglasses on, I slam my purse down on my office desk, late, and drop my bana into my chair. I'd still be asleep if Nana hadn't rung one of her collectible bells outside my door this morning. She has one from each of the fifty states, the US territories, and most of the countries in Europe. Her entire side of the duplex is decorated in bells. She carries them with her when she goes out to check her crops. I assume it's so she can ring for help if something happens to her.

"The onliest reason for lying about be if youse ailin', and we both know you ain't. Quit your lingering and scatter, girl." She keeps ringing at the door until I stumble to it.

I shield my eyes with one hand and hold my head with the other, careful so my brains don't spill out. "Quit your racket, old woman, or I won't let Ginger come visit you anymore." She's brandishing a Grand Canyon bell today, pewter and engraved with a canyon view. I'm very familiar with it, just not this early in the morning.

"Me aine afraid a'you a'tall," she declares, laughing as she walks around back, moving at her own pace.

After that wake-up call, I'd made it into the office in record time. Friday mornings after a gig always blow, and they blow harder when you've just discovered your nice new Indiana Jones boss is pimping you out. The urge to march into Harry's office and quit is powerful, but I resist. In only twenty-four hours of having this better job, my aspirations have already risen to meet my means. Jah willing—I rotate my deities, hedging my bets—I can help my parents, do more than just unburden them and provide for Ginger.

I hunch over my desk so no one can see me sans makeup and contacts. I drank too much last night. I have an uncomfortably sad memory of taking a late-night call from Collin, but I'm not clear on how it ended. Maybe it's just part of a nightmare, the whole night.

I decide to ease into the day slowly, and boot up my laptop. First, a horoscope for my inner lioness:

Stay centered when dealing with a personal matter.

Okay. That's referring to Collin, probably. I can do that. But that's like the big easy in horoscopes. It would fit any person on any given day. It's not real guidance. I continue reading.

Some of you might want to take your time to evaluate a real estate proposition.

Real estate, me? Ha.

Your instincts will guide you through some difficult decisions.

No, or I'd have already fouled the kettle of fish this morning when my instinct was to tear Harry a new one.

Try not to sit on your feelings.

I snort.

Tonight: home is where the heart is.

Well, yes, because that's where my daughter lives. Duh.

I don't know why I bother with these things. Today's is especially bad, but they're rarely insightful. I've pissed the universe off somehow, and she's deserted me. I recycle. I conserve. I use earth-friendly products except for my stinkin' lipstick. And she can't even throw me a useful horoscope anymore. No help. No damn help at all.

I type angrily, pulling up the *Source*. The unsettlingly familiar photo of the missing blonde woman tops the lead story, pushing Lailah lower in the scroll. My stomach plummets. I do know her. Maybe it's because of all the resurrected St. Mary's connections—it's the girl I babysat after the bell released her from St. Mary's, for years, until I got too busy in high school. Lailah's friend. By then she was old enough to be alone a few hours, anyway. She cried when I told her I was quitting, and the memory of that angel face, tears on her cheeks, is like a mallet to my already-pounding head. How could she end up a dancer in a seedy club, much less disappearing?

It's too disturbing to ponder without coffee. I walk to the break room, mulling it over, and I have a glimmer of hope. Nevaeh, the *Source* called her. But that hadn't been the name of the girl I babysat. Even though I'd remembered Lailah's name instantly, I blank out on the girl that was like a little sister to me. All I know is that it's not Nevaeh. I set to convincing myself it's not her, that it isn't and can't be.

The break room is empty, and there's no coffee made. I stand beside the coffee maker as it brews, tapping my nails. *Shit.* I'd chipped my special one last night, with the fifty-dollar VI flag painted on it. *Me and my big problems, while women are dying and disappearing.*

It's while I'm scrutinizing the nail, seeing if I can fix it, that I become viscerally aware of the absence of sound in the office. According to the clock on the wall, it's eight forty-five. Our start time is eight-ish. Where is everyone?

The emptiness of the place crawls across my skin with light fuzzy steps, like a wolf spider had once when I was a girl. I jump and spaz a little, a reflex to the memory. I'd thought *I* was late. Maybe there's a lateness epidemic today.

I pour my coffee, then call, "Hello?" When there's no answer, I repeat myself, louder. "Hello—anybody here?"

Silence, except for some bumping sounds coming from the other side of the office, behind the locked door of the Odd Pod. Okay. So maybe I'm not here completely alone.

"Hello?" I put my lungs into my shout, moving to their door, where I'm now loud enough to be heard by anyone back there. "Please answer if you're in there."

Silence.

We in the Virgin Islands are proud of our public holidays—eighteen of them, to be exact—but this day is not one of them. So, yeah, I'm wigging out. Like is it Saturday, and I've been hungover and missed

Friday? Did the rest of the world die in a nuclear explosion or alien invasion last night? Or did—

Far behind me, the interior entrance door opens, and I crouch, nails flexed instinctively. A tiny woman walks in, dwarfed by a waterproof-looking bag hanging from her shoulder. She has lustrous black hair and skin a few shades lighter than my cappuccino color. When she turns, her almond eyes widen. I stand up and loosen my hands, pretending I hadn't just been in a ninja posture in my high heels and mid-thigh skirt, like a *Charlie's Angels* reject.

"Oh!" she squeaks. "So sorry." Her accent isn't local. It's not really continental, either.

We eye each other, and she looks as wary as me. I half-expect her to pull some James Bond shit. It's that kind of feeling.

"Can I help you?"

"My name's Noni. With Green Thumb. I do the plants."

Of course. I'd seen her at ABC. She's even got on a version of the shirt she wore then. This one is green with GREEN THUMB in white letters across her chest. Jah knows this office needs her. It's fancy-plant central.

She goes on. "I come some weeknights, but also on Friday mornings, when the office is closed."

Fridays . . . when the office is closed. *When the office is closed.* Which is why there's no one here and all the lights are off. I smile, relieved, then excited. A bonus day. If I was at ABC, I'd be eyeing the clock until five, but M-Squared has Fridays off. Another reason I have to find a way to forgive Harry.

I offer her my hand. "I'm Ava. I'm new."

Tension visibly slips from her, relaxing her face and shoulders. "For a minute I thought I had the wrong day."

I catch her scent. It's fresh and clean, but then I get a whiff of the undertone. Cigarettes.

"Nah, it really is Friday. I just made coffee if you want some. I'm about to leave." Now that I know I can.

"Great, thanks. Nice to meet you, Ava."

"You, too, Noni."

I watch her from my desk as I load up my things. She opens a supply closet and comes out wearing green rubber gloves and carrying a watering pot and some plant food. I wave goodbye as she moves down the hall from pot to pot, watering, feeding, and picking off dead leaves. I decide to take a bathroom break before I go. While I'm washing my hands, my phone buzzes. I accidentally see the text, because my phone is on the countertop and I'm looking at it when the picture of an enormous bouquet of flowers takes over my screen. Then one that shows the card that came with them. MCKENNA: THANK YOU FOR EVERYTHING. I OWE YOU BIG. LOVE, AVA

McKenna: *Thank you for the flowers!!*

I smile, dry my hands and exit. I hear Samuel's voice. I whirl to its source. He's standing in the doorway to the Odd Pod talking to Noni, standing close-close, his posture and arm movements personal, his face angry looking. Has he been here this whole time, while I made a fool of myself hollering around looking for people?

"Samuel?" There's some anger in my too-loud voice. He's Harry's colleague. I'm a new employee. I need to calm down. He hasn't done anything to me. Not really. Except shake my trust and hurt my feelings last night, and now there's . . . this. Whatever this is.

Noni and Samuel startle, jumping apart.

Noni answers even though it's his name I called. "I thought you'd left." She laughs, and it's the sound of a little girl, busted when her mother walks in and the chores aren't done and the TV is on.

"This area is strictly off limits in the future," Samuel says to Noni, his voice stern.

"Yes, sir. I'm sorry."

Samuel strides toward me, letting the door to the Odd Pod shut. "Ava—"

"Have you been here this whole time?"

"Um, yes."

"I called out."

He takes off sunglasses, and his eyes are blood red. "Sorry. I had a long night and rough morning. Just stopped by to pick up some files."

I point to the Odd Pod. "In there?"

"I had to check on some things. For Harry."

I don't respond, but I think it's weird that he has a key to it when he doesn't work there. And that Jarod would let anyone outside his band of misfits near Amphy.

He touches my wrist, and it's soft and tentative, which is so unlike him that my antennae quiver. "You really were magnificent last night." Then he whispers, more like himself, "And so fucking *fine*."

Noni hasn't moved. She's standing about ten feet behind us, hanging on every word. But Samuel's given me an opening to bring up the topic I really want to talk about, so I don't hold back, even though the flower lady is within earshot.

I cross my arms over my chest. "And luckily not on the menu."

I could swear his dark face reddens. He grabs my elbow—which shoots sparks to my girly parts (thanks for nothing, Artemis)—and guides me out the interior door, to the vestibule. "About that."

"Was Harry trying to put me on the menu?"

"Wait, what—Harry? God, no." Now he smiles, his face aghast and entertained at the same time. "Harry is like Man of the Year." He guides me to the outer door, then through it. "Here's the story. One of my clients owns entertainment venues."

"Strip clubs, you mean?"

He winces. "Amongst other things, but yes. They can be—"

"Jackasses?"

He smirks. "They're my clients. Not my choirboys. They demand entertainment, whether I approve or not. It's all legal, don't worry."

I'm leaning against the wall, the bright morning sun flooding the atrium through the branches of the tree. "Whatever."

He puts a hand against the wall beside my head. "Did I mention how much I enjoyed your performance? I've never heard a voice like yours. You've got something special."

I sniff. "At least you have a good ear."

"I've got other good body parts. I promise. Give me a chance to show you some of them."

"I'm not completely opposed."

His smirk morphs into a sexy grin. "I'm thinking of hosting a dinner party tonight." He pushes a lock of hair away from my face— I'm wearing loose curls this week—and tucks it behind my ear, pressing in so close that his lips tickle me as he speaks. "Come. As my date." He slips my glasses off. I'd forgotten I had them on.

I'm still feeling fractious and mistrustful of him, but his heat is thawing me quickly. "I'm not—"

His warm, soft lips cut me off. They're full, insistent. When my response is wooden, it doesn't stop him, and he teases my mouth open. He sucks my upper lip between his, nips gently, and growls into my mouth. "God, you are one sexy woman."

I can't even thank him, his lips reclaim mine that fast. This time he runs a hand down my arm to slip over my hip. Beside us, the door opens.

"Sorry. So sorry," Noni chirps as she walks around us. The sound is false and brittle, and her face is in harmony with her voice.

Waves of humiliation surge over me. I've just been caught making out with Samuel, a colleague, in broad daylight outside the office, on my fifth day of work. Sure, it's by the plant lady, but she seems to know her way around here, so who knows who she'll tell?

"I've got to go," I say, ducking out from under him and snatching back my glasses, which I stuff in my purse.

"Me, too. I'll walk you to your car."

Noni scampers down the stairs ahead of us and is out the door before we reach the landing. Samuel makes plays to reclaim me, his lips landing everywhere from my ear down to my shoulder. I'm not having it, and I pull him down the stairs with me.

"You're going to ruin my fine reputation," I say, my voice scolding.

"I can be a gentleman." He opens the door for me.

I parked streetside today, feeling lucky to find such a good spot. Now I know it was because the office was closed. I open the door to the Rover.

Samuel cups my bana as I climb up.

"Is that what you call being a gentleman?"

"Only if you like it."

I shake my head at him. "You're bad."

He growls—for a moment he reminds me of a werewolf, with his red eyes, dark skin, and large size—and I feel it in my core. "But I'm good when I'm bad. Pick you up at seven?"

I shut my door without answering him. I don't have to. He knows the answer is yes. He walks away, and I put on my glasses and seat belt, checking my phone before I put the Rover in drive. When I look up, Samuel is opening the door to a black Lexus convertible. It could have been the car I saw yesterday when I was talking to Rashidi, maybe even the one I saw when I was toting around that baldhead earlier in the week. Tinted windows. New and shiny. But I hadn't noted the make and model before, so I can't be sure now.

He fires up the convertible's engine and speeds away. My own signals are misfiring, haywire, and I don't know up from down. But as I drive off from West End toward my parents' to get Ginger, I realize Samuel left without the files he said he'd come to pick up.

WITH HIS PARKINSON'S, Dad locks up mostly on his left side. If he's stationary, he can still operate his right hand on his good days. Today is a good day. When I enter the kitchen, he's pouring milk into a sippy cup for Ginger. His hand is shaking, but he doesn't spill a drop.

"Hi, Daddy." Careful not to mess him up, I skip touching him for now. I reach my arms toward my daughter. "Ginger Thomas flower."

Ginger bear-crawls over, one-armed, and head-butts my leg, never losing grip of her Elmo.

"P-U. Someone stinky."

She slumps over onto her bana. I cringe, thinking, *Smush.* Dad lowers the cup, and she stretches for it, fingers opening and closing in a *gimme* gesture accompanied by little panting grunts of frustration. When she finally grasps it, she jams it in her mouth.

I take a moment to marvel at her. She has curls like mine. Dark, thick curls I can already wrap around my fingers. Jet lashes frame her eyes like butterfly wings. Her rosebud lips beg for mommy kisses. Maybe, just maybe, I'm biased, but she's luminous, even with a rank diaper. Her sperm donor is a beautiful man, I'll give him that, if not the time of day.

She smiles around the mouth of her cup, and it wheezes as the suction releases. A little milk dribbles down her chin and onto a purple polka-dotted dress. She shakes the cup at me, offering me a drink, and more drops spill, this time on the tile. I grab a wet rag to wipe the milk up. My mom keeps a spotless kitchen.

But today I notice the floor needs mopping, food residue sticks to the countertops, and dishes overflow the sink. Cabinets are ajar. Old issues of the *Bahama Catholic* newsletter are scattered on the table. Ginger's toys are everywhere. Oversized quilted blocks. Cardboard picture books. A rubber ducky that she insists on playing with outside the tub instead of in it.

"You're home early for lunch." Dad begins his journey back to his recliner in the living room. I get a whiff of weed as he passes me.

"Turns out we have Fridays off."

If I had one wish, it would be to give him back his vitality. He is fierce, though, and I don't shame him by staring at his jerky gait or offering to help. The day will come when he has to accept it, and none of us want to rush him. I do, however, walk over to the stereo and turn on his favorite scratch CD from Stanley and the Ten Sleepless Knights.

He grunts. His gait becomes easier, more rhythmic. The power of music. "Thank you."

As he settles slowly, painfully into his chair, I scoop Ginger off the floor and carry her to a changing pad that's a semipermanent fixture on an old indoor-outdoor love seat. It's the only waterproof, stain-resistant piece of furniture in the house. Bouncing on my hip, my cherub leans her head over backward like a pairs ice-skating move, giggling at the thrill of her maneuver. I kick her toys out of the way as I go. When I have her settled, she tosses Elmo and goes two-handed on the sippy cup.

"You like the job?" Dad pushes back in his chair. It's plush green velour. New. As a contractor and builder, he was always too active to need a comfortable chair, until recently.

I pause, holding Ginger's ankles up. "I think so. Full time, full pay. That a lot to like." I leave out long days and the uncomfortable encounter last night.

"Mahogany Management."

"Yes."

He finally has his chair adjusted to his liking. He sighs. I glance over, and his eyes are closed and his seat tipped back. I finish cleaning Ginger and the pad. I stuff the dirties in the Diaper Genie—best invention ever. I fasten Velcro on a new diaper and tug her dress down, then lift her under the arms and set her bana-first on the floor.

"I've been hearing some weird things," he says, eyes still closed.

Sensing he wants to talk, I pop in a *Veggie Tales* video for Ginger, feeling only a little maternal guilt at neglecting her. Dad needs me, too. As the opening music plays, Ginger squeals and kicks her feet. She tumbles over and laughs at herself. I push the STOP button on Stanley and his Knights.

I ditch my sandals, losing three inches in height, and curl up on the couch with my legs under me. I take Dad's right hand. "What you hear, Daddy?"

"People are talking about seeing lots of Feds down here lately. They say change is coming for the EDCs."

Dad still spends Wednesday mornings with his cronies over long breakfasts at The Golden Rail. If they were a bunch of women, what they do would be called gossip. They claim it's "talking business," but not a one of the old fools knows how to mind his own. Still, they count business owners, executives, and former senators and governors in their number. They know people who know people.

I squeeze his hand. "They always saying something like that."

Dad opens his eyes, turns to look at me. "Maybe so. Maybe not like this, though. There's talk about money laundering and black marketeering."

His words make my tummy do the limbo.

The side door bangs open.

"Gill? Ginger?" Mom's voice is strained. "Who that parked out front?"

I jump to my feet, letting go of Dad's hand. I'm surprised she doesn't recognize the car, but she's only seen it in the dark. "In here, Mommy. It's me."

"Oh no," she says. I hear cans shifting in bags as they clump down on kitchen counters.

I head her way. "What?"

"You fired?"

"No, no." I can't fault her reaction. Mom is playing the odds based on a long track record for me. "Fridays off. Only they forgot to tell the new girl." I join her and place canned soup on the pantry shelf. Eggs in the refrigerator. Bananas in a basket.

"So you free today?"

"As the wind."

She pins me down with a look. The circles under her eyes are dark and large, the skin baggy. "Good. Rent's due."

Rent collection is a full-day task once a month and involves a strong stomach, a flair for negotiation, and the occasional barter-and-transport transaction, which can involve anything from a bag of oranges to a live pig. Usually this is done with Dad's truck, which is in the shop.

I think about the messy kitchen, the fragility around Mom's eyes. She works so hard. And she kept Ginger last night. "Say no more."

The M-Squared Range Rover probably isn't set up for livestock hauling. I'll need something to protect the interior. I grab a blanket from the hall closet and return to the kitchen.

I stop to ask a question. "Mommy, you remember the name of that girl I used to babysit after school?"

She's applying elbow grease to the countertop. "Heaven."

Heaven. I smile. Not the missing dancer. "Thanks."

I bestow goodbye kisses and head for the Rover, my finger poised on Porky's number in my recent calls. Lailah's guardian angel will be using her drive time to check in on his progress.

All I get is his voicemail. "Porky, what the progress on finding Lailah's killer? I'm gonna keep calling until he behind bars, so get used to my voice."

I hang up, frustrated, and add Porky to my favorites in my contacts.

SEVEN

THAT EVENING as I stand in the entry to Samuel's place, I trail my fingers over a sleek jade elephant statue that's three-feet tall. I'm wearing a fitted fire-engine-red halter dress, I know I'm looking my best, and I'm rocking my first-date stilettos.

Just the thought of them brings an unwanted flashback.

"Your shoes are ridonkulous, you know that, right?" Collin had once said to me. He was sitting on the couch in his living room, a Lone Star beer in one hand.

I'd lifted a leg so he could get a better look at my four-inch stilettos. It was our first date, so I was wearing the same shoes I have on now. I call them my *fuck me pumps* to make Katie cringe.

"Seriously, I once had a domestic where the wife put one of those all the way through her husband's package. It stuck and hung there. Now every time I see one of those shoes . . ." He made a sound like he was shivering with cold and fear at the same time.

I tossed the shoe off by my toes. It landed in his lap.

"Whoa, that was a close one," he said, and gently removed the other one. His hands massaged my feet, and I lay there in bliss.

Yeah, well, the shoes are invited to Samuel's tonight, but he isn't. *Shoo, Collin, shoo.* Easier to say than do. The memory tries to dig its fingers in and cling to me, but I brush it off roughly. *Be present,* I admonish myself.

I inhale and smell something woody, clean, and slightly astringent with a hint of sweetness. It's coming from near me, and I spy the telltale curl of smoke. Incense is burning in a tripod cast iron pot on a black lacquer table beside the elephant. A man after my own heart. Music pipes out of speakers, soft strings that sound Japanese to my Caribbean ears. Samuel's fingers are lava hot against the bare skin on the small of my back. If I incline my head, it will fall against his chest, even with the extra height my heels give me. I don't, though. Instead, I survey the scene of his dinner party.

Guests mingle through the house. Out the wide-open French doors at the back of the great room, I can see more people gathering on the back patio. A woman passes by, serving tiny skewers of yakitori.

Samuel increases the pressure on my back, then circles around me, fingertips trailing my waist. Ivory buttons hold the fronts of his black silk shirt together, but there's plenty of sculpted chest showing out the top. "Let me get you a drink." His voice is velvet. He holds out his hand for my purse, and his biceps flex. "I'll put this away."

The man is sex walking tonight, a black Fabio with a Barry White soundtrack synchronizing to his movements. I put my hand on my bag. It's a tiny satin number on a long chain, perfect to keep my lipstick and mace with me at all times. "I'll keep it."

He shrugs, one shoulder lifting almost imperceptibly. "Your choice."

I follow him the rest of the way into the house and onto the back patio, murmuring, "Good evening, good evening," to people I know.

The patio is enormous, easily as big as the footprint of the house. Multiple levels stairstep down to a black-tiled swimming pool, which is positioned like a long-vowel symbol over the U made by the patio. A magical sound draws my attention. There's a turquoise wall built on the far edge of the pool, like a waterfall, and from it a giant concrete koi leaps, water spouting from its mouth. I freeze like the fish, feeling caught in something beautiful that I don't understand.

This is no impromptu gathering, not the small dinner party Samuel had represented it to be. This is a preplanned fete. For a moment, I stiffen. It bothers me some, but I've only known him for a few days. We've never even gone out, so I can't expect him to have asked me earlier. I'm no stranger to partial or reshaped truths, when they make the best sense. It's just that his subterfuge seems unnecessary.

Samuel's voice breaks my trance. "Champagne? We're having sake with dinner."

We've arrived at an outdoor bar. A young man smiles at me. He's wearing a tuxedo shirt with frayed ends where the sleeves are torn away. His bow tie is askew. It's quite a look.

I don't answer Samuel. "Ordy Jones, you moonlighting, what?" The last I'd seen the ambitious young man, he'd been working a sound board at the Yacht Club.

"Ava." He says my name in the way that horny young men do, and I feel Samuel's hand on my shoulder. "Times dem tough." Ordy's eyes cut to Samuel. He straightens and looks down. "Champagne for both of you?"

"Yes," Samuel says, even though I haven't answered him.

Ordy hands Samuel two champagne flutes, and Samuel hands one to me.

To me, champagne is about those first few moments, and the feel as much as the lovely taste. I put the glass under my nose, enjoying the tickle as the bubbles pop. I let the first drops seep into my taste buds. It's dry with a hint of pear, and feels like swallowing a sparkler. "Delicious. Thank you," I say, aiming between the two men.

Ordy nods, wiping a hole in his bar top.

Samuel says, "I'm glad you like it."

Movement catches my eye, foreign and familiar at the same time. It's Harry, his wheelchair breaking away from the group he's talking to. He dodges people in a graceful dance, his arms moving powerfully and smoothly as he propels, turns, backs, and wheels like Fred Astaire moving across the floor to Ginger Rogers. But it's us he's coming toward, and I fight a flare of anger inside me. Samuel says Harry is Mr. Clean. I want to believe him, but I've watched wealthy men exploit local women all my life. I hide my misgivings behind a smile.

"Ava, don't you look beautiful. Samuel, great party." He shakes Samuel's hand.

"Thank you, Harry," Samuel says.

"So, how was last night?" he asks us.

I feel like I've just sucked a lemon.

Samuel answers, smooth and easy. "You should hear this siren sing."

"I'd love to. Didn't you say you were a voice major at NYU, Ava?"

"No, theater. But music is a passion."

"Do you have any albums or . . ." His voice trails off.

I know what he's asking: "Are you for real?" *Almost,* I think, *if Katie hadn't left me high and dry when our big break came.* "I focused on musical theater in the States. After I came back to St. Marcos, I recorded a demo, but it's hard to break into the business from here."

Samuel said, "She's got the talent, stage presence, and sex appeal. The right person just needs to discover her."

A look passes between Harry and Samuel that excludes me, yet seems about me, heightening my suspicions again. For the first time I wonder if there is a Mrs. Harry. I don't see a ring on his finger.

"Thank you." I hear the tightness in my voice. *Stop with the paranoia,* I chide myself.

Whatever the moment was about, Harry lets it pass. "I hear that you're friends with the Kovacs, Ava. I was just speaking with them."

My voice squeaks. "Katie and Nick?"

"Yes. Delightful couple."

I hadn't called her today. I'd promised, and I hadn't done it. Cell service is so bad on most of the island, and it's nearly impossible to make calls when collecting rents. But that isn't the real reason I've put off calling. I don't want to talk to her about Collin. I don't even want to talk to Collin about Collin.

I'm about to ask Harry where exactly he was speaking to them, when a loud handbell rings, making me think of Nana. Voices quiet. There's no time to quiz Samuel or Harry about the Kovacs. A very young local woman in a short kimono is on the highest level of the patio just outside the door. "Dinner ready." She curtsies and holds out the sides of her kimono, bell still in one hand.

The buffet is assembled on the far side of the patio. From the looks of it, Samuel has had a team rolling sushi all night. A chef in a boxy red shirt and black pants with a short apron tied around her waist is slicing ribbons of sashimi from an immense yellowfin tuna at the end of the table. Samuel gestures for me to precede him, and we join the line. Harry navigates to the side where there's a ramp connecting the levels of the patio, then rejoins us.

All negative thoughts—about last night, my noncareer in theater and music, dead and missing girls, my family's problems, my man troubles, and Katie and Nick—vanish. I'm a sucker for sushi, and for everything that comes with it. It's the inception of every multi-orgasmic sexual experience of my life. A tingling sensation builds inside me, slowly, steadily, deliciously. I take one of everything and double the sashimi, and Samuel raises an eyebrow. I smile like a madonna. The man has no idea what he's in for.

Floods spill artificial moonlight over the pitch-black patio tile. Samuel chooses a table at the far end of the pool, next to the sound of water as it tumbles from the koi's mouth. A tiny bonsai tree is the table's centerpiece. Around it are the keys to heaven: tiny ladles protruding from black lacquer bowls of soy sauce, ginger, wasabi, and sesame seeds, with a stack of square plates. I take one and reverently arrange an assortment of the enhancements, ready for baptism, communion, even confessional; hell, bring it all on, plus some ganja, crystals, and a chicken foot. I'm just this side of ecstasy.

"You like?" Samuel asks, a grin on his face.

I moan, because there are no words.

He's catching on to my mood and pulls my chair over to him, rough and urgent. He takes a moment to study my eyes before lowering his lips to mine. His mouth is sweet with champagne, his lips warm, and a breath catches in my throat.

A waiter materializes, and we break apart. She removes a chair. Harry slides into the spot on one side of me, and then a tall couple takes the two chairs beside him. Nick and Katie, which answers my unasked question about where Harry had been talking to them. Here. Jarod, the geek from the Odd Pod, grabs the last chair, completing our table and looking uncomfortable in another of his button-cuffed shirts in the summer heat. He sees me, looks at Samuel, and his eyes widen. I feel a little bad for him. It's hard competing against a man like Samuel for the attention of the woman you're crushing on.

The waiter fills sake glasses for everyone. Samuel leans back. I move my chair a few inches away from his and take a slug of the sake. Warmth infuses me, and the cup and my hands hide my face long enough for me to regain composure.

Katie looks up to greet the others at the table as soon as she's arranged. Harry introduces the Kovacs to Samuel. It seems they already know Jarod. I'm on the darker side of the table, and her eyes move to me last.

"Ava!" Her smile is strained, and her voice polite.

I raise my sake glass, holding it by the bottom. "Kanpai. Katie, Nick. Good evening."

They exchange a quick look, full of secret meaning. It's like a bucket of ice water on the flames sushi and Samuel have lit inside me.

Katie bats her eyes at Samuel. "You don't mind switching with me so I can chat with my best girl friend, do you?" she asks.

Samuel raises a brow at me. I shrug. I won't make a scene, even though it's not my preference. He stands, backs away, gestures for her to take his seat. "Of course."

He and Katie exchange places, moving as yet untouched plates around.

She gushes to Samuel. "Thank you, thank you so much." It's her thing. Southern, she calls it. She turns to me. "I had a long call with my brother today. When I didn't hear from you."

I sigh.

She waits, pushing the sake glass back and drinking from a water glass.

I nibble tekkamaki.

Her voice rises, just a touch. "He's really hurt and confused."

I don't look at her. I keep my voice light, but with an edge. "That's between Collin and me, not you, the table, and the party."

She lowers her voice. "What's going on with you, Ava?"

"I'm the same me I've always been. I made no promises to him." The words are ash on my tongue even if they're true.

The night I'd run into him in New Mexico last spring, he'd

reminded me that we'd shared a stolen kiss at Estate Annalise, under the stars, to the music of coqui frogs, one that had stayed our secret. He told me he'd never gotten it out of his head. I'd admitted I hadn't either. We'd stayed up talking all night—just talking, about our lives, our dreams, our families, our fears—and finally kissed once at dawn, a soft, warm kiss that set my heart on fire instead of the places I was used to burning up.

I add, "He needs to move on."

Tears shine in her eyes. "This is my brother we're talking about. You can have your pick of men." Her sad voice sharpens. "You should have stayed away from him if you didn't want 'you being you' to impact me. To impact our friendship."

I put my tekkamaki roll down. It's less appealing with a side of tongue-lashing, even deserved. I soften my voice. "You're right. It was my mistake."

Katie locks up, like she expected me to argue and now doesn't know what to say or do next. Then she picks up her fork and moves her sushi around on her plate. *You don't eat sushi with a fork, Southern girl,* I want to tell her. Very softly, she says, "So, you're with him now?"

Samuel, she means. "Just hanging out. No big deal."

"He has a reputation."

"So do I."

She laughs, one huff. "True. Be careful, though. Please."

I nod, keep nodding, little ones. "Collin was special. It's better this way, Katie. It hurts less."

"Him or you?"

Jarod interrupts from across the table, a little drunk and oblivious. I'd kiss him if he wouldn't get the wrong idea. "So, Katie, do you feel like an expert in virtual currency now?"

She smiles at him, all manners. "Before, about all I knew was that bitcoins existed. After yesterday I at least understand SeaCoins, but Amphy's more Nick's thing than mine."

So Katie and Nick have been working with Jarod. Doing what, exactly? I knew Harry was a client. I'd assumed Stingray did background checks and other bread-and-butter PI work for M-

Squared. And maybe that is what they do. Maybe Jarod is helping them understand the industry and its risks.

"You catch on fast, then." *The flatterer.*

"Well, we've talked about it before. I understand they're the future. Decentralization. Anonymity. Fast, secure, no middleman. I get all that. I worry about fraud and theft from hackers."

Nick jumps in. "That's one problem. A bigger one, as I see it, is the association, perceived or real, with illegal transactions. That money can be laundered with or without suds."

Jarod puts his palms up and shrugs. "Guns don't kill people. People kill people."

"Yeah, yeah, I agree." Nick deadpans to Jarod. "I'm still depressed Kanye got the whole Coinye currency tossed."

Jarod laughs. "Kanye thought they were getting bit on the side."

Nick slurps a pot sticker into his mouth, chews, and swallows. "The pleadings alleged it was a bit dodgy." He grins.

Jarod slaps the table. "And nothing but a bit of fluff."

I interrupt, my tone harsher than I intend. "More like a bit of nonsense. What are you even talking about?" It isn't just the confusing terminology and industry-insider jargon that's irritating me. Jarod's starting to ring my guardian angel bell with his sexist comment about bits of fluff on the side. Maybe I'm hypersensitive to stuff like this right now, especially since Porky left me a voicemail while I was collecting rents. There's been no progress on Lailah's case.

"Digital dollah humor," Jarod says.

"Under the SeaCoin," Nick sings, a la Little Mermaid. He and Jarod bump sake glasses.

"Everything's better, down where it's wetter." Jarod's voice is suggestive and his face a leer.

This brings laughs from the rest of the table, so I decide, again, not to make a scene. I just shake my head.

Harry acts the diplomat and changes the subject. "Katie, Nick says you and Ava used to perform together."

Samuel piggybacks. "How about a few songs, ladies? The ambiance is perfect for a capella."

Nick's eyebrows shoot up. He knows how resistant Katie is to performing these days. Like if she does, her resolve will crack and her world will crumble into an endless string of bright lights, late nights, and bar fights. It's his fault, though. If he'd've stayed in Texas and let her get over him, she and I would be in New York, recording albums, living the life. Instead, he comes here, sweeps her off her feet, saddles her with his dead sister's kid, and she gives everything up. Everything of hers and everything of mine. *Look away from the abyss*, I remind myself. I love Nick and Katie, and I can be happy for them. Most of the time I can. But sometimes the blackness calls to me.

She surprises me, takes my hand and squeezes it. "Might be fun. What do you think?"

The ugliness lapping at my feet resettles. I know it's getting awkward, and I feel the tick-tick as seconds pass with every eye at the table on me. I remember the horoscope from this morning: *Your instincts will guide you through some difficult decisions. Try not to sit on your feelings.* Maybe my horoscopes aren't completely worthless. Katie's trying. Doing something she knows will please me.

I can try. "Yah mon," I say.

The tension breaks. Harry and Samuel grin. Nick laughs, and Katie hugs me. Something breaks inside me. I hate getting crosswise with Katie. I hate when the past jams me up. I hate that I'm such a shitty person and don't deserve a great guy like her brother. Who I miss. Oh, crap, it's true. I miss Collin. I push past it, hard, willing it and him away from me, more determined than ever to squeeze all the spice and fireworks I can out of this night. *Sushi, Ava. Think sushi.*

I stand and hold out my hand. Katie grabs it. "The Wood?"

"Perfect," she says.

"Do you want me to introduce you?" Samuel asks.

I shake my head. "Nah. It ruins the mood. Just turn off the other music between songs, and we'll pick up like we're the next track."

Samuel flags a waiter, who nods and scurries off.

I'm still holding Katie's hand.

"I love you, Ava."

"Yah, I know you do."

She sticks out her tongue.

"I love you, too."

"Irie," she says, in her bastardization of the West Indian accent.

"Let's warm up, soft."

We run through the song, fast and low.

When we're done, she looks at me, her heart big in her eyes. "If you ever want to talk about it. Collin. Or anything. Anything at all."

I raise a hand, smiling. "I know."

The canned music ends.

I count aloud, and my hand pulses the rhythm by my hip. I start to sing. Katie's voice joins mine as we near the end of the first verse, then we soar together in a harmony that aches with bittersweet memories. Standing beside the pool at Estate Annalise, after the rehearsal dinner for Katie and Nick's wedding. Where I'd first met Collin, who'd taken my breath away. An impromptu performance for friends and family. Katie and I'd sounded good then, and we sound good here tonight. Our voices fill the space by Samuel's pool now, electrify it, vibrate it.

The din of the party has ceased. Heads turn, faces tilt toward us. Katie's twang is higher than my voice. Most people say mine is resonant, rumbly, raspy even. Whatever it is, we sound better together than apart.

The song ends, and applause erupts on the patio. Even the waitstaff stop what they're doing and cheer. A tear slips down Katie's cheek. She laughs as she wipes it away. She's the emotional one of us. I squeeze her other hand.

"One more?" I ask her.

She nods, dislodging more salt water. She catches it with her finger. "I Believe."

The Dixie Chicks song is her favorite. I count out the intro, and she leads off, silencing the patio again. I watch her, even when it's my turn to sing, even when we sing together, never looking away.

Love confuses me. I love my Pollyanna friend so much, even though she's hurt me. We continue, with our mutual pain between us, but I can't give that same trust to a man. How can I believe in this love with her, in it being real and strong, and not in the love Collin has for me?

I don't have an answer by the time we finish. I've never had an answer.

"Leave them begging for more?" she says, winking.

The applause is thunderous, helped along by the great acoustics of the U-shaped, pool-capped patio. We've surprised them.

"Always."

We return to the table, waving to acknowledge the friendly requests for more.

Nick folds Katie into his arms. Samuel licks his lips, and looks like he wants to eat me.

Harry beams. "Marvelous. Both of you." We thank him. "Katie, do you still have an interest in performing?"

"Lord, no," she says, and leans into Nick. "I like my life just like it is."

"Well, that just makes you performing for us tonight that much more special, and the world's loss." He then turns and speaks directly to me. "Samuel's right. I had no idea. So many people sing, but so few are the whole package."

Samuel nods, not taking his eyes off me.

I know something, too. I've gotten better in the last two years, since Katie and I quit singing together. I've worked at it, in musical theater, in online courses, in long hours of practice. I've really come into my own.

Harry wheels his chair over to me, and I turn to face him. He lowers his voice, so it's just the two of us. "I have part interest in a recording studio in New York. My wife, God rest her soul, was a ferocious patron of the musical arts. We have a strong Caribbean presence." He whispers, "Shakira and Rihanna both record with us from time to time." I gasp, and he smiles. "Maybe you'd like me to set you up with one of our producers to record a real demo?"

There's a loud ringing in my ears. My pulse takes off like a rocket. I can't believe what I'm hearing. I can't speak.

He goes on. "I can't make any promises, but if it turns out well, maybe we could get someone to listen to it. What do you think?"

I realize Katie is eavesdropping when she squeals, "She thinks she can be on a plane first thing in the morning."

I don't argue. I'm already planning what to pack.

EIGHT

AFTER I FINISH my sushi and a lot more sake, I excuse myself to powder my nose. Katie is on her feet instantly, floating behind me in her white sundress and flats. I'm buzzing hard and we laugh at nothing as we break off from the crowd, in search of a bathroom. We stumble into the house, and, in the hallway, we pass a closed door with three women outside it.

"There's a line," one says.

I raise my eyebrows at Katie, wiggling them. Or I think I wiggle them. I can barely feel my face. She giggles, and we move farther into the house. It's hotter in here than outside. A house like this is bound to have split-unit air conditioners, but all the doors are thrown open, and no air is on.

At the end of the hall is the entrance to a suite. We enter, and it's scrumptious, with an enormous scrollwork of black headboard over an emerald green and sapphire red satin coverlet. Floating black-enameled side tables. A huge painted fan over a chest of drawers that matches the rest of the furniture. The scent of lemongrass and cigarettes. I follow my nose to the open French doors, which Katie doesn't seem to notice. She disappears into the en suite bathroom. I let her do her thing and exit toward the sounds of the party outside, wiping beads of perspiration from under my hair on the back of my neck.

I step onto a patio ringed by tropical plants, including delectable night-blooming jasmine. On one end is a showerhead and drain. On the other, a chaise lounge. A cigarette smolders, stubbed in an ashtray on a round table beside the chaise. The greenery looks near impenetrable, but when I bend closer, I see an imprint of the forefoot and spike heel of a woman's shoe. A small foot. I step back, pick up the ashtray. Red lipstick on the butt.

"Ava? Your turn." Katie joins me on the patio. "What are you doing?"

Her warning from earlier about Samuel's reputation replays in my head. "Nothing." I set the ashtray down and follow her into the bathroom.

Bamboo, black marble, and stainless steel. Katie hops up on the counter, chattering about Taylor's latest claimed conversation with their big jumbie, Annalise. Just your normal, everyday island stuff. I half listen. I'm tuned in with all my senses to Samuel's room and whoever was in here before us.

When I'm done with my business, I notice there's a closet entrance through the bathroom, and I poke my head in, turning on its lights. Men's clothing, including the clothes I'd seen Samuel in earlier that day at the office, in a heap on the floor. No women's things. But there'd been a woman hiding in here during his party, clearly. Could have been a guest taking a break from the scene. If so, why push off through the bushes around the patio? Unless maybe it's a worker hiding for a smoke break.

"What is it?" Katie asks, coming up behind me.

I'm serious, pretending to be kidding. "Snooping."

I turn off the lights and return to the mirror. I freshen my lipstick, adjust my dress, reposition my girls. "Is it just me or is it Hades hot in here?"

"Mmm, it's warm. Ish." Katie isn't sweating.

I blow upward on my forehead, creating a small cooler spot. Outside the hubbub of the party, I feel drunker. I decide to slow down on the sake when we get back.

I catch a glimpse of Katie in the mirror. She's frowning. "On the subject of snooping . . ."

"Hello, ladies." Samuel's voice booms in the small space, and we both jump.

"The hall bathroom had a line," Katie says in a rush. She's always filling in the blank spaces, making other people comfortable at her expense.

I nudge my purse with my hip accidentally on purpose. It clatters to the floor, my lipstick and mace rolling out. I retrieve them and take my time standing, showing the full package off to its best advantage. "I'm tired out, Samuel, waiting for you to show me around. Privately." I think about pouting without doing it, which has the desired effect.

Samuel's eyes gleam.

I look at Katie, who is oblivious. The girl's never had a lick of sexual savvy. I sidle up to her, press my body into her arm, run my fingers across her cheek and tuck her silky sheet of red hair behind her ear. I lean in and whisper loud enough for Samuel to hear, "Order me a sake when you get back to the table?" I nudge her with my knee toward the door.

She loses her balance a little, and I catch her without impeding her progress. Her green eyes are startled, and something else I can't quite read. But I'm not going to let how she feels about her brother and me ruin this night, this moment. I'm on a high I don't want to come down from, and I wrest my gaze from her to Samuel before she's out of the bathroom.

Samuel backs to the bedroom door and closes it behind Katie. He turns the lock and flips the light switch to off. I do the same in the bathroom. The lights from the patio twinkle through the privacy border outside his room. The expanse of floor between us is charged with electricity, and I feel its energy on my skin, I feel his energy slipping under my dress, up my thighs, and I tilt my head back, my bana against the bathroom counter, letting his current wash over me and into me. I laugh softly, eyes closed.

"What?" His voice is thick across the room.

I open my eyes and face him. "My friend doesn't approve."

He doesn't move. "It's not her I want to fuck."

"Mmm, good thing. Because I'm ready for my private tour." I lift my hair off my neck and fan with my hand. "Which I do hope includes an air conditioner." I drop my hair and pull the bodice of my dress out, which doesn't do much good, as it's fitted, other than to let some air touch my sweaty breasts for a second.

Now he closes the distance between us, moving fast. He walks straight into me, his erection cupping me between my legs, and he lifts me with a hip thrust, right onto the cold marble. My dress slides up, exposing my silk thong. The scant material is no match for his bulge, and it slides to the side. I can feel his heat through his pants, and I'm so wet for him that he could probably shove his way in without taking off a thing.

"Oh my," I say in a breathy tone, holding myself up on my slick palms.

"This is my bathroom counter."

"Nice."

After a few moments with me on the counter, we're both panting, and he says, "There's more I want to show you."

I bite his lip, swallowing his words, and suck his mouth dry, one hand behind his head, pulling his upper body against me, encouraging him to get a little dry-hump out of it, too. If he keeps talking, he might stop hand fucking me, and there's no way I'll let him out of me until I come, because I've never had an orgasm during intercourse. We grind against each other, primal and wild. I feel the waves building, and I buck against him until lights explode in my head.

I scream into his mouth, "Collin, Collin," and drop my hand to catch myself.

Shit. Damn Collin. Damn him for being the one in my head.

But if Samuel hears me, I don't know it, because I'm not the only one screaming, and the lights aren't just inside my head. Someone has turned on the bathroom light, the bedroom light, and the porch light, and she's shrieking like a banshee.

Smack! Something cracks into the back of Samuel's head, knocking his forehead into my teeth and busting my lip.

"Shit." Samuel jerks out of me and reaches behind him. He stumbles backward, then spins and runs into his bedroom.

I grab my mace. I hear the sound of retreating footsteps, the rustle of bushes, and then silence. I drop the mace back in my purse and jerk my panties over me and my dress down. Samuel is silent, his back to me.

"What the hell just happened?" I ask.

He doesn't answer. His hand is pressed against his scalp and blood seeps out from between his fingers.

"Want me to call the police?"

He shakes his head, winces.

"Who was that?"

He shrugs. "Hurts like a motherfucker, though."

I draw closer, get a better look at the gushing blood. "Maybe I should call an ambulance."

"I'll deal with it."

"Let me help you." Head wounds bleed badly, I've heard. His injury might not be as bad as it looks. But the man clearly needs first aid.

"No, I'm fine." His voice is harsh. I recoil. He regains control of himself. "But you'll need another ride home."

Of course. He can't drive now. Something catches my eye on the black floating night stand. It's a white coaster. I walk over, pick it up. The XXX Club. I frown, remembering an unbroken black surface. It wasn't there before.

Samuel snatches it from me.

"Where'd that come from?"

He throws it in a trashcan by the door. "I have no idea."

I stare at the trashcan, feeling lots less drunk than ten minutes ago.

My phone buzzes in my purse. By reflex, I pull it out.

Harry: *Can you catch 6 am flt tmrw for Sun appt w/producer? Stay a few days at my condo, work w/him.*

"Yes!" I say, speaking aloud in a whispering shout.

To heck with the God of all who is not Catholic and the heck with Jah. It's time to pull out the big guns of voodoo: praise be to the Holy Virgin Erzulie Freda, loa of beauty and art.

I need to get out of here, and I need a ride. I feel awkward about dismissing Katie so I could get with Samuel, so I don't want to ask her, not if I can help it, but there's no Uber on-island.

I text back: *YES. Thank you.*

His reply is instantaneous: *I'll email your ticket.*

I text again: *Can you help me get home from Samuel's? Now.*

Again, he texts instantly: *Out front in 5.*

I look up from my texting. Samuel is watching me, his face like the drama mask of tragedy. "Tour over," he says, and goes into the bathroom, shutting and locking the door behind him.

NINE

THIRTY-SIX HOURS LATER, I'm in a different world.

"Eff me." I gape at the silver plastic chairs, perched on single shiny chrome legs over a turquoise sea of carpet, like oysters on the half shell, swiveling back and forth in the current of energy coursing through the recording studio.

High-tech gizmos line the console, and, behind soundproof glass, an aquarium teems with musicians schooling, packing up their instruments. A singer exits a smaller tank—glass within glass—leaving headphones perched on a stand and a microphone hanging down from the low ceiling. Her hair is tucked into a ball cap and sunglasses obscure her face. She and the other big fish swim toward me noisily, and I stare at the empty space left behind, wondering if maybe a little fish like me is in over her head.

The tiny singer passes close enough for me to smell coconut and lime. She whips off her oversize sunglasses for a second. Honey skin, warm brown eyes, perfect lips.

"Is that—"

"Shh," Kenny says, cutting me off before I can say "Shakira." "You didn't see her. And if you say you did, you can forget about recording here, no matter what Harry says."

Kenny is the producer, and he doesn't have to tell me twice. His meaty hand and fat sausage fingers cup my bana. I'm wearing black spandex leggings under a hot-pink scoop-neck top, and the thin cloth is not much of a barrier between me and his hand, which feels hot, sticky, and all around nasty. I turn to him, dislodging his creeping fingers. *I want this. The time at Poseidon Studios, where Rihanna and Shakira cut songs. The demo. The potential of a recording deal.* I want it so much. I muster up a smile with no fangs. I punch his arm—it jiggles—and sidle closer.

"You." I slide my arm through his cushiony one, so I can keep it away from where it has no business. "When you think I get a chance at that?" I play up my island accent, a reminder that this studio is friendly to singers south of the border, sly-like.

"A fine piece like you has ways of getting what she wants." Kenny clears his throat, phlegm rattling. The rattle gives way to a wheeze, then to racking coughs. His pasty jowls quiver. The man looks like he's going to croak any second. Cholera, maybe? TB. Ebola virus. Something deadly and probably contagious would be my luck. Come all the way from quasi-third-world St. Marcos to New York and catch a dread disease *here*. Exactly like my mom was always afraid of during my New York years.

Harry hadn't told me Kenny was in such rough physical condition. All he'd said when he'd come with his driver to fetch me home from Samuel's was, "Make us proud, girl. Stay as long as you need to. Your job will be here when you get back." Then he'd handed me the keys to his Central Park condo, which rivaled Samuel's place for luxury. The whole Boardwalk thing is behind us, as far as I'm concerned. Harry's a saint. First time a man other than my dad has been so nice to me without expecting something back.

So with Kenny hacking up a lung, I start praying to my God-of-the-day (I'm sticking with Erzulie, since she brought me here) that he won't die before we cut my demo. I'm only a little ashamed, because, really, I'm sure he doesn't want to die either.

Kenny taps his throat, then mimics drinking from a cup.

"Something to drink?"

He nods, his bulging eyes watering, showing their popeyed whites.

"Sure." I have zip idea where to find anything, but off I go. There's got to be a break room or kitchen or bathroom in here somewhere. Where else is the caterer going to set up all the sparkling water and tropical fruit for my girls when they're in the studio? Someday that's going to be me. I ain't having no water. Caviar and Cristal. Moet and mango. Brut in Baccarat, baby.

I scurry off, daydreaming and a little wobbly in my spike-heeled, peep-toe ankle boots, checking my phone as I go.

Collin, who's moved past "fuck this" and is back to "what the fuck," not giving up.

Harry, checking on me.

Samuel, apologizing.

Mom—biting back her disappointment and disapproval—sending a cute picture of Ginger captioned *Good luck, Mommy!* Which reminds me that I need to stop and get a thank-you gift for my parents and for Nana, who's caring for Elvis.

Katie, asking me to call for something "important." I thought we'd just finished that discussion?

I file them away in a mental do-not-disturb-Ava file. Response not obligated. RNO. RNO.

It's a Sunday afternoon, and the studio has cleared out since the musicians left with she-who-will-not-be-named. I turn away from the entrance and head down a narrow hallway on a foaming river of aquamarine carpet. Red and black paintings that remind me of Rorschach ink blots hang one after another on the left side of the hall. There are black lacquer doors, all on the right, with waves in their surfaces like old glass, from layer upon layer of clear coat. I open the first one.

An enormous man stares past me, mouth open, eyes vacant. *What the heck is wrong with him?* Before I can ask, I see a bobbing black ponytail, crotch-level to him. It stops and the owner of the tail turns. I catch her profile. Beard. Moustache. Oh. She's a he. He runs the back of a hand across his mouth, and I throw up a little in mine. Why is it that sex is so yummy when it involves me, and so nauseating when I see someone else doing it?

"Sorry." My voice comes out like a squawk. I shut the door. I half laugh, realizing I forgot to look inside for cups and water, but I'm not going back in there.

At the next door, I knock, because Mom didn't raise a fool. No answer. I knock again, then enter, eyes half-closed, but it's empty, save for a kitchenette in gleaming black with two round tables and silver chairs, cheaper versions of the ones in the waiting area. The blue carpet is gone, replaced by glittery black tiles on the diagonal.

I pull a paper cone from the bottom of a dispenser. The water tank is almost empty. I tilt it, and it glugs at me, spitting out enough water to fill the flimsy cup. I hustle back to Kenny, still wobbly, holding the cone high so I won't spill.

I reach Kenny, but he's not alone. Two men are standing with him. I recognize them, and I feel heat in my cheeks, happy that my skin is too dark to show a blush. They give me the once-over as I hand Kenny the water.

Kenny nods and gulps.

Black ponytail speaks over Kenny's drinking noises. "You're the singer keeping me from religious observance today." His voice is squeaky, his tone not a question.

Suspecting we didn't start on the right foot, I refrain from an observance of my own on how he's spending his Sunday. "I apologize."

Big guy rumbles, and it sounds like, "You some kind of island pagan?"

Why, yes, I want to say. Instead, I go with: "I'm a Catho-Rasta-voodoo-New-Age-ian."

"What's that?" Black ponytail narrows his eyes at me. I notice the cross hanging from a chain around his neck.

"It means *confused.*"

"Seriously. Is that some kind of radical?"

Kenny saves me, having recovered from his bout of pleurisy. "Ava, this is Big Mike," he says, gesturing to the guy with the scrawny black ponytail, "and Yarrow," indicating the big man.

The names were going to be hard not to mix up. "Nice to meet you."

Big Mike crosses his arms and Yarrow salutes. I already know my particular wiles will be useless with them, so I nod instead of flirting.

"Big Mike is our sound engineer. Yarrow plays every instrument in the known universe. These guys work well together. Twice as good in half the time."

"That sounds great."

"My job is to size you up, figure out your sound, and direct the project. Your job is not to waste our time. Questions?" He coughs again, but recovers.

A million, all idiotic. I pick the least. "When do we start?"

TEN

I CURL my feet around the chrome legs of my chair and shovel shrimp lo mein into my mouth with chopsticks, soaking in the world outside, five stories up, and a half-dozen blocks away from Poseidon Studios. Across the street, I see flickering images animate TV screens in room after room across multiple floors. Light poles cast shadowy circles in either direction, with Central Park just past the one to the left. Despite the late June heat, I have the window open. Horns blare. The stench of garbage rises like a green ghost wafting in over the sill. I'm done in and energized at the same time.

I've missed New York. NYU, the classes, the relationships, the performances, the nightlife, the food, the cabs, the parks. All of it. And today? Today feels like I've reached a destination after a journey worthy of Odysseus, one that started and is ending in the same place.

I hum a few bars of "I'm Just a Girl," reggae version, reveling as I replay the day in my mind.

Kenny kept his fingers off my bana long enough to talk through my musical interests—reggae, hip-hop, rock, R&B, even some folk (thanks, Katie). Yarrow proved he could play anything in any style on command, and the drum machine helped pull the sound together so I could really visualize it, hear it, feel it. Enough that I laid down vocals for four "Ava-style" covers before we called it a day. Kenny and Big Mike holed up, replaying my vocals and talking outside my earshot.

Yarrow was packing when he told me, "Hold on to your ass, little lady. Kenny's about to launch you into the stratosphere."

"What do you mean?"

"I've known him for a lot of years. He's into your sound." He fastened his guitar case and put the strap over his shoulder. "You're just right for right now."

I hadn't been sure how to take that, but I'd thanked him. I sure hadn't been just right two years ago when I came to New York. Styles change, I guess. People's tastes change, and I want to believe.

Kenny walked me out behind Big Mike and Yarrow. It was way past sundown, and we stopped on the sidewalk outside the brownstone housing Poseidon.

"My man Big Mike and I think you're a fit for a songwriter we work with. She's agreed to sit in with us tomorrow. Maybe we can come up with something fresh for your demo. We'll have enough by end of day tomorrow if we work it *hard*."

I tried to ignore the slight hand gesture and hip thrust with his final words. He just can't help being a troll. "That sounds great."

"You down for a photo shoot Tuesday?"

"Sure." My lip is puffy from where I busted it on Samuel's head a few nights ago, but that's in style.

"I'll hook you up with a makeover and wardrobe in the a.m., photos in the p.m. We've got to take five years off you." He steps back and looks me up and down. "Ten. Rihanna, before she got old." My heart threatens to explode out of my chest, and I need a paper bag to breathe in. I'm older than Rihanna now. "We're selling the Caribbean, youth, and sex."

I repeat, "Caribbean, youth, and sex," silently, over and over. I feel very out of my league, and my head swims. "Thank you."

"Wednesday Yarrow will record whatever else we need, and we'll mix and master and all that shit."

"Do you need me for that?"

He gives me a look like I ride the short bus. "That's when it all starts."

"It's just, I have a daughter, she's with my parents, and my job . . ."

He lifts a shoulder, purses his lips. "Yeah, sure, go home, take care of things. You can come back if we get any interest." The odious fingers reach for my bana again. "We're going to peddle this ass hard, though, and you snooze, you lose." Suddenly he starts coughing again, doubling over.

Maybe Erzulie smote him. I pat Kenny on the back a little too hard, hopeful I'll leave bruises. *Peddle this ass.* I want to show him an ass-peddling. My quick anger brings Lailah's face to mind. I can't get much further away from being her guardian angel than here in New York, and she's yet another reason I need to return home quickly. I'm going to go visit Porky, see who's speaking up for Lailah, first thing. A girl living the kind of life she led might not have family. A sadness squeezes my chest. I might be more than her guardian angel. I might be all she has.

I keep patting, patting, patting, and thankfully Kenny's driver arrives, sliding a black limo to the curb beside us. The driver gets out, opens the back door nearest us. He ducks back into the car and comes out with a water bottle. He hands it to me, and I nod thanks.

My anger in control and game face back on, I hand Kenny the water bottle. "Thank you so much. See you tomorrow morning."

Last thing I'd seen was his fat face covered by a fist, his eyes on my backside as he drove away, leaving me to walk or find a cab. I walked. Stopped for souvenirs and thank-you gifts. Listened to people talk presidential race. Picked up Chinese takeout on the way. Bid the doorman a good evening.

And here I am.

But I can live with Kenny's rude behavior. I have to. This is my dream coming true and I cannot wait for tomorrow. Except for the part where I'm supposed to be Rihanna, only younger. My adrenaline rushes, and sitting here doing nothing in Harry's fancy condo isn't an option, so I pull up Facebook on my laptop. It's too late to call anyone back home. I post a status: *nYc, I cUtTiNg A dEmO, pInCh Me.*

Likes start to hit, then a comment. The Real Zach Ringo: *That's grate. Would love to see you. Send detales.*

My stomach does a flip-flop. My ex, Zach, Mr. TV Star. Well, he never was a speller, but he's gorgeous as sin and talented. Really talented. Like I expect him to leave *CSI* behind and take over the action-adventure flick world any day. Sure, he hurt me and I'd sworn to never see him again. But he might be a good person to reacquaint myself with, just in case this music thing needs a few good connections.

Katie comments, too: *Girl, you better answer my texts and voicemail. And I can't wait to hear all about it.*

Someone clicks LIKE on her comment. I click to see who. It's Collin.

I put my hand over my mouth. No. I have to keep him blocked from my mind. It's bad enough when I scream his name while climaxing against another man's hand. I have to focus on moving my career forward. This will either happen fast or not at all for me, because I have to get back to St. Marcos and my job and baby girl. Everything else can wait. Everything else has to wait.

Other commenters post, but I ignore them. RNO. I press PLAY on a voicemail from Katie.

"Call me ASAP. It's about Samuel. And Mahogany Management."

I sigh. Thank God it's too late to call.

I send Zach an inbox message: *Hey, stranger. Are you in the City? I'm only here a few days. Working crazy hours on this demo. Hope you're doing great!*

Just as I'm about to close the tab and shut the laptop, his answer pops up on the screen: *Hey yourself sexey. Yeah I live here, overlooking the Park. Its sweat. Meet me for a drink. Tell me all about youre demo.*

My heart pounds. He's probably only five minutes away, but it's a bad idea. I Google him in another tab. Didn't he get married? I scan the top hits. Yep, married . . . and divorced. I rub my chin, torn. I'm not interested in reliving our past. But I know he'll put the moves on me. It's in his DNA.

He sends another message: *Ava? You their?*

I type: *When and where?*

ZACH IS at a round table for two in the Cuba Lounge at Victor's Café. He jumps up to greet me, lifting me and spinning me around in a bear hug. The salsa band announces a break literally seconds before I reach him, so our voices resound unnaturally loud, like we're onstage. It's not a large space, just tables, chairs, a long bar top, and a space to mingle. The delectable smell of meat frying in grease, the sounds of cutlery knocking against plates and drinks against tables, and the aroma of freshly chopped citrus are dear and familiar to me.

"What the hell—whoa, whoa, okay now, Zach." I laugh. The man still smells like baby powder, his obsession as long as I've known him.

When he sets me on my feet, he shakes his head, his blue eyes amused. "Damn, Ava, you get better looking every year." I start to protest, but he holds up a hand. "Scout's honor. But you don't have to take my word for it. The guy following you couldn't take his eyes off you."

I rubberneck, trying to see. "Who?" It's dark in here—cozy—with wood paneling, Saltillo tile, and potted palms. I don't see any men looking at me.

Zach purses his mouth. "Some older guy. Not your type at all. I think he's at the end of the bar over there."

I crane my head, seeing men at the bar, but their faces are turned away.

Zach pulls my chair over to his side of the table. Now we'll be sitting knee to knee and thigh to thigh. He takes a seat. "Trust me, I'm far better looking and much better in the sack."

I snort.

Before I can sit, a woman scrambles between us. She's very eager, and appears quite nubile. "Zach Ringo?" she says in a breathy voice.

He nods, a serious look on his face. "Yes, but I'm with a friend."

She doesn't even glance my way. "Can you sign something for me? Like an autograph?"

He says, "Sorry, Ava, just a second." To her, "Okay."

"I'm Tanya. If you can make it to me." She lifts the front of her shirt, exposing small, bare breasts, and hands him a black sharpie. "Go slow, and make sure you write across my nipple, please."

His face registers no surprise at her request. He takes the Sharpie and scrawls his name across her.

"Ahh, umm, yes," she says, wiggling a little bit.

I stick my finger down my throat to pantomime retching.

"Have a nice night. If you'll excuse us, please, so my friend can sit."

"Good night, Zach."

He lifts a hand to wave, but doesn't look at her.

Tanya backs away, pouting.

I slide in beside him. I wave to Tanya, too.

She ignores me and rejoins a table on the restaurant side closest to the bar. She starts slapping high fives with three other young women. My eyes move from them to the twinkling lights in the palm trees and the colorful mural of all things Cuban.

"What's the world coming to, meh son?"

"God, I've missed that voice." He slides an arm around my shoulders, pulling my chair even closer. Now I'm basically in his lap. "Does this bring back some good memories or what?"

His body is warm, and he smells like a Johnson & Johnson poster child. There's sangria in front of me. His teeth do something brilliant with the light. Yes, it does bring back good memories.

Suddenly as two men pass our table, one pulls out a phone and starts shooting pictures, using a flash. The flash on the other phone is continuous, making me think video. It happens so fast, my jaw drops and I squint and cover my eyes. One of the men starts firing questions, but I'm blinded and can't see which one it is.

"Zach, who's the new woman? Does this mean you and Rachel McAdams are done? Will you be bringing your mystery girl to the wrap party for *CSI* this season? How do you respond to allegations that you're glorifying gun violence with your trigger-happy character? Does your new squeeze know about rumors you've been sleeping with Jason Harden?"

Zach grabs a menu and opens it, holding it up in front of both our faces. He scrunches toward me, eyes wide, voice deadpan. "When attacked by the North American grizzly paparazzi, play dead until they go away. Never run."

I laugh. I can't help it. Zach grew up in Montana, near Glacier

National Park, and he's full of little tidbits like this (and learned to shoot before he could walk, salute the American flag, and pray in school—if he hadn't become an actor, he'd probably have enlisted in the Army to be a sniper; yes, opposites attract). I had forgotten how he made me laugh. "Jason Harden? I didn't know you like basketball."

"Once you go black you never go back."

"I think it more, 'Once you try Ava, you favor the flava.'"

Zach hoots. "There's no one like you, baby. Red, white, black, yellow, or green." He lowers the menu until it rests bottom-on-the-table and top-against-our-foreheads. "How long has it been?"

"Since you cheated on me the last time, and I dumped you for good?"

He winces, his actor's face wringing all he can get out of the expression. "Straight to the heart."

I get a whiff of spearmint. I don't smile, don't break eye contact. "Yes, it was. And it's been eight years."

He swallows, and we're so close I can feel the vibration of his Adam's apple. "I'm sorry. I was an idiot."

I make my eyes big and bat my lashes. "No argument here."

Zach leans the inch toward me. Watching him play a cop on TV these last few years has enhanced his sexiness quotient, and he never lacked in that regard. For the briefest of moments, I give in to the urge to see if his lips are as soft and plump as I remember, if he still jump-starts my battery. I catch him by surprise, but he rallies and holds me to him for long seconds.

They are (soft and plump), but he doesn't (jump-start my battery). Instead, a single word jolts me: Collin. I duck away, knocking the menu into Zach's lap. A waiter is standing where the inquisitors were a moment ago, shifting from foot to foot.

"You ready to order?" he asks, not making eye contact.

Zach coughs and nudges my knee with his. "Tapas?"

"Nothing for me."

Misunderstanding me, Zach grins. "Check, please."

The waiter tears a sheet off his pad and hands it to Zach, who already has a credit card ready and hands both right back to him.

I test my sangria. The wine is still good, but I miss my island painkillers, my rum and coke.

Zach grabs my hand. "Tell me about your demo."

"It went well. We'll see what we've got in a few days, I guess."

"I never understood how you'd throw away your career and head back to the islands."

I feel my eyebrows stretching for my hairline. But I'd never told him about Dad's Parkinson's, and I don't now. I grunt. "I'm doing a lot of theater and playing solo gigs every weekend. My parents help me with my daughter. And I have a great job."

"Really? Doing what?"

I decide to skip the Island Liaison part as that might sound too much like an escort, which would send me to fretting about last Thursday night's Phil encounter again. "I work for a company that, amongst other things, has its own digital currency system. They're called SeaCoins. It's a big interisland network."

"Wow, how cool is that? Our season finale is on virtual currency."

"Really?"

"Yeah. Only the human traffickers called their currency SexCoins and used them as a way to launder money from the sex trade."

"Ick."

"And your daughter?"

I grin. I can't help it. I show him a picture. "She's one. Has us all wrapped around her little finger."

"She's beautiful. Like you." He puts his hands on either side of my face. "You're going to make it big now. And I'm going to help."

I smile between his hands and around my tiny cocktail straw, draining my sangria. "Thanks."

The waiter returns with his card and a curling white strip of paper. Zach signs, we stand, and he puts his hand at my waist, warm fingers against bare skin between my stretch pants and demi-top. He keeps them there as we wind our way to the exit. Conversations hush as we pass, and I hear his name whispered over and over. I see iPhones rising.

This is nothing like my college memories.

At the door, I turn to him. He pulls me in, pressing our bodies together under a red awning with VICTOR'S CAFÉ in white script. I know this man and his angles and bulges so well, it's like puzzle pieces coming together. And that face. The expressions. I see the hunger in his eyes, but something else, something that actually has the power to surprise me. I see happiness there. Is that happiness about seeing me, about the attention he's getting, about life in general? I refuse to consider it, afraid of what it could do to me if I'm the reason.

I disentangle myself and take a step back, aiming my gaze lower than his. "Thanks for the drink."

"You're welcome." His voice holds the confusion I expect to hear over rejection, but I also hear the hurt I'm afraid will reel me in. "You're leaving?"

A man and woman walk by, and the man says, "Zach Ringo, my man, love you on *CSI*." He holds up a fist.

Zach smiles and lifts his, a motion that looks reflexive. They dap and the couple moves on.

"Ava?" Zach's attention had never wavered from me. "Don't kick fate to the curb here." He smiles, the face that graces magazine covers everywhere, the one I'd once loved. When I don't respond, he says, "Dinner tomorrow night?"

Yes buys me time to think about it and still leaves room for no. I nod, just once.

"You won't regret it."

I shake my head.

"Give me your number?"

A sense of tumbling through darkness washes over me as I type my digits in his phone. Instead of taking it back from me, he covers my hands, pulls me in, and his hand cups the back of my head, his fingers weaving into my hair.

"I love that you grew your hair out." He lowers his mouth to mine and kisses me, no tongue, just pressure, like he's falling and I'm catching him, holding him up. He lays his face against my forehead. His voice is soft, so soft I almost don't hear him when he says, "Just one chance."

There's a part of me that wants to give it to him, the part that loved him when I was eighteen, when I was twenty-four. There's another part of me that knows my heart is taken, but wouldn't mind the kind of help a man in Zach's shoes can provide. There's still another part that is disgusted with Ava Butler. I ignore that one. Men have taken what they want from me since I was a girl, Zach included. Maybe they owe me back a little. Or a lot.

Then he releases me, and I walk away without speaking, acutely aware of eyes watching me. At the corner, I turn to wave and realize it's not Zach's eyes on me but a man from the restaurant. An older guy.

I walk faster and clutch my purse hard to my chest, hoping this guy doesn't force me to defend myself. It's only when I shut the door to Harry's condo and throw the deadbolt that I remember I left my mace at home in the duplex because of airport security.

ELEVEN

LUNCH the next day is New York-style pizza, delivered so we can take the shortest break possible and get back to work. I've never been so on fire, even on opening night of my one very forgettable off-Broadway leading role my senior year at NYU. In fact, today may be the first time ever in my life I arrived anywhere early.

The songwriter Kenny brought in, a dreadlocked woman with more piercings than I've got teeth, is unbelievable. Louella—that's the name she goes by—gets me, and Yarrow gets her. During the morning, we narrowed it down to three original songs, and we're ready to record after lunch. Kenny wants to have at least seven songs to pick three from for the demo.

I can barely eat. Partly because I'm excited, and partly because I know tomorrow I have to look younger than Rihanna. I take tiny bites of honeydew melon from the fruit salad ordered specially for me and read the *St. Marcos Source* on my phone, skipping my horoscope since it's already clear the stars are aligned for me today. I miss home until I see the headline: ANOTHER STRIPPER MURDERED, with Nevaeh's picture. It's eerie how familiar she looks, her eyes drilling into me with a thousand-yard stare. She was garroted and sexually assaulted, like Lailah. No witnesses. No leads. No new information about her. Porky's name is given as the officer to contact with information. The piece is so brief I suspect they just found her, just posted it. It doesn't give me anything to go on except a certainty that my guardian angel duties just doubled.

I forward a link of the article to Porky with a quick message: *What's going on with her and Lailah???*

I do the same to Katie, thinking it more likely she'll fill me in. I remember she wants to talk about Samuel and M-Squared and add to my message: *Back Wednesday nite. Talk then?*

She replies: *Nice of you to answer, finally. Wed nite OK. Taylor said to tell Auntie Ava that Annalise thinks she should be careful of the bad man. I have no idea what that means, but it's good advice in general.*

I smile. Taylor and his Annalise.

A receptionist I'd met first thing that morning walks in, a young man who looks like rock star Joe Slither did back in the days I'd known him, from his times on St. Marcos, before he ended up in a federal penitentiary for drug trafficking: heroin slim, greasy long hair, overwrought tattoos, and pale skin.

Slither's younger brother (he could be, after all) is balancing a clear glass vase filled with water, rocks, and water lilies, biting his lip, trying not to splash on the floor. "Where can I put this?"

Yarrow whistles. "Wowee, those are classy."

The young man juts out a hip. "C'mon, man, clear me a spot?"

We push pizza and fruit boxes aside, and he sets the arrangement on the table, sliding it toward me. There's a card jutting out of the flowers. AVA BUTLER.

"For me?"

"Du-uh," he says, and leaves.

I caress my ring.

Kenny groans, then hacks like a cat with a world-record hairball.

"What?" I ask, reaching for the card.

"You're giving your finger a hand job. Don't be doing anything for yourself you're not willing to do for Uncle Kenny later."

I shake my head, but I pretend to find him amusing. "It's a ring, Kenny." I've put up with more for less. I tear open the sealed envelope.

Trust fate.

Zach

Louella looks up from her phone. She's been fiddling with it for the last few minutes. "I'll bet I know who those are from."

Kenny does a few hip thrusts in his chair. He's less amusing with every passing moment of our acquaintance.

"How's that?" I ask her, arranging the wet blossoms. The flowers—purple-tinged petals, lightening toward the bright yellow head—are basically floating in their own self-contained boats of greenery. The scent reminds me of home. Lemony, a little watery, and sweet.

Louella turns her phone toward Big Mike and Yarrow. They stare, then turn to me. Big Mike looks at the phone again, then wobbles his head side to side. Yarrow leans back, his expression smug, hands behind his head with his elbows out.

"What?" But I have a suspicion, and I want to see the picture without acting like I do.

Yarrow says, "You've got it made, don't you?"

Big Mike looks impressed. "You're only in town one day, and you've bagged Zach Ringo?"

Kenny sits up. "Give me that."

Louella holds it away, saying, "Don't open any porn." Then she glares and hands him the phone.

I squeeze in beside her, and we look over Kenny's shoulder. It's a series of shots on TMZ.com. My deer-in-the-headlights stare, Zach nonplussed and gorgeous beside me. Zach and me behind the menu. Us walking out with Zach's hand on my bare midriff. Yeah, I figured those would be the ones. And then—the surprise—our kiss outside the restaurant. My insides stir. Damn. Pretty sexy, actually. I scan the short narrative. ZACH RINGO AND MYSTERY BOMBSHELL OUT IN NYC.

"Mystery bombshell." Kenny rubs his chin. "I can work with that. Louella, got anything we can record with that vibe?"

She sits with her eyes closed, seeming to forget Kenny and the rest of us. She starts swaying, then humming, then slapping the table in a one-drop rhythm. When she opens her eyes, she's smiling wide. "I've got a start, I think." She hums a few bars. "Ava, help me with the lyrics?"

THAT AFTERNOON, Kenny sends me home in a Town Car. The driver pulls out in traffic, his face forward, and asks me if I want to listen to anything. He's wearing a limo-driver cap and a uniform. I feel glamorous and successful.

"No, thank you."

"Knock on the glass if you need something," he instructs me. Then he raises a tinted window between us.

I love the privacy, and I settle into the plush black leather seat. I push PLAY on my phone for the rough cut of the last song we recorded, and I put it on a loop. I'm getting writing credits on it. *Writing credits.* My blood is pumping harder than I've ever felt, my excitement explosive. I've never recorded an original before, much less an original I cowrote, even less one so effing awesome.

Every cell in my body is a live wire pulsing to the strong backbeat, and I wish I had someone to burn with. Throw you against the wall, rip out your hair, howl at the moon kind of burn. I think about Zach, about dinner. Maybe. He's better than a stranger, but I don't want him getting the wrong idea.

I wriggle in the seat. If Samuel were here, we could finish what we started Friday night. It had ended weird, but I'm not mad at him. All I want is someone for right now, someone to keep my edge honed.

What I sure as hell don't want is the vise of a relationship.

The driver isn't watching me, so I put one of my heels up on the armrest of the door. I keep my eyes on the mirror, but the driver is ten and two, eyes on the road. I've got five minutes until we get back to the condo, maybe more with traffic. Plenty of time.

I start humming, my hand closing over my mound, squeezing, then opening. I relive the day, revel in it. We finished the songs for my demo, and "Bombshell" is the song I was born to sing. I swear, Kenny had tears in his eyes when I recorded the vocals. I have tears in my eyes now.

"Money, baby. Money," he'd said.

I sing it, my breath hitching as my imagination shifts. Now Collin's teasing me with the pressure of his hand.

"Bitch a bombshell, blowing up on me. You the ignition to her TNT. Mortar flying, I the enemy. Bitch a bombshell, but she ain't the half of me." A heavy crash of instrumentation and percussion in the chorus on the word *bombshell*: "Bitch a bombshell, baby. Bitch a bombshell, baby."

I sing until the spasms rip through me, and then I smile, sighing and pressing my fingers into the pounding of blood in my clitoris. *Thank you, Collin. Now get the eff out of my head.* I still want a good romp with someone other than my hand, but this will hold me over, keep me from doing something tonight I'll regret later. Maybe.

For the first time, the driver flicks his eyes, and they meet mine. He stares at me, hard. Maybe he saw me. Can't be the only time something like this has happened in his car. He looks familiar, in the way that so many ordinary white guys look alike. I wink at him. He jerks his eyes away, and I laugh aloud. Each laugh pushes outward from the inside, putting pressure on the good spot my fingers are hooked over.

"Why, thank you," I say to him, but he can't hear me.

When the tremors stop, I put my foot down and release my still-throbbing crotch. I plug in my phone, which is on fumes, and once it's charging, I turn off airplane mode, which I'd had it on since lunch. It starts blowing up with messages from basically everyone I've ever known in my life about the pictures of Zach and me. Still singing, still tingling, I read them.

Harry: *I hear you're a celebrity. How's it going?*

Emily: *OMG. Zach Ringo. You dog.*

Katie: *Isn't that your EX?*

Samuel: *Should I be jealous?*

Mom: *Ginger misses you. And what are you doing with Zach?*

Porky: *Officer Bachoo is out. This is Winslow. Why you so interested in dead hookers?*

That one has me seeing red. I wonder if Bachoo knows his partner, Babyface, is answering for him. Another text appears in the string.

Porky: *Hot Rod, your ass better deliver my package today if you don't wanna be box up.*

I respond: *What?*

I stare at the screen until an answer appears: *My bad. Thought you someone else.*

I close the string with an angry swipe.

Collin: *I get it. You'd rather be tramping around with your famous new boyfriend than with me.*

The music stops, the curtain drops. Collin. I'd known I would hurt him. Well, this would have been the moment he dumped me, which means it's a damn good thing I'd backed away first. I turn my screen off. Buzzkill.

RNO, baby. *RNO. RNO.*

———————

ZACH TEXTS that the paparazzi are on his tail, so I adjust my makeup for floodlights. I pick through my cosmetic bag in a daze, my energy and excitement sapped by Collin's message. Bobbi Brown liquid liner to my upper lids, drawing them out with a halfhearted flourish to the end. Mascara—three coats. And lips—base, a rich MAC plum called Commotion, and a sparkle from a mostly clear lip gloss. My plum push-up top is squishing my girls, so I rotate them nipple-up. But my heart's not in it. I sigh. At least I'd straightened my hair this morning, so I shape the angle against my forehead and jaw and call it George.

A buzzer goes off. I remember the security downstairs and realize I don't know how to admit guests. I've never lived anywhere this posh.

I find an intercom by the door and push a button on it. "Come up," I say into what looks like the microphone area, trying to force some life back into my voice. I expect to hear an answer. Nothing. I don't know who it is or whether I let him in, or if the darn thing's even working. I press the button again, perplexed, but I'm careful not to wrinkle my perfectly painted brow. Crease marks make a woman look haggard in pictures.

I gather up Harry's keys, my phone, the lipstick and lip gloss, and my wallet, stuffing them into my tiny black shoulder bag. I hurry, afraid I didn't succeed in letting Zach in, on the one hand, and afraid I did, on the other. Honestly, I want to keep us as far from a bed and privacy as possible, but I don't want to leave him stranded with grizzly paparazzi either.

There's a knock. Okay, my intercom operation worked. Showtime. I close my eyes and take a deep breath. As I exhale, I lift my shoulders, coax my mouth into a bright smile, and open my eyes. Then I throw the door open, ready to barge out and barrel Zach back down the hall to the elevator.

Only it's not him.

It's Samuel, in the flesh, smiling like he's crafty, holding a single red rose, the kind men buy from street vendors as an afterthought. Why not, they think. Might round her heels a little.

I feel the shock registering on my face, and I wipe it away, leaving neutral in its place.

"Wow," he drawls. "You look so"—he pauses, shakes his head like he's clearing cobwebs—"goddamn fuckable."

He could have been describing himself. He's in all black, from his laced pointy-toe shoes up the creases of his slacks, across the bulge of his thighs and his . . . above-thigh area. I'd describe the rest of his outfit, but that's where my eyes stop.

I lick my dry lips. "Samuel. This is a surprise."

He nods. "Whoa, I'm not the one you're planning on doing tonight, am I, Venus?" He holds up the flower. "I should have bought out the cart."

I ignore his words. "You're a long way from St. Marcos."

"I'm in the City on business."

"Mahogany?"

"Yes. A presentation on Amphy and SeaCoins to some potential clients and investors."

"More rejects from the church choir?" I picture him in front of a room of gangsters. No, not gangsters. Sleazeballs. Sexual predators who expect redheads for dessert and would like me on the menu, too.

His forehead wrinkles, then his eyes light up with understanding. "Yeah, something like that. I didn't know you were here, too, until I saw the pictures." He says "pictures" like they're scandalizing. "Then I talked to Harry."

Damn that Harry. "Last I saw you, someone gave you a headache. A girlfriend?"

He shrugs, laughs, shoots a glance back down the hallway. "No girlfriend."

I cross my arms. "No answer, either."

Beside me the intercom buzzes again. Samuel looks at it and me.

"That's my date."

He rolls the stem of the rose between his fingers. "I fly back tomorrow. You?"

"I reach the next day."

He smiles. "I actually know what that means."

I press the button and hold it, letting whoever it is in. Zach this time, I hope. I withhold further comment and inspect a fingernail.

"Damn, Ava, you're not making this easy. Now I've got a time bomb ticking on me." He grabs me, pushes me against the door, backing me into the room. He crushes his mouth on mine, and I hold my own. When he lifts his mouth, he eyes me. "Come straight to my place when you get on-island. I want to take you someplace nice, after I fuck you far better than your date will tonight."

I reach in my purse, pull out my lipstick, put fresh on. I wipe a little off his mouth. "I'll think about it."

He snorts and holds out the flower.

I shake my head. "Nah. I think you'll do better next time."

The elevator at the end of the hall dings.

I shoo him with my fingers. "Go along, boy, you're cramping my style."

Samuel's eyes flit down, his grin sardonic, and he saunters off toward the emergency exit sign and stairwell, in the opposite direction of the elevator. My pulse is racing, and I'm glad for a second to catch my breath. The man is a hell of a kisser, I'll give him that.

Two men get off the elevator. One is Zach. He waves. I wave back, slicking on a layer of lip gloss while he walks toward me. The other man looks both ways, pauses, then follows Zach.

Zach is carrying more roses than I've ever seen one person hold. I hear a door open at the other end of the hall, and I hope Samuel sees how it's done. Zach hands the flowers to me and swoops in to kiss my cheek. The man behind him is beside us now, and his eyes flick up to mine from behind horn-rimmed glasses just as Zach's lips leave my skin. He's older than me with gray at his temples, medium height, wearing a boxy open-collar golf shirt. He has a haircut like an accountant. Hackles rise on my arms and neck. His eyes leave mine as he passes.

I've seen him before. It hits me like a ton of bricks. He was at the Cuba Lounge. "Hey," I shout. "Why are you following me?"

I turn and he's walking backward shooting a picture of us on a phone.

Zach's voice is amused. "I think he's following *me*. You'll get used to it."

Damn grizzly paparazzi. Zach and I are easy prey out here.

I pull Zach inside. "Let's get these in water."

TWELVE

I'M a hostage the next morning in an off-Fifth salon so big on minimalism it doesn't even have a name, on the receiving end of a once-going-on-thrice-over from an Asian stylist rocking skinny jeans with no room for anything above his thigh bones. I know, because I checked from every angle, and there's no evidence of junk. I'd say he's a she, except there's no trunk, either. Tape job, I decide. Has to be. I pray to Mother Earth (she's on duty for me today) he waxed first.

Chen—that's his name—tilts my head, scrutinizing me under harsh light from every angle, like he's a proctologist looking at the sorriest ass he's ever seen. My face is bare of the makeup he'd removed first with something that makes paint thinner seem like some pansy shit. It could burn right through the ozone layer, now that it's laid waste to my face. But I stand my ground to the violation. Then he holds up his iPhone, where he's enlarged a *New York Daily News* full-color photo of me with Zach from the night before in Dirty French—which is the name of a restaurant, not a sexual position. Chen purses his lips like he's channeling Angelina Jolie and gives his chin-length, straight black bangs a head toss.

"You sleeping with Zach Ringo?"

I'm not sure how this is relevant, but I answer anyway. "I did for six years, but I'm not now." Because I hadn't slept with him. A slide show of images from last night runs through my head. Dirty martinis at Dirty French. Zach, full of ideas about how to make it big in the Big Apple. Heavy petting in the back seat of the Town Car. Zach, knowing full well my difficulties with intercourse and climax, going down on me for a second orgasm in a cave of black-tinted privacy glass while his driver smokes a cigarette on the other side up front. (Really, if *the* Zach Ringo is offering another go-round, who in her right mind would say no?) Me only mouthing Collin's name instead of screaming it. Me telling Zach we have to take it slow as I zip him up, my lipstick around his bamboo an oxymoron of sorts juxtaposed to my words.

It's not that I'm patting myself on the back for staying out of the missionary position with him. I'm just glad the photo in the *Daily News* isn't Zach's head buried between my thighs, my ankles locked around his back in my four-inch heels.

"*He* must see something in you." Chen doesn't look at my face, still staring at the *News* picture. "Kenny's asking for a younger, edgier Rihanna. I'm not frickin' Annie Sullivan. You're what, twenty-five? Twenty-six?"

I bite my tongue. Thirty-one and eleven-twelfths, but I'm not giving up that information without a court order for my birth certificate.

He shakes his head, muttering, "He must be blind."

Not only is he making me feel like I'm repulsive, he's scaring me. I need phenomenal pictures today, and Chen is in charge of my hair, makeup, and wardrobe. If he has no faith, this will be a colossal failure. Anger ignites in me. I'm not letting this Pete Wentz-wannabe screw things up.

I toss my hair, lift my breasts, and spit my words at him creole-style, which men always seem to find more intimidating than baloney-sandwich yank speak. "Kenny blind? How 'bout you? I expect more." I get to my feet, rough, sending him flying backward on his rolling chair. "He say you the best, but no reason I can see. You got no imagination. I calling Kenny." I grab my phone out of my purse.

Chen's look of distaste changes to surprise and then delight. "Yes! I see it now. But it's not Rihanna, and it's not about age as a number."

He claps his hands twice. "Inspire me. Show me." He raises his voice and his hands. "Show me, girl, show me."

I'm on to him, and I don't let the grass grow on it. I hit PLAY on the rough cut of "Bombshell" on my phone, and turn the volume all the way up. The music starts, tinny and thin from the phone speakers, and I straddle the rolling stool, half of it warm from Chen's insubstantial tush on it a moment before. I'm flashing my dark twat barely covered by a scrap of red silk, but I don't care. I lean one shoulder down and move like I'm going frontways under a limbo bar as I roll forward toward him. I sing my lungs out, and I'm a bombshell, blowing up this place, blowing up his face.

Chen's eyes are wide, his mouth an O. "What the fucking fuck is that?" he says, shouting over me and the music.

I ignore him, into it now, showing him, showing everyone who has ever doubted me that I can *bring it*.

"Rock? Hip-hop? Reggae?"

Between verses, I say, "It Ava, bitch. And this what she look like."

"Give me that." He holds out his hand for my phone.

I twirl on his chair. *Bombshell, baby.* I thump my fist three times over my chest. I toss the phone over, still deep into my role. *Bombshell, baby.* I thump harder.

Chen stalks over to the sound system. He turns off the background music, which I hadn't even heard, I was so into my own groove. There are moans and groans from the other stylists who are setting up their stations, along with a few early-bird clients drinking mimosas, Irish coffees, and Bloody Marys, looking like they came here straight from closing time at the clubs. He turns off "Bombshell." I grind to a halt. He messes with a cable, which he plugs into my phone, then turns a few dials.

"Everyone, listen up." Chen gestures to the disgruntled room at large in a "shut it" motion, all snap and attitude. "This is Ava." He points at me. "She's about to become a huge fucking star. I'm going to prep her for her breakout photo shoot, and you're going to be the first humans in the world to hear her new track." He lowers his hand. "Look her up on the *Daily News* website today. You're welcome." Heads duck to phones and fingers and thumbs fly. He presses PLAY on my phone, and "Bombshell" floods the room in surround sound, full blast.

The explosive heat in my cheeks is immediate, intense. I am one part wanting to duck my head and hide and another wanting to jam to my track. People are silent, listening and scrolling the *News*. I keep my eyes on the floor. My face feels like it's under a broiler. By the end of the first verse people are starting to jam, making the kind of sounds that I think mean they like it. In the middle of the chorus, the place erupts. It only takes one iteration of the heavy "Bombshell" lyric for combs and brushes to bounce in trays on rolling carts and people to jump to their feet brandishing their morning libations.

Chen pounds his chest like I'd done a moment ago. Then he leans over to me and yells in my ear, "Show *them*."

I'm on my feet and the rest of the song is a blur as I sing and move to the music, going by pure animal instinct. Everyone pounds out "Bombshell, baby" with Chen and me to the chorus. When it's over, my head slumps. I'm panting, sweat in a river between my breasts, heart tripping, afraid of people looking at the real me instead of the other Ava. But there's no time for that. They're all over me, touching me, talking to me, excitedly conferring with Chen about what he's going to do with me for today's shoot. It's a small crowd, but it's my first taste of what making it big might be like, and I like it.

Chen propels me back into the chair I'd started in. He crosses his arms.

"So, what you think?" I ask, batting my eyes.

His smile is one of triumph. "You're about living without apologies. Wide open. Yesterday's clothes and the walk of shame. Crow's-feet showing. Smudged makeup and bed head. Chipped fire-engine-red nail polish. Sexy like the earth on fire, and ready to chew up the next man and spit him out."

I glance at my nails quickly. I'd painted them that morning, but, sure enough, chipped.

I see his vision, and I'm so in sync with this role that I taste the morning breath and long for Tylenol. "It's not what Kenny asked for."

"Ah, but it's what he wants. Patron saint of sinners. Goddess of the morning after. He just doesn't know it yet."

IT'S LATE, nearly ten p.m., and I'm coming off shots of Jack during the shoot and bubbly after we wrapped. Kenny is reviewing the proofs on a file share while Chen and I cluster around the speakerphone with the photographer, Jose. Someone smells rank and I suspect it's me; I danced my bana off today. We're in Jose's office above his studio, which is only half a block from Chen's salon. Proof sheets litter every surface, giving off the faint chemical smell of ink. Framed photographs of the current who's who of the music world adorn the walls at eye level, with stark white walls shooting up another ten feet above them. I wonder if Jose changes them out on a weekly basis. Then I wonder if any of my shots will ever make the wall. I bite my knuckles to contain myself. Mother Earth did me right today.

Jose—whose last name is Stein, wears a Jewfro, and has a schnoz big enough to shade Rockefeller Plaza—is basically creaming over his work, and I'm not far behind him. The pictures are masterpieces, and the way he and Chen are presenting them is like a music video. Chen knows he kicked ass. They're his vision, from giving me the motivation for the part I played, to the set, to the storyline, to the instructions he gave Jose, to the male models who Chen dressed, prepped, and posed. My favorites are the ones where I'm in a blonde wig—Deborah Harry, 2015 version.

"You like?" Chen asks Kenny.

"Hold on, Jesus, I'm still jacking off to them."

While it must be a joke, it sounds like that's exactly what he's doing. Jose and Chen laugh. They both claim to be straight (but my money's on bi for Chen), and they discuss the shoot and their reactions like I'm not there. I'm glad their women aren't. It's not news that my sexuality is an asset, but, in going for tainted, tattered, and a little past prime, they made even my liabilities into assets. I'm not ugly. I know I'm an attractive woman, but my appeal is in the active, in a Lady Gaga or Madonna sort of way. It's in the release of pheromones so intense they burst into a photo shoot and the frame, and Chen and Jose know how to work with that. Some of the shots border on blurry, but it works.

Now, though, listening to them, I feel weird about it. Or maybe it's just the thought of Kenny ejaculating across his office, and the cleaning staff having to mop up after him.

Seriously, I'm worried about how women will react to them, and there's no one here to speak to that perspective. My hope is that women will relate, whether it's because of a one-night stand they've always regretted or a dirty fantasy they've never admitted. Or how they feel the next morning after one too many at the office party where they finally make a pass at the hot coworker who says, "I don't think so." But maybe they'll hate our concept and me. They may think it's slutty. I don't want it to matter to me, but I think it does. I wish Katie was here to give me her opinion.

The conversation turns technical, about which shots to use for what purpose and how to process them. I scroll my messages, which I've ignored all day. It's mostly the usual—one from Collin (still pissed about Zach), Samuel telling me he's home. Zach smarting because I didn't call. Katie asking if there's any way we can talk tonight, because there's another dancer gone missing.

WTF? I browse the *Source* quickly. Nothing about a new girl.

The last text is part of a long string from my mom. I save her for after I answer the rest. To Zach: *Still on set. So sorry. Busy but great. I'll be in touch soon.* To Katie: *Ran too late. Sorry. Has to be tomorrow.* Nothing to Collin, who I care about the most. To Samuel: *Wednesday. You ready for me?*

Then I open my string with Mom:

You there?

Ava?

I need to talk to you.

I call, you don't answer.

Call. Please. I have bad news.

My heart jams itself up in my throat, and I can barely choke the words out. "Excuse me. I have to make a call."

I vault into the narrow hallway outside Jose's office and hit speed dial for Mom. The wood floors creak under my feet as I shift around. "Come on, come on," I say, as the connection seems to take forever.

Mom answers on the first ring. "Ava? That you?"

"Yes, Mommy, what the matter? Daddy okay? Ginger? You?"

"Yah, we all fine, it the girl you ask me bout. Heaven McAllister. The one you babysit."

I'm so lightheaded with relief that I see stars. "Yes?"

"It seem she change her name. You remember her parents move to the States when she in high school?"

"No, I didn't live on-island then."

"Oh, well, they move and she stay with friends. Her parents send Christmas cards for a while, but you ever notice no one send them anymore?"

I'd never sent Christmas cards, so I keep my mouth shut and let her go on.

"She go a bad way, and she change her name."

I slump against the wall. "Oh no, don't tell me."

"Nevaeh. She change her name to Nevaeh Allen. Nevaeh is Heaven backwards. And she turn up murdered. There a memorial gathering tomorrow afternoon at St. Joseph's."

"Heaven. Nevaeh." A life turned around. I'm stunned, numb.

"I so sorry, Ava. I know you love that girl."

I had. I'd loved her like a favorite doll or pet at first, like a little sister by the end. I'd kept her safe, those couple of hours each day when her parents trusted her to me.

"You be back for the service?"

"Yes. Yes, I will."

We talk a few more minutes, but I can't find any words that matter, other than to tell Dad and Ginger I love them, and that I love her. After we hang up, I squat on my heels, drop my head in my hands. I'd been off in New York. Colorado. Texas. And Heaven had fallen into one of the rabbit holes the islands are known for: drugs, alcohol, abuse, mental illness, poverty, homelessness. People get seduced by the idea of paradise, by the illusion of beauty, and they fail to see the ugly. Sometimes because they're blind to it. Sometimes because they choose not to. But I'd known it was there. Even as a child, I got my taste of it.

A memory surfaces, powerful and fresh. Heaven, asking me why the Mother Superior punishes girls for being pretty. Showing me the raw flesh in her palm from the ruler strikes. Me holding her, rocking her, and telling her she's done nothing wrong. The old woman thought she could stop the inevitable with her cruelty, maybe she even thought she was doing us all a favor. Lashes with a metal-edged wooden ruler doesn't stop the bloom of youthful allure with its intoxicating scent. After Heaven's tears dry, we make ice cream sundaes and do our homework. I don't think she has anything to worry about from Father Jerome, just the meanness of nuns. I put on glittery white wings from Heaven's Halloween costume and wave a magic wand. I promise her that everything will be all right. She giggles and tells me I'm her guardian angel.

And that had started it. Heaven told her two best friends. Three little girls looking like a Neapolitan sundae of one chocolate-brown head, one white blonde, and one strawberry red, Lailah the chocolate brown. For a while, I'd smart off in algebra or social studies to earn detentions so I could be present and protect Heaven and the others from cruel nuns and unholy acts. And for each day of detention, I'd earned Heaven's grateful hand in mine as we walked home together after I'd been released.

Even knowing what I'd been through, and what Heaven and other girls likely went through, too, I left island to pursue my dreams and adulthood, and she'd never crossed my mind again. Not until that picture nudged my brain back to her.

Why had I not remembered this before? I'm so good at burying the bad stuff. Maybe this is what I am blind to. Maybe I blocked it out on purpose. Maybe it's that I've come so far from glittery white guardian angel wings, to a place in my life where the angel is in a red boa and mermaid-cut dress, flicking an ivory cigarette holder, flashing bedroom eyes rimmed with thick black eyeliner.

But I realize there are others, even with the girls I thought I was guarding dead and gone. There have to be others, just like there were back at St. Mary's. If I don't let this go, if I don't succumb to the inertia of lazy, corrupt island cops who don't care about a few dead prostitutes, then it's possible I can keep them—these others who are surely out there—from ending up dead and gone, too.

It's an enormous thought, almost too heavy to carry. Before I can change my mind, I pull up the last message on my string with Porky, the one from his partner, Babyface. He'd asked: *Why you so interested in dead hookers?*

Now I have a response for him, and I send it: *Because I knew Lailah, and I knew Heaven McAllister very well. I owe them. I can help. Please let me.*

Chen sticks his head out. "Hey! You coming back in?" He takes a closer look at me. "Are you all right?"

I stand, pat my cheeks hard to bring myself back. "Yeah, wow, too many cocktails today. Tired."

I follow him back into the office, my mind half in the present, half in the past.

"I found her." Chen puts a hand on my shoulder. He shows me their selections and explains them quickly. "You did great, Ava."

"Thank you." I slip into creole, a fist on a cocked hip. "My flight at six a.m. If everyone here through with his jollies, how 'bout we wrap this up?"

Jose says, "I think we're done, if Kenny agrees."

Kenny coughs roughly, then his voice is normal again. "Feel like celebrating, Ava?"

I roll my eyes, and Chen and Jose stifle laughs. "Next time." He'll probably be dead from whatever his awful disease is by then, anyway.

"That's okay, I probably couldn't get it up again."

I feign retching to more stifled laughter.

"We'll finish the tracks, and I'll start shopping your package. Unless you want me to wait for you to get an agent."

I look from Jose to Chen. They shrug. I've already waited so long for this. "Nah, go ahead."

"And I'll transfer SeaCoins to your accounts, boys. With a little bonus."

I can't help it. That gets my attention. "You guys use virtual currency?"

Jose and Chen exchange a look, and Chen answers. "Not all the time. But when we work with Poseidon."

Kenny snorts. "Play with the big boys, play by their rules."

When Jose turns to me, his hair sways. "It's cool, kind of like gaming. You point, click, and it's done."

The speakerphone crackles. "It's fucking great, like *Grand Theft Auto*. I like to buy a blow job then cap the bitch so she won't go all *Fatal Attraction* on me."

Jose grimaces. "Uh, I was thinking more *Super Mario*."

I'm thinking *whatever*, and my face must show I'm done with Kenny, because Chen says, "Okay, well, thanks, and I guess we'll sign off."

We end the call. I pack and make my way out after thanks-yous, congratulations, and goodbyes.

Chen runs after me, catches me before I can call for the old-fashioned cage-style elevator. "Hey, I have to tell you something."

Expecting more praise, I muster a smile. "Yes?"

"When we were doing wardrobe, I couldn't help but notice your lump. On your breast. Not that I was looking. It was just right there."

I take a step backward, feeling a familiar girding. "Okay." I punch the down button.

"In case you hadn't noticed it."

"I have."

"Well, then in case you haven't had it checked out."

"I have."

His nervous frown loosens. "Oh, good. My sister had a lump, and her first biopsy, this needle thing, missed the cancer cells. It was pretty advanced by the time they figured it out. She died. Only thirty-five years old. I, well, I just had to say something because of her."

I put my hand on his arm. "Your sister. I'm sorry."

He nods, quick. "Thank you."

The elevator comes, and I get in. It descends, and my stomach plummets with it. My doctor had done a needle biopsy. Is it possible she'd missed something?

There isn't only one way for a former St. Mary's girl to end up dead and gone, after all.

THIRTEEN

MOM AND GINGER meet me outside baggage claim at the airport midday on Wednesday.

"Gah." Ginger coos when I scoop her from Mom's arms and crush her to my shoulder. She's in a navy sailor outfit, dressed for the memorial, as is Mom. As am I, per Mom's instructions last night.

Still no walking, no words. I try not to blame myself, but after how little I've seen her in the last week, it's hard. Maybe if I was around more? Her scent of No More Tears and sweet baby girl mingles with what I suspect is eau de smashed peas and rice with soured milk.

"My sweet Ginger Thomas flower." I lean and hug Mom with one arm.

"How it go?" Mom is elegance and steel femininity in a black linen sheath with a round scalloped neck. Her sandals have square two-inch heels and look older than she does.

I smile, my face pressed into Ginger's hair. "Better than I ever hope, Mommy. Really."

A man walking away from baggage claim catches my attention. He's graying at the temples and looks ready to tackle a Form 1040 and itemize my deductions. It's the damn photographer that followed Zach when he picked me up at Harry's. He avoids eye contact, but I know he's following me. I'm just glad he's not snapping shots of me with my family. Now what I do reflects on Zach, I guess. I wonder if I'm cut out for this crazy life.

Mom unsnaps the clasp on her black vinyl clutch and retrieves keys. "I pray for you, night and day." She looks both ways then crosses the street to the parking lot.

I pull my rolling suitcase with one hand and balance Ginger on my hip with the other. She's twining my hair through her fingers, which is warming me up from the inside out. "Those be the nightmares I having, then."

Mom doesn't even glance back at me, used to my mouth. She clicks her keys, and lights flash and a horn honks on the far side of the next row. We reach her Buick. Dad is in the front seat. He nods and I nod back, my hands full or I'd blow him a kiss. We settle in the car, and I rise and lean over the front seat to buss his cheek. The scent of pot permeates everything around him these days, but it's not too strong today.

"Hi, Daddy. You look handsome."

He does, wearing a sports jacket and pressed navy dress slacks I haven't seen him wear in years. His thick hair is still rakish, though long-since white instead of blond, standing up and flopping to the side.

"Hi, Ava girl." His mischievous blue eyes sparkle and a smile twitches the right side of his mouth upward, gathering creases like shock waves across his cheeks.

Even though I look like Mom, I get my smile and voice from him. If he hadn't raced cars, he could have been one of the Beach Boys, I've always thought. I buckle Ginger into her car seat then retrieve two small items from my purse. "Thank you for keeping Ginger, Mommy and Daddy." I hand Mom a small bottle of Opium, her favorite perfume. Daddy gets smoked salmon, vacuum-sealed.

"I raise you right," Mom says.

Dad holds the package of salmon to his chest and smiles, his eyes floating. I know he's gone a few thousand miles away to New Brunswick, where he grew up.

Mom pulls away from the airport and proceeds five miles per hour under the speed limit, a velocity which leaves her white knuckled, all the way to downtown Taino and St. Joseph Catholic Church. The service today isn't a funeral. It's more of a gathering of mourners who knew Heaven back when. I guess her real funeral will be in the States, wherever her parents are.

My hands are sweating. I hate this place.

The lot is full. Mom drops Dad and Ginger, and we park two blocks away. I get out, tug my stretchy black dress longer, then upward at the neckline.

Mom unlatches the trunk. She retrieves a black cardigan and hands it to me without a word. I slip into it, and it's just long enough to cover my T&A. The Mother Superior would approve.

Thinking of her inevitably makes me think of her partner in crime. "Is Father Jerome on staff these days?" I tense, hoping for a no, I think, but I feel so unsettled I can't be sure.

"Father Jerome pass ten years ago."

"What?" My voice breaks. Now I'm sure. I needed to see the man. I've dreamed for years of confronting him and the Mother Superior, calling them out, demanding apologies for how they treated us. For what they did to us, most especially to what they did to the younger girls. Now I'll never get a chance with him.

"Yah. Poor man. He walk in on a burglar, who cut him up."

"How did I never hear about this?" I subtracted years and realized it was during my NYU days.

"It in all the papers. He mutilated. Very sad."

I don't feel sad, I realize. Just cheated. "What do you mean, mutilated?"

She shakes her head in rapid micromovements, like the thought of elaborating is too horrible to bear, which tells me it was sexual.

And I smile. I cover it up quickly, but I smile, because I'd bet my bana that was no burglar in his house. That was island justice.

"What about the Mother Superior?"

"She around. Retired. I see her at mass."

I decide right then and there to pay her a long overdue visit.

Mom starts walking, and I follow. We make our way back to the church, passing a Rasta man screaming obscenities—Tourette's—and a few homeless women curled up under the shade of the overhang in front of an abandoned building, using their hands for pillows, half-empty plastic grocery bags pressed between their bodies and the wall. Their outfits are skimpy, and with a jolt I think of Lailah and Nevaeh/Heaven. I'm staring, almost swiveling to keep looking at them, and I make myself stop, to not rob them further of their dignity.

Dad is standing inside the gate and Ginger is playing on the sparse front lawn of the church. Several of his cronies are gathered around him. Most of their faces are familiar, road maps of their generation. He's the only white man in the group, as usual. He draws people in with his sly wit and ready laugh, and the black local power structure has always accepted him, which is rare. I'm proud of him.

Other people are hanging around the entrance, too. One gives me pause. It's the damn photographer again, and it's about time to give him a piece of my mind. This is a memorial service, not a see-and-be-seen New York club. But I can't yet, because the old farts with Dad are making a big deal of Mom and me. I let them fawn and tease and compliment, my eyes on my parents.

When they met years ago, Mom—as the newly crowned Miss Bahamas—had presented a car race trophy to Dad. That picture of the two of them hangs in a bi-frame with their wedding portrait. Watching them together, I realize she still gazes at him like the champ and he at her like the prize. She wears the passage of time better than he does, but then, she hasn't spent it working outside. In years past, he would have stepped over and pulled her in under his shoulder. Now, he stands rigidly, but she closes the gap and claims her spot anyway. My chest feels tight and funny.

"Ginger pie, how you doing, sugar?" Katie's voice chimes.

Katie is leaning over, arms out to Ginger. Behind her, Harry stops his chair. Ginger bear-crawls over to Katie, and I get there about the same time.

"Harry."

He wheels forward to me. "Ava. Glad you made it back safely."

"You knew Heaven?"

"Um—"

"Nevaeh, I mean. Did you know her?"

"Not really." I stare at him until he goes on. "She worked for a company that owns clubs. I own a company that works with a company that owns that company."

If he just said something that meant something, it went right past me.

Katie hefts Ginger, swooshing her and making airplane noises. "Whoa, she's getting heavy, Ava."

I turn my attention from Harry. "Twenty pounds."

Katie is dressed for the service, too. A page from my mom's book, or how my mom would have dressed at her age. A black dress with a belted waist and slightly full skirt, scoop neck and short sleeves, little black pumps. Red hair in a French twist. All she needs are elbow-length gloves with lace trim to complete the look.

"How was New York?" Katie plants a smooch on Ginger's cheek. Ginger giggles.

"I feel like a rock star." I smile at Harry.

Katie bounces Ginger. "That good?"

"Better."

Harry grins. "Much better. Kenny said you killed it."

Katie wipes imaginary sweat from her brow. "Phew. You can't imagine how happy and relieved I am to hear that."

I'm sure. "Maybe everything was for the best."

"I'll have twinges of jealousy, I imagine."

"More than that, probably."

Katie throws her head back and laughs, an honest sound. Ginger, intrigued, copies her, and we all laugh.

Mom and Dad interrupt us to greet Katie. Hugs and cheek kisses are exchanged.

When they're done, I say, "Harry, may I introduce you to my parents, Anita and Gill Butler? My boss, Harry Darnell." Harry can't hide his reaction fast enough, and before he can speak, I add, "My dad is white. I've had him since I was born. Yes, it's weird and I consider myself black. Everyone is curious. Best to just get it out of the way so it's not a distraction."

"Well done." Harry laughs. "Very nice to meet the two of you."

"Inside joke," I explain to my curious parents.

They shake hands and start a conversation.

Katie pulls me away by the arm. "How about I take you and Ginger out for dinner after the memorial? For our talk."

There's a long, awkward pause.

"Hello, Ava?" Katie pretend-knocks on my head, down to making a chucking noise with her tongue for each knock.

"Can I ask a favor?"

"You can ask."

"I have somewhere I have to be for a few hours." There's no way I'm telling her I'm meeting Samuel. Guilt sneaks in, but I backhand it away, sharp. I'll spend the whole weekend playing with Ginger. We'll go to the beach. Run in the surf. Fill buckets with sand. Have a picnic. Take a long nap together in the hammock on the porch. "Mom needs a break from Ginger. You keep Ginger, I promise we'll talk when I come for her tonight."

"Well . . ."

I salute crisply. "I swear. Or give my oath. On my honor."

"Okay, but this is important—it's about Samuel. And those three girls."

"Samuel? And what do you mean, 'three girls'? There's nothing in the *Source* about a third girl."

"Someone with a lot of stroke is keeping a lid on it."

"Like Samuel, you're saying?"

"I don't know. But I do know he's been linked to all three of them. There's talk he's a suspect."

"Linked how?"

"They each performed privately for clients he had on-island."

"So, not linked like fingerprints or DNA."

"Well, no, but—"

Which means anyone else present at the "entertainments" had a link, too. "We'll talk." But first I'm going to talk to Samuel. I have my ways of getting information, and if those girls were on the menu for his gangster friends, I'll find out.

"I'm serious, Ava. And worried about you. You can't put this off any longer."

Does she not even know me? I think. But I say, "Yah mon."

KATIE DRIVES GINGER and me back to the duplex. We traipse inside. I drop my bags—one of mine, one of Ginger's—and flip on light switches. Elvis runs up to us like a puppy, but he's all cat, biting my ankles.

The little booger draws blood. "Ow." I swat at him, but he ducks away, running to Ginger.

Ginger coos to him, and he purrs. She pulls his tail, and he doubles back and walks under her arm, giving himself a back scratch.

I hustle into Ginger's room and pack her a bag with a clean outfit, swim togs, fresh pj's, and diapers.

Nana's voice crackles through the house. "Ava, you home?"

I return. Katie is giving Nana a hug. I take my turn. "Hi, Nana. Thanks for taking care of Elvis."

"Yah mon."

She's wearing a cotton work dress, threadbare and permanently darkened at the knees. Her floppy-brimmed hat is snugged under her chin without a wisp of hair to be seen, shading her thin face. She's barefoot—which is not unusual for her—and her feet are worn smooth and white from working outside.

I dig in my luggage, retrieve a gift bag. "For you." I hand it to her.

She peeks inside, pulls out a layer of tissue, which she sets on the table with the bag beside it. She smooths and folds the tissue in quarters first, then digs in for her gift like she digs in the dirt in her tubs. She pulls out a white ceramic bell with a picture of the Statue of Liberty and the Twin Towers in the skyline behind it. I know she's been wanting one with the fallen towers.

She rings it, holding it up by her ear to hear the little tinkling sound. She grunts, smiles. "My peace. This a fine bell."

"I'm glad you like it." I turn to Katie. "Here's Ginger's bag."

Katie accepts it, deftly throwing it on her shoulder as she leans over, one leg up like a counterweight, and scoops Ginger into the crook of one arm. "Don't be so late we can't talk."

"I won't." I give Ginger an Eskimo kiss. "Bye Ginger Thomas flower."

Katie heads for the door and I follow them out. Ginger blows me smooches with her fingers so straight they're curved outward at the tips, kissing her palm and flinging her arm, then catching mine and planting them on her cheek. We play the game until Katie's Montero disappears at the end of my drive.

It hits me for the first time that she didn't know Heaven. Why had she been at the memorial? I'll ask when I see her later.

I close my eyes. The service hangs on me, a lead weight hooked into my heart. Heaven's face imprints on my mind. Nevaeh. Heaven. At Ginger's age, blonde wispy hair and big blue eyes. As a toddler, with bruises and pigtails. In grade school, donning the same plaid I'd worn, her hair now in a bob, her eyes blue and bright. I'd babysat her after I got out of school, from sixth grade until I was sixteen, and known her since her birth. What had gone wrong in her life that she'd ended up dancing nude and prostituting herself? But I know the answer to that question. Or suspect I do. I force my eyes open, dislodging the image of a nine-year-old Heaven with braces on her teeth, who looks so different from the photographs of grown-up Nevaeh.

My date with Samuel will help remove the clinging weight of death and unwanted memories from me. Katie's warning still rings in my ears, but I'm not scared of Samuel. I don't like that he's under suspicion, but I'm sure I'd get a bad vibe if he was up to no good. The tie to the girls just means he may have something I want besides a way to scratch my itch. Information about Heaven and Lailah, and maybe this third girl.

As I reenter the living room, Nana scares me out of my skin when she speaks. "You pushin' Ginger off already so's you can get you some feel good with the charcoal man?" She's sitting at the table, partially in shadows.

I squawk. "I forgot you here, Nana."

"Well?"

"Samuel. His name is Samuel." And he is rather dark-skinned. "Where you hear 'bout him?"

"Bush got ears." She gets to her feet, slowly, leaning her weight on the table through her palms.

"I, uh,—"

"I hate seeing you an outside woman."

"But he not married."

She harrumphs, shuffling away from her chair. "It the nature of a pussman."

I rub my palm on my breastbone, thinking. I remember the lipstick on the cigarette I found on Samuel's patio. The blow to his head when we were en flagrante delicto. The evidence does suggest that Samuel has other women in his life. Maybe even Heaven or one of the other dancers. But so what? I have other men. It doesn't really matter to me. Maybe it mattered more in Nana's day.

"Stop you going on," I say. "We just breezin'. No bacchanal and no bullin'."

I remove Mom's cardigan, fold it, lay it on the table. I notice Nana has tucked the tissue and bell back in her bag, which she slips over her wrist by its string.

"All right, all right, all right." She walks out, bag swinging.

"Good afternoon, Nana. Thanks again."

"Good afternoon." The screen door slams behind her and she disappears in the direction of her front door.

Trust Nana not to mince words. She tends to leave me feeling unsettled. More unsettled in this case.

I strip out of my black dress and panties, tossing them toward my bedroom with my toe. They fall short by six feet. I twist my hair up to keep it dry and jump into a quick shower in my little underwater bathroom. It has Caribbean blue walls with embedded seashells that I arranged in a Nautilus pattern. It's the symbol of multiplicity in creation from Hindu mythology, and a perfect example of elegance in nature, and I did it all myself. It's my favorite room in my house, even if it is tiny.

I'm careful not to disturb my makeup. When I'm out, I brush my teeth, rub coconut oil all over, and spritz perfume on my pulse points: wrists, above the slit of my buttocks, at the top of my inner thighs, behind my knees, at the back of my neck, and between my breasts. I touch up my makeup and release my hair, fluffing it. It still looks good from Chen's trim and styling yesterday, if a little wilder and sexier than I'd normally trouble myself to do. He'd ruined my manicure, but I'd repaired it last night. I add dangling gold hoops and march nude back to my bedroom, picking up my discarded clothing and dropping it in the dirty clothes.

I decide on a pair of denim hot pants, a white wraparound halter top, and espadrilles. Sexy, not slutty, so I won't look like something on or off the menu.

A thought stops me. I haven't heard back from Porky. Or, for that matter, Babyface. I could drop in on them this afternoon, let them know that I'm going to hound them until they find whoever is killing these women. What's one more afternoon, though? I decide I'll do it in the morning on the way to work. Like my conversation with Katie tonight, I won't put it off any further. I stand in front of my bedroom mirror, two fingers up like the Girl Scout I never was. "I swear," I tell myself.

I grab my purse and a bottle of merlot, and bolt for the Range Rover before another wave of guilt sidelines me. I plug my phone in to charge, and see "Bombshell" saved to my desktop. I route it through the Rover's stereo and crank it all the way up. It begins to work on my mood, empowering me, emboldening me, enlivening me. I am not a bad mother. I am not a bad person. I will visit Samuel, keep it short, pick up Ginger, talk with Katie, and crank up my crusade tomorrow.

I decide not to text Samuel to confirm I'm on my way. He showed up unannounced in New York. I'm expected; he just doesn't know the exact time. The drive is short—ten minutes—and when I reach the grounds of his estate, I turn off the car and lean my seat back. I'm nervous, I'm sober. I pull an unmarked vial from my purse, rolling it between my fingers to warm it. It's my homebrew, all-natural stimulating concoction: borage seed oil, evening primrose oil, angelica root extract, coleus extract, and ground "herbs" from Nana's tubs.

I squirt a dab on my finger, slip it up the leg of my short shorts, and under my panties. I tease my dry lips apart, protecting the feel-good potion until I reach the right spot. I stroke it onto myself, not for the feel of my fingers, but for the transfer of the joy juice. Just enough to get the party started. The stuff is gold, so I cap it and stow it back in a zippered pocket carefully. I'm already feeling warmer in the desired location, and that relaxes the rest of me. I sigh, releasing more tension.

I make my way to his big front door and knock. No answer, but his spiffy car is in the drive, in front of the Rover. I try the doorknob and find it unlocked, which is normal in the islands. I open the door, stick my head in. "Samuel? You here? It's Ava."

He doesn't answer, but the sound of water running is coming from the direction of his bedroom. Aha, he's in the shower. I let myself in, and see red rose petals so thick they make a carpet that starts at the front door and turns down the hall toward the master suite. What's more, the air conditioner is cranked so high I almost see frost in my breath.

The man shows a capacity for learning. I'm a little relieved after all. Nothing sinister here. Just a straight-up, full-on seduction scene.

I bite the inside of my lip. Since he's still in the shower, I have time to make a side trip to the kitchen. There, I rummage until I find wineglasses. They're fine, like real crystal. I flip one and read BACCARAT on the base.

"Shit. Be careful, girl."

I don't have to snoop to find the wine opener because it's right out on the counter, one of those clamp kind on a standing black granite vase. It's sleek and modern. I pour the wine. The liquid glugs into the glasses. It sounds gauche and overly loud in the quiet. I want to wrap my hands around the flow to muffle it.

I freshen my lipstick one last time, grasp a stem in each hand, and leave the kitchen. Each step feels great now that my DIY love potion has had five minutes to work its magic. My espadrilles are silent on the tile, crushing rose petals with each step. My smile grows as I get closer to the sound of his shower. There's easily five dozen roses out here, scattered petal by petal on the floor, and a gorgeous naked man behind the door in front of me. If the flowers are any indication, he's ready to try hard. Real hard.

I push the half-closed door open with a toe. Loud enough for him to hear me over the water, I say, "All this for me?"

Inside the room are twice as many petals as in the hallway. Samuel has done more than buy a street vendor cart's worth. He's bought up every rose on this island. Candles flicker on the floating side tables. On one satin pillowcase lies a single flower with white petals and filament-thin stamens with gold filigree tips. I've only seen them in pictures, and I smile. Myrtle. The flower of Venus, a potent aphrodisiac, and an ancient name for the clitoris. And who says a classics education isn't valuable? Steam softens the air from the direction of the bathroom. He has some kind of greenish-gold light thing going on around his headboard. The effect is very exotic.

He's putting on a performance worthy of a return engagement and we haven't even started yet. There's no music, so I start to hum the opening to "Bombshell." The feel-good mixes with my own wetness, and a tingle spreads down my thighs to my toes, up my belly, my breasts, my neck, and flushes into my face. For a split second I teeter on the edge of a decision: strip and join him, or tease him from the doorway?

Easy answer. I'm always the tease.

I take a deep breath, straighten my shoulders and lift my girls, and lean around the bathroom door, planting my back against it and lifting one leg in a pinup pose. Then I look in the shower.

My scream shatters the glasses in my hands. I'm falling, falling, falling, and everything hurts. I pick myself up off the slippery floor. There's red everywhere. *Merlot*, I think. Yes, but blood, too. I've fallen into the shards of crystal, and they're embedded in my knees and palms. My white halter top is streaked and splashed.

I scream again as I walk, a big shard of Baccarat sticking out of my knee. I ignore it, trying not to fall again as I make my way to the shower. It's not just my blood now. There's far too much of it. The shower door is partway open and the interior mostly steamed, but it isn't enough to keep me from seeing what flattened me a moment ago: a trail of blood, bloody streaks on the glass, and a large body on the floor, one foot out. My eyes dart around me, looking for someone else, someone who could have done this, but the only thing they find is a blurry image of me in the fogged-over mirror.

I think about my purse. The mace. In the kitchen. No, at home. I hadn't returned it to its proper place yet, post-New York trip. I have nothing, just myself, and an enormous dread of who or what's in that shower.

"Samuel?" I gasp, opening the shower door the rest of the way.

Maybe it's not him. Maybe it's a stranger. Maybe even now he's down at the police station reporting an intruder. Maybe this is the person who assaulted him last weekend.

Or maybe it's the third girl. Oh, Venus, Zeus, and all the gods above, don't let it be a young woman.

It's not.

Samuel lies crumpled, a stream of his blood mixing with the water and circling with his life down the drain. He's lying facedown, and I scramble in, forgetting my own pain.

"Samuel, can you hear me? Samuel?"

I'm fighting déjà vu of the most terrible kind. It seems like only yesterday, even though it was several years ago, that I found the slashed and bloody body of Guy Edwards. *I was the outside woman*, I think, remembering Nana's words.

I reach for Samuel's wrist to search for a pulse. Nothing. More déjà vu, this time of Lailah. I'm no doctor, I don't trust myself, so I feel for his carotid. I find blood and open flesh. I probe and realize my fingers are inside his throat.

I scramble back, falling over on my bana, and then my head hits the step at the mouth of the shower. Roman candles explode before my eyes, then blackness.

FOURTEEN

THERE ARE people all around me when I wake up, close-in, crowding me. The shower's no longer running. The faces and bodies come into focus. Police officers. Emergency medical techs. Other people doing official things, I don't know what, gathering evidence? Piecing Samuel back together? My head clears a little and my field of vision widens.

Samuel is still beside me.

"No, no, no, no, no." I'm keening, frantic, and I struggle to get up.

A hand on my shoulder presses me back down. A woman in a tailored uniform shirt with official patches on it is kneeling over me. It's her hand restraining me, and I fight panic. I see spots, my chest tightens, and my breaths become short and shallow.

"You've had a bad fall, and you're cut up. Give me a second and I'll get you out of here."

"Your hand. My shoulder. I'm feeling claustrophobic." My heart tries to batter its way out of my chest, to escape like I want to.

She lifts it. "Sorry, miss. I'll keep it off you if you'll just stay down a moment."

"But Samuel, right there, he's dead. Samuel." My voice trails off. I stop fighting. My breathing eases. Samuel is dead. I had found him. I hadn't gotten to ask him about the girls. If he knew something, it's gone now.

"I understand ma'am. I'll hurry."

"I'm cold," I whisper.

She nods but doesn't answer. Her hands move quickly. I feel a sharp pain in my knee. I ignore it. I turn my eyes to her face. Crow's-feet in cocoa skin, coal-black eyes, and thick lashes curled tight. Her lips pressed together. No makeup. Hair as short as I wore mine in my twenties, which is to say she has almost none.

Two men maneuver a stretcher through the bathroom door. "We're ready for her."

The woman says, "We're going to lift you out of here, then we'll get you to the hospital."

Terrified, I shout, "No hospital."

"Ma'am, you need stitches."

I start to sit again. Has this woman never been in a St. Marcos hospital? I'm not dead. I don't want to be dead. "NO. HOSPITAL."

The woman glances at the two men, one dark, one more Hispanic-looking, both young. They lift shoulders, say nothing.

"Fine," she says, "but we have to get you safely out of this bathroom. I'll patch you up outside. There's a lot of glass in here, and it's very slippery."

The woman backs out of the shower. One of the men steps over me. Someone grabs me by the shoulders as the stretcher slides under my head. The man who entered the shower lifts me under my knees. He's the one who says, "This may hurt a little, but we'll move fast."

Both things are true. They have me on a sling-type stretcher, and they lift it, one on each end—I can see the Hispanic guy at my head now—and carry me into the hallway. They transfer me to a wheeled stretcher, then roll me into the great room. The woman reappears at my side. When they've set the wheel brakes, the two men leave without another word.

"Thank you," she calls after them. To me, she says, "Okay, let's see what we've got here." She has some kind of kit or bag with her, but she sets it on the couch and the stretcher is too high for me to see it.

Behind her, a man appears, his face in shadow, late-afternoon sun streaming in the entrance door behind him. *Air conditioner*, I think. *Someone needs to shut it off or shut the door.*

To the EMT, he says, "A word with the patient, please." His voice is authoritative.

"Are you okay to talk to the police?" she asks me.

"Yes."

"Alone," he says.

I see her eyes narrow, but I'm not dying and Samuel already has. She doesn't argue. "Please let me know when you're done so I can resume her care."

He doesn't acknowledge her as she walks away. He moves closer to me, and his face slips into light.

"You." I recognize him. It's the photographer from New York. I prop myself up on one arm, put the other over my face. "No pictures. This has nothing to do with Zach. No pictures!"

"I'm not here to take your picture." He's wearing a Hawaiian shirt instead of bean-counter clothes.

In a flash, I know I've seen him several times, in different outfits, hats, and glasses, even before Zach. I've always had a gift for faces, even if this man dresses to be a chameleon.

"You weren't following Zach."

"No."

I'm confused and at a tremendous disadvantage after hitting my head. I sit the rest of the way up. The room spins, and I feel nauseous. "You've been following me. Here. In New York. Now. Before."

"We need to take a drive."

I point at my legs. "I'm hurt." And don't want to go with him, but I don't say that.

He looks down, picks something out of the EMTs bag, and before I can say a word in protest, he leans over and tweezes. It hurts. A lot.

"Hey!"

He keeps scanning the surface of my skin. Tweezes again.

"Are you a doctor?"

He ignores me. After a few more tweezes, he says, "Anywhere else?"

I hold up my palms.

He works them over, raises my arms, inspects them, and takes something out of one elbow. He quirks an eyebrow. "Okay?"

I nod.

He digs in the bag on the couch again and comes up with hydrogen peroxide and gauze, both of which he uses liberally. It stings like a jack spaniel wasp. Next he slathers on antibiotic cream. "No, I'm not a doctor."

"I figured that out."

"Let's go." He gives my elbow a tug.

It hurts. "Show me a badge."

"When we get outside."

"Uh-uh."

"It's in my car."

I cross my arms, realizing my white top with no bra underneath it is sopping with water, wine, and blood. I'm just a few bread crumbs short of profaning the holy sacrament.

"I not going anywhere with a stranger." Stranger comes out "strain-JUH" in my irritation. "And I'm freezing my ass off."

"You're a suspect in a murder investigation."

"Suspect? I'm a witness."

"You think?"

"I did nothing. Nothing."

Looking bored, he says, "You were found with the broken glass and victim whose throat was slashed with it, his blood all over you."

Voices audible from a few rooms away reach me. They're talking about Samuel, and about . . . me.

I hear one of them say, "Ain't she the one murder Senator Guy Edwards awhile back and get away with it?"

Several people chuptz.

A female voice says, "Pretty convenient her men dem keep winding up dead."

More chuptzes.

A man says, "True dat, mon."

My chest is tightening again. "That's crazy talk. They're worthless," I say, worthless coming out "WUT-liss" as I lapse into a strained blend of yank and island patois.

"Maybe. But things will get really unpleasant if I leave you here with them." Hawaiian-shirt guy pauses. "Unless that's what you want."

I ignore the last part. It's just rude. But I'm convinced that listening to him outside may be in my best interest. I swing my legs over and stand, wobbling a little.

"Oh no, no, no," the female EMT says from the kitchen, where she's holding her cell phone against her chest, like she's pausing a conversation.

I wave her off. "I'm fine. Really. I'll go to my own doctor tomorrow."

She presses a button on her phone and scurries over. In a soft voice she says, "Have them take a look at that lump on your breast while you're there."

I feel a stab in my gut. "Yes," I say. "Thank you."

Hawaiian-shirt guy watches us, impassive.

"My purse." I hobble painfully to the kitchen for it then follow him to the front door.

Porky and Babyface are entering as we exit. Behind them, a rooster struts across Samuel's front yard, a bevy of chickens pecking their way along behind him.

"Bachoo, Winslow," Hawaiian-shirt guy says.

Porky grunts. "Where you taking our witness?"

Hawaiian-shirt guy shakes his head. "My witness now. I'll give you a copy of her statement."

Porky holds up a hand, moves closer. "This a murder investigation."

Babyface puts his hand on his gun, his voice dripping with attitude. "We got a right to question her, Galindo. She may be a suspect."

Galindo smiles. "Only if the FBI says so."

FIFTEEN

"SPECIAL AGENT GALINDO, FBI." Those are his first words, and we've been driving for five minutes.

I've turned the heater on, but my teeth are still chattering—from fear and the cold—and my arms are tight across my chest. "Can I get a sweater or a dry shirt?"

Without answering, he turns his dark sedan left at the next corner. "Samuel worked for us. The FBI."

His words hit me like a sledgehammer to my already tender head. But Samuel was a businessman from South Carolina. I turn to Galindo, fierce. "Show me your badge."

He points to the glove box in front of me. "It's in there."

I pop the door, and a leather badge holder falls onto the inside of it. I pick it up, flip it open. The badge is intimidating, gold with the letters FBI across the center. His ID card is above it. Department of Investigations. Special Agent John Galindo. It looks authentic enough, but I don't know if it's real. Porky didn't dispute he was FBI, though.

My head is a bowl of spaghetti, limp, useless, and tangled. I'm out of my depth. "Can I call someone?" I'm thinking Collin, if he'd pick up. Or Nick and Katie. This is their element. They'll know what to do.

"You need to listen to me first. Because my offer won't be good after."

"Your *offer*?"

"The offer to keep you out of jail for Samuel's murder."

"I didn't kill him." My voice is shrill and I twist toward him. The seat belt cuts into my shoulder.

"Says no one but you. You heard the police. I'm not so sure you didn't do it, myself. But I can make that go away."

Galindo turns onto a dirt road. My dirt road. We're headed to my house, and he didn't ask for an address or directions. I feel seasick, like the ground is heaving under us. He stops in front of my door.

"How? How can you make it go away?" My voice is shakier than Nana's. I'm close to losing my shit completely.

"Samuel was undercover. We need somebody in Mahogany Management. We need you."

My jaw drops. "You want me to work for the FBI undercover?"

He nods, curt. "Go get a shirt. You've got five minutes to change and come back with your answer."

I get out and slam the door. Walking hurts. I will my brain to function and head straight for the bathroom. Elvis is all over me while I inspect the damage. I look a wreck. The goop Galindo used on my wounds is staunching blood flow, but I cover a few of the worst cuts with Band-Aids and pop four ibuprofen.

I stare into my eyes in the mirror. Samuel is dead. Someone murdered him. I found him. The police are set to blame me. Samuel worked for the FBI. The FBI wants me to work for them, and promises to keep me from taking the fall for Samuel's death if I do. Implied: that Galindo will make sure I am a suspect if I don't. Which is blackmail, and the anger in me builds along with the questions. What *exactly* do they want me to do? What *exactly* did Samuel do?

It seems like working undercover is a good way to get killed, and I don't feel like dying. But I also don't want to go to jail. Just being charged before nearly ruined my parents financially. It was terrifying, and I only escaped conviction because Katie and I figured out the real killer. My reputation was left in tatters.

And I have Ginger to think of now.

A horn honks. My eyes are burning. I take out my contacts then run to my bedroom, grab a bra, dry underwear, a pair of short multicolored yoga pants, white Keds knockoffs, and a large white T-shirt. I change quickly, shrugging Elvis off me several times.

"I'm sorry." I dump some food in his bowl, and that placates him.

I grab my glasses from the bedside table before I trot to the car. It's not my signature look, but that fits, because I know when I get back in that car I will become whatever person Galindo tells me to be.

GALINDO DRIVES me back to Samuel's at dusk. The crime scene is still buzzing with activity, but no one pays us any notice. Galindo parks his sedan and leaves the motor running. It reeks of aged KFC from the bags of half-eaten chicken on the seat between us. At least he got me food. At least he's using the air conditioner. At least he hasn't burned me with cigarettes. I'm a Stockholm-syndrome case in the making.

Galindo says, "I called Bachoo and Winslow while we were at your house. I told them you were under surveillance and vouched for you. They agreed to accept the statement you gave me."

It's hard to believe they'd roll over with no questions, like what the surveillance is about or what he saw. But I let it go. I'm bushed.

I stare out the window at the twilight view of the Caribbean Sea. The blues are dark and merging colors rapidly. "You really have no idea who was here before me?"

"How could I? I was following you. Honestly, I don't even know if there was anyone here before you."

I cut my eyes at him. "How convenient."

A stretcher rolls out the front door of the house, an EMT at either end, one pushing, one guiding. It's a large body, covered crown to sole with a sheet. One big black hand hangs off the side of the stretcher. Samuel. I hate the thought of him spending hours naked, broken, bloody, with bright lights and a small room full of people working on and around him. The EMTs load the stretcher into the waiting ambulance, close the back doors, then take their seats. The emergency vehicle leaves. No flashing lights, no sirens. Nothing that gives a clue to its cargo or the violent scene it's leaving behind.

"So you know how to activate the wire." Galindo's tone is hard, yanking my leash to direct my attention back to him. There's no good cop in his repertoire.

I hold up the ballpoint pen that doesn't write. "I click the push button." I demonstrate. "If the point's showing, it's on. I click it again to turn it off."

"And what are you going to record?"

"Conversations with anyone related to M-Squared. Mahogany Management, I mean."

He'll hear the audio through a wireless connection and capture it to the great cloud drive in the sky. And I'm not having sex again until this is over, just in case of accidental activation.

"Record as often as you can. If you get into trouble, we'll get there as fast as we can, although you signed a release." He hands me a baggie of packaged batteries. "Change these out every day."

The Feds and about half the agencies in the federal government suspect M-Squared is laundering illegally obtained money of their own or of their clients or other users of Amphy and SeaCoins. Earlier, Galindo had rattled off a list of agencies from the IRS to the SEC to the DOJ, ATF, FCC, and all the letters of the keyboard. Their problem is they don't *know* anything: what kind of illegal activities (although he gives me examples of possibilities: drugs, gun sales, human trafficking, prostitution, and fraud, to name a few), when, or who's involved, if anyone. But to them it's a foregone conclusion. A person (Harry, in this case) doesn't move to the islands and set up a virtual currency system if he's honest. Guilty until proven innocent, only they want me to hand them evidence of guilt.

I am so out of my element. My ring feels tight, and I twist it. My fingers are swollen.

He makes me recite my other tasks, again. Look for ways to see Amphy users, transactions, and details. Develop relationships with Harry and those who work closest to the numbers (i.e., the people in the Odd Pod). Copy files. Take pictures. Record conversations.

"Understand?" he asks, when I'm through.

"No."

He raises a bushy eyebrow, apparently too disgusted to use his voice.

"How could Samuel tell me Harry is Man of the Year material if he was trying to prove he wasn't?"

"Undercover, remember?"

He seems sincere about it. Amused that anyone would think otherwise. But whatever. "He was trained for it. I'm not."

"But you're already inside, and you're local. He wasn't."

I remember Samuel's prospective client presentation earlier in the week, and his nasty clients last week, the "not choirboys" who reminded me of gangsters. "Wait a minute. Samuel was drumming up undesirable business partners for M-Squared, right?"

"Yeah, so?"

"So isn't that entrapment?"

"Not without coercion or fraud."

I'm no lawyer, so I can't argue the legal points with him, but—not that I'd admit this to just anyone—I watch enough of Zach's *CSI* episodes that I don't like Galindo's answer. "Even if it's the FBI's idea and they convince him to do something illegal?"

He sees through me. "This isn't TV, Ava."

But it isn't right, either.

He pulls out a sheet of paper I signed earlier and waves it. "I keep the St. Marcos detectives off you as a suspect as long as you produce for me. You check in daily, you produce results. If I don't get them, I turn you over to the police any time I want. And give them motive, means, opportunity . . . and a witness."

"You don't have a witness."

"Don't I?"

I stare at my knees, feeling them tremble. I hate this man. I hate what he's forcing me to do. That he's trapping me and making it hard for me to breathe. That I'm so scared. "I can't guarantee anything. All I can do is my best."

"You're an actress, I hear. That's all this is, acting."

Easy for him to say. "If that's all, why is Samuel dead?" Seconds tick by, uncomfortably. When I can't stand it anymore, I say, "So, you're undercover, too?"

"Yes."

I snort. "Only a Statesider would think the way to go undercover in the islands is to wear a Hawaiian shirt and drive around in a dark new sedan. You look like you've been fired from *Hawaii Five-0*."

His eyes look offended. "I'm a tourist."

"Uh-huh." I gather up my purse and put my hand on the door handle. "Can I go now?"

"Yes, but remember we're monitoring you and have a GPS tracker on your vehicle. If you don't record when you should, I'll know it. If you don't make attempts to do the other things we've talked about, I'll know it. I'll know everything you do, before you do it."

This is *Twilight Zone* stuff, and I don't know who to trust. I wonder if they have me bugged, and if there are more Feds in M-Squared, but I know he won't tell me if I ask. I let myself out, feeling conspicuous, and walk to the Rover.

Before I can get in it, Galindo shouts after me. "Do you carry a gun?"

"I hate guns."

He shrugs. "Your call."

Damn right it is. I don't need someone incapacitating me or worse with my own weapon. I get in the Rover and start it. It hums to life and I slip away without anyone trying to stop me. No matter what Galindo says, I'm sure the local po-po will be on me likes flies on a rotten mango soon. Unless he's paying them all off individually, someone will break ranks and harass me.

I turn the car west, toward Estate Annalise, my daughter, and Katie, and try to think of which cops I've pissed off lately and which will stand by me. I've rebuffed advances from half the force, without respect to gender. It's a given that most of the women hate me on principle. Some officers hold a grudge that I wasn't convicted of killing Guy. I suspect the rest will rally around their brothers and sisters in blue. And with the Jacoby brothers dead, I've got no friendlies on the inside.

Come to think of it, I've got no one on the outside, either.

I BOUNCE DOWN CENTERLINE ROAD, awash in memories and self-pity. Before, when I was charged with Guy's murder, I felt alone, but I could talk to my attorneys, Katie and my parents' friend Duke Ellis. Rashidi. Jacoby, eventually, once he figured out I was innocent. My parents.

This time, I'm alone. The irony isn't lost on me. The woman who always runs off, RNOs her messages, bags out. And in this, no matter how badly I want to talk to someone, I can't. Not for support or for guidance, even though the man who is in love with me is a cop, his sister—my best friend—and her husband are investigators, and my old boyfriend plays a cop on TV (which has to count for something).

How did I end up like this?

After a few hairpin turns, I catch air on a speed bump as I rocket through a shanty town and past the cement plant, then start the uphill climb. Darkness swallows the Rover and me whole. No moon, no streetlights. I roll down the windows so I can rely on more than my eyes. I've been driving, straining, for about five minutes, when I round a curve, and a piece-of-crap Coupe DeVille darts out across the roadway, its chassis rocking as the driver slams its brakes, blocking my path.

No, no, no. Land pirates.

I've always been safe in my local junkers, and I've never driven M-Squared's fancy Rover up in the isolated rainforest at night before. Forewarned is forearmed, though, and I'm not stopping for anyone or anything.

I accelerate, thinking I can squeeze through behind the Coupe, on the right, which is the opposite side of the road from me. I try to take a deep breath and come up empty. Stars crowd the edges of my vision. My heart bangs in my ears. For a split second, I ponder what lies hidden in the vegetation: culverts, stone ruins, or dead falls. It's not going to be fun if I hit one of them head-on. I swerve, hard to the right, then jerk the wheel back to the left. The Rover tilts, and I'm sure it's going to roll, but the expensive suspension proves its worth. It grips the road, and I bust through branches, grazing the bumper of the Coupe.

I catch a glimpse of red. Backing lights. The driver has thrown it in reverse, but he's too late. I'm clear. I gasp for a breath, then another, and another. The stars vanish.

Take that, sucker. I stab the air with my middle finger. It's dark—he can't see me, but I feel better.

I steer back to the left. He won't be working alone. Maybe there was just another dread-headed thug in the car with him, but there could be someone laying a trap ahead. Or his second might have been in the bushes. I think of mowing a pirate down and it makes me smile. Yeah, I'm losing it. I need to just focus on productive breathing and trying not to pant, as I navigate the curves as fast as the Rover and I can take them.

I'm approaching the road to Estate Annalise. I don't signal or tap my brakes, not wanting to help anyone who might be following with their lights off. For now, there's nothing between the Rover and our turn. At the last second, I brake and turn sharply to the right. The surface is asphalt but it's covered in dust, and the Rover slides to the far left side of the road before regaining traction. Almost immediately, the roadbed becomes gravel. Rocks ping like gunshots, fraying my nerves further, and I flinch and jerk. I correct back to the middle. I just need to put a few turns between the main road and me. The bandits don't usually target the less-trafficked roads, like this one. But still.

My pulse roars in my ears, and they're hot as fire. I want to clap ice over my ears, and I promise myself that as soon as I get to Katie's I'll at least splash cold water on them. Until then, I can't do anything but drive like my dad would. I know this road by heart—the S curves, the overhanging trees, the potholes, the junkyard dogs guarding houses. I am aggressive, reckless. I count down the switchbacks. Suddenly, there's a car on my left facing me, with no lights on. I veer to the right, realizing as I do that the car belongs with a house at the end of a jungle-like path that starts nearby.

I'm past it. I wipe sweat from my eyes. I gather my hair in one hand and fan my neck. I only look away for a second, just a dashboard check, but when my eyes return to the road, headlights are bearing down straight at me.

"No!" I shout.

I pray the driver is local, and swerve left back to my side of the road. If this is a tourist, we'll meet head on, as most everyone reverts to habit in driving emergencies. My luck holds. The driver of the pickup honks at me in the typical island greeting as it passes by.

Two more turns to go. I make a bouncing left onto an unnamed lane leading to the Estate Annalise entrance. Inky outlines of flamboyant branches crisscross the road overhead. The headlights freeze their orange blossoms. The lowest hanging fronds scrape across the roof, raining fireworks of flowers onto the windshield. I can smell them through the open windows, as well as the dust I'm stirring up driving so fast. Despite my best efforts, I hit a pothole so hard my head knocks against the steering wheel, just like it did a week ago in Dad's truck. My forehead remembers the pain, and I know I'll have a wicked headache tomorrow.

The Rover stalls from the impact. In the quiet left behind by the Rover's engine, the noises outside are deafening. Coqui frogs screech, bats shriek, and the birds sing their eerie night songs—*kikidoo-kikidoo-kikidoo*—like a horror movie soundtrack. The vehicle's electrical system is still working with the key turned on, so I roll the windows up, but it's like slow-mo.

"Come on, come on," I beg, expecting an arm to shoot in and choke me or slice open my throat.

Finally, they're up. I hit the locks. Sweat rolls down my face. My eyes struggle against the darkness, and I'm conscious that my peripheral vision has been stripped away. A tiny island deer leaps into my headlights. I scream, and my hand flies to my chest. The deer nibbles something, then walks off, taking her time. I spend long seconds motionless, just breathing and trying to get control of my pulse and brain.

When I feel calmer, I put the car in park, turn the key off, pause and count to three, then twist the ignition back on. The Rover roars to life like nothing happened, blasting cold air in my face.

I close my eyes and swallow. I ease down the pitch-black,

overgrown lane. At the gate, I punch the numbers for the code. I drive in, down and around the sweeping turn, half-expecting to see the Headless Horseman galloping through the spooky trees, although I know this is nothing but a harmless orchard around me, at least by day. Even with the windows up, the scent is pungent with its overripe fruit and rot. I accelerate to get away from it. The Rover fishtails. I round the last curve, and there's the house, lying ahead in the darkness, save for one light on the driveway.

"No," I shout.

I hadn't imagined they wouldn't be home.

I park as headlights from behind me sweep across the yard and pin me in their beams.

SIXTEEN

I WHIRL, trying to see the approaching car, but I can't identify it in the glare of its lights. It could be the pirates. It might be Samuel's killer or my FBI minder. Or most likely, Nick and Katie.

But I don't stick around to find out. I have a key to the front door. My un-Ava-like outfit makes it easier to run, and I sprint toward the porch steps. Halfway there, I trip over something hard and scratchy, landing on it like a bag of cement. For a moment, I'm confused, but then I remember that the Kovacs planted baby palm trees. I pick myself up, but discover I've dropped my keys and my glasses have flown off. I crouch and feel around on the ground but can't find either.

"Son of a motherless goat!" I scream. I don't know what to do next. Run and hide? Bad idea in that bush. Just the thought of diving into the thick, scratchy darkness raises a silent scream inside me. Return to the car for my phone so I can use its flashlight? But if I do, whoever is coming up the drive will be on me before I can escape. But something changes before I make up my mind.

I feel her.

It's a warmth, an energy I've experienced before. But, while I've sensed her presence, I've never glimpsed the jumbie Annalise. Sure, Katie has told me all about her, but that's different than seeing her with your own eyes. And I do. I see her, right in front of me, standing in front of the door to the house. She's a lovely young woman, dead since the seventeen hundreds, yet undoubtedly here, right now. Annalise. And I can really see her, even without my glasses or contacts.

"Oh," I whisper. She's beautiful, as dark as the night, with a headscarf covering her hair, her feet bare, white blouse tucked in a plaid skirt that skims her ankles. I want to stop and drink her in, to marvel at this moment, but I don't have time.

She's waving someone toward her, and I look behind me. She's Katie's jumbie, not mine. Or maybe she's more Taylor's these days. Regardless, neither of them are here, so at first I can't believe she's motioning to me, but she is. Her mouth moves, but I hear no sound. I try to read her lips.

"Come," she urges. Or at least I think that's what she's saying. "Hurry."

I rise and discover a reserve of speed I never knew I had. I'd passed on soccer and track in high school, and sex is about the most exercise I take. I'm way out of breath as I reach the top of the steps. *I should work out. I should drink less. Just say no to reefer.* My thoughts are buckshot, random, unhelpful. I'm out of control, and when I hit the porch, I barrel into Annalise. A cold shiver and the scent of cinnamon and vanilla engulfs me, and then I'm warm again on the other side of her, which freaks me the hell out, and I yelp.

The door, closed a moment before, is wide open.

I don't need an engraved invitation. I duck inside, slam the heavy door behind me. There's about five million doors and windows in this damn place, and no time to check any of them. I throw the deadbolt to the front door anyway, the little Dutch boy with my finger in the dyke.

I leave the lights off. I'd lived here for months a few years ago, and I know every nook and cranny of this place by heart. Hands out in front of me, I make my way down the hallway between the great room and dining room to the kitchen by feel, staying out of direct line of sight to the driveway, but trying to keep the car in view from different windows and angles. It's gray or silver. Small in a tin-box sort of way. An old Saturn or something. A short figure with dark hair climbs out.

I curse myself for taking out my contacts. Man or woman? I can't tell. The person steps out of the bright light and into its shadowy edge, body leaning forward, shoulders bowed like a miniature ox pulling a cart.

The doorbell rings. It's a civilized sound, and I'm struck by my vanity. I've been assuming whoever-it-is out there is here for me. Four adults live in this house, plus a toddler and two babies Ginger's age. The person could be here for any of them, I think. Again, I know I'm losing it when a voice in my head says, *The babies probably don't get a whole lot of visitors, Ava.*

There's a banging on the side-entrance door, three times. Not a knocking. A banging. WHAM! WHAM! WHAM!

Aggressive, whoever the person intends to visit.

"Ava Butler, I know you're in there." The voice is an angry, sexless roar.

Or the person could be here for me. Dammit. But if he or she knows my name, it's not a pirate. Not that it makes me feel any better knowing that. The doorknob rattles but holds. I swallow a huge dry lump. I crouch behind the kitchen island, cursing the panting breaths that immediately plague me. *No,* I order myself. No panicking.

I'm only fifteen feet away from whoever it is. And there's no way in hell I'm answering. I concentrate on regulating the ins and outs of oxygen into my lungs, and I hear a whine. I realize it's me, but it's better than a full-blown attack, so I forgive myself and try to soften it.

The voice lowers. It's midrange leaning toward feminine. Still hard to get a definitive read on gender. "We need to talk. I know you were there today. At Samuel's."

Shit, shit, shit. It could be the police. Off duty. Plain clothes. Or the witness Galindo hinted at.

Or the killer.

I hear footsteps, soft, purposeful. The person is changing tacks. I risk standing, sensing movement around the corner to the front of the house. I tiptoe back into the great room and see a dark figure lurking outside the dining room window, a place sheltered from the lone outside light on the driveway. I strain to see better, but it's fruitless. I decide it's a woman from the voice and the frame. She walks to the front door. I can't see her now, so I watch from the inside. She doesn't bother knocking, just checks the massive latch and shakes the door. It doesn't budge.

I'm not sure when she reappeared, but I see Annalise standing by the door latch on the inside, head cocked toward it like she's listening. I rub my eyes.

More lights bounce up the driveway. Let it be the Kovacs and not reinforcements for this woman, please, please, please. One set comes toward the house, then two. When I tear my eyes away from the lights and back to Annalise, she's no longer there.

I see the woman outside, though, moving quickly back to her car. I track her, my tennies slapping the tile on the way back into the kitchen. I'm desperate to see her face, to learn the identity of the person who knows I was at Samuel's today. I'm running, but so is she, and by the time I get to the bay window looking out onto the driveway, her back is to me as she slips into her car. She guns the tail of her vehicle toward the front entrance of the house, slinging the car's nose toward the gate. Now the arriving vehicles are clearly visible. It's Katie's Montero and Nick's truck. The Kovacs. They pull across her headlights into the driveway and park.

Nick is out of his car, fast, as is his father, Kurt, who's basically his twin except for their thirty-year age difference. They're staring at the woman and her car as she accelerates and heads for the gate. Nick scowls. Kurt wears an expression that makes Nick's scowl look like a bright smile. The woman waves to them, a casual, friendly gesture. Nick raises his hand, a partial wave. The Saturn-or-whatever-it-is drives away, now at a sedate pace. The two men share a look. Nick shrugs his shoulders in a move that lifts his whole body onto his toes.

It's over. I'm safe. I crumple back against the island, a hand to my mouth. I have to pull it together. I have no explanation for what just happened, but I need an innocuous one, because I can't tell the truth. Not about anything, anymore.

Katie's voice rings out. "Ava's here. Ginger, honey, your mommy is here." She opens the back-seat door of her Montero to retrieve children. To Nick, she says, "Who was that, honey?"

"Must be a friend of Ava's. I didn't recognize her."

Good, yes. A friend of Ava's. A work friend. That's what I'll go with.

Katie puts a hand on her hip. Now she's watching the car retreat, too. "Maybe. But no one from this island would come up here at night and not say good evening to the owners of the house."

I know she's right. And I realize, suddenly, that I could have turned on my wire and talked to the woman. Had the cavalry at the ready. Created evidence, in case this was Samuel's killer. This thing with the FBI might have its advantages, if I keep my head about me next time, if there is one.

FIFTEEN MINUTES LATER, Ginger is tucked into her car seat, asleep. I have the Rover running and AC blowing. Katie and I are sitting on the front steps where I can see the car while I give the version of the afternoon's events I'm allowed to tell.

"I'm so sorry." Katie takes my hand and squeezes it. "How awful for you to find him, too."

"It was bad." I didn't love Samuel, but I liked him. I was sad for him. As sad as I was for Lailah and Heaven, almost. And I was sad for myself and the situation I was in. I was—yes, I admit it—sad that the joy of New York had worn off so quickly.

"Do the police have a suspect?"

"If they do, they didn't tell me." Because overhearing them discuss *me* as a suspect isn't the same thing.

Katie wipes invisible debris off the step with her palm. "I wonder if it was the missing girl. The redhead."

"Why would it be her?" My brow furrows in on itself. I don't have a big forehead to begin with, and when it does this, it's like the whole thing disappears. I consciously release it.

"You know, if she was, uh, trying to escape, or something."

I'm flummoxed. Katie really believes Samuel is a kidnapper and a killer. I just don't see it. I want the killer found. I want him locked up. But I don't see how focusing on Samuel will make that happen.

So I just say, "Uh-huh," and join her in wiping invisible debris. It's strangely soothing.

Katie shakes her head. "Okay, I want to tell you something, but you can't tell anyone."

If she only knew how good I am at that. "Yah mon."

"We've been hired to look into this. Stingray, us, I mean. For our client."

"The triple X Club?"

She ignores my question and continues with what she wants to tell me. "Samuel has been booking these girls as entertainment for his clients."

"Riiight. You told me that." Samuel booking sex acts for clients was only slightly less troubling than if he'd booked them for himself. And I was only assuming he wasn't participating. I could be wrong, but I really don't want to be.

"And the third missing girl?"

"Yeah?"

"She was the entertainment last Thursday, and no one has seen her since then."

"Oh no." I close my eyes, thinking back to that night. Thursday. When I'd seen Samuel and his not-choirboys at the Boardwalk. Samuel had said something to Phil about the dessert being a redhead, and Phil liking redheads. "A redhead, you say?"

"Yes."

A picture forms in my mind. Heaven's house. Three little girls in plaid St. Mary's uniforms. One blonde, one brunette, one redhead. Heaven, Lailah, and . . . what was the other one's name? I'm concentrating, tuning Katie out and getting nowhere.

She's still talking about the redhead when she recaptures my attention. "The police are releasing her name and picture to the public tomorrow, so it's okay to tell you. Did Samuel ever mention anyone named Shayna?"

I'm on my feet. "No, never." I back toward the Rover. "Or Nevaeh or Lailah."

"Where are you going?"

"I just heard Ginger cry. I've got to get her home," I lie.

Katie stands. "Okayyyy."

"Thanks for keeping her."

I dive into the Rover and peel out on the gravel and dirt. I can't get gone fast enough.

Shayna. Shayna was the name of the third St. Mary's girl in the picture.

SEVENTEEN

IT ONLY TAKES a few phone calls the next morning to line up my day. To Harry, first, letting him know I'll need the morning off to go to the doctor. While I'm talking to him, Ginger starts throwing Cheerios at Elvis. She's squealing with laughter. I put a finger to my lips, but it doesn't do much good. I walk out on the balcony overlooking the harbor, leaving the door open behind me. Better. I briefly tell Harry about the afternoon before, and he's horrified. I practice using the wired pen during the call, to avoid having to call Galindo and get his permission for my doctor visit, too. And to keep him happy, prove to him I'll use the damn thing.

I pop back in and add a chopped banana and sippy cup of milk to Ginger's high chair. She grabs a handful of banana, squishes it between her fingers, and holds it up for me to try.

"Nom, nom, nom," I say, and pretend to eat it.

She giggles, then talks in gibberish to the cat.

As per usual, I'm getting bombarded by texts.

Mom: *When you and Ginger reach here?*

Zach: *Everything OK back home?*

And, yes, Collin: *Katie told me. That blows. If you need me, you know how to reach me.*

Collin. He's rough and rude and kind and sweet all in one, even when I've done nothing to deserve it. I can't let myself get soft and sentimental, though. Thinking about him will weaken my ability to get through this FBI ordeal. Plus, I'm supposed to quit thinking about him anyway. I broke up with him.

From behind the wall separating our side of the duplex from Nana, Bob Marley croons "One Love."

I'm a believer in One Love, just like Marley taught us. That One Love is wrapped in the arms of one God. I know this deep in my core. But from there it gets fuzzy. I'm not sure who's got it right about what to call him or her. Every religion has its drawbacks, even atrocities for many. That's why I rotate. I trust that the one God sees me, loves me, knows me, and understands the reasons in my past for my confusion now. So, all kidding aside, I rotate my deities not out of sacrilege, but because I have no idea how else to handle it. So it's the one God I'm praying to now, no matter how I mask him for my sanity (and, yes, sometimes for my entertainment). And right now, my sanity is borderline.

My go-to in times of trouble has always been Dionysus: god of wine, theater, and religious ecstasy. I'm a huge fan of wine, theater, and ecstasy. But now I need something grittier, tougher, and stealthier. My classical education is invaluable at these moments, and it's thanks to my Roman mythology classes that I zero in on Minerva. Goddess of wisdom and war. Today, what I want from the one God are the qualities Minerva has in spades, so I trust the Big Guy knows when I call out to Minerva, I'm calling to him to help me be more like her.

Okay, Minerva, do your thing. And hurry, because Ginger has thrown cereal and bananas all over the kitchen while I've had this episode of introspection.

I pour myself a third coffee, heavy on the cream and brown-sugar cubes, and pull my wallet out. I notice the mace isn't in my purse, so I retrieve it from the bathroom counter and replace it in its rightful spot. Then, from a number on a business card I've kept for years, I dial my second number: Dr. Megahy. Who it turns out retired a few months ago, selling her practice to a man. Truth: I hate doctors. I hate male doctors most, but female doctors, too. I hate them all.

When a rude voice answers, I jump, sloshing in a complete mouthful of coffee instead of blowing and taking baby sips. It scalds me, I spit it out, and it ruins my nightgown. Somehow I manage not to hang up. I book a visit for later in the morning, keeping my explanation of the reason for it general. I'm pretty sure I get chuptzed for it too as I hang up.

But I don't even care.

Because it's my next call that has me agitated. I call the number for the Mother Superior, which I look up in an old-fashioned St. Marcos phone book. There she is, just one in a long list of names in a sans serif font—Mary Catherine Flaherty—with an address and phone number. Mary Catherine. Sister Mary Catherine, earlier in her career. Mother Superior and Grand Poobah of St. Mary's Catholic School by the time I met her. A pretty fancy name for a plain ole headmistress, if you ask me.

The phone rings once, and someone picks up.

A tremulous voice says, "Hello?"

I'd know it anywhere. Before I can say anything, though, there's a crash, a caterwaul, and Ginger's scream shattering the peace for ten square miles.

I hang up. Milk is splattered from floor to ceiling and a lot of in-between. Ginger, apparently, had practiced her shot-put skills with her sippy cup, and its lid came off on impact. Elvis is drenched, there's a puddle of milk soaking into the throw rug and milk dripping down the pedestal leg of the kitchen table. Elvis yowls and swats at me when I reach for him. He disappears into Ginger's bedroom, where he'll transfer his soon-to-be sour smell to something I won't find for weeks.

I start cleaning while Ginger continues to voice her displeasure. I'm not feeling very "bombshell" at the moment.

But that's okay. A guardian angel is going to see the Mother Superior this morning for a long overdue chat, after dropping off her own little angel with the real mom superior.

THE MOTHER SUPERIOR'S house is not what I expect. Well, what I'd really expected is that she'd move back to the States into a convent when she retired. Obviously she had not. I'd heard talk about an inheritance. I suppose this house must be part of it. Anyway, she'd always been so bottled up, so contained, that I'm gobsmacked to discover a riotous garden of tropical plants in front of a bright pink masonry home.

I walk up stones toward the door, just as a dark sedan pulls over on the side of the road one hundred feet back. My phone makes a hissing noise like a snake. I'd given Galindo a text tone that I'd had to download special, but it was worth it.

Galindo: *State your business.*

I reply: *None of yours. I have a life.*

Galindo: *Correction. You used to.*

I shoot daggers at him over my shoulder then send a reply text: *An old teacher from my school.*

I flick the switch to silence my phone, and I stuff it into my purse, knowing he can see me. Taking pleasure in knowing he can see me. I put an extra measure of sway in my bana. *Kiss it, Galindo.*

Birds chirp and insects buzz over the flowers. A meager woman in a sun hat with insect flaps comes around the side yard. She stretches her steps to reach from one flagstone to another on a path of them. Long sleeves dangle over her wrists. She clutches a trowel in a gloved hand. When she sees me, she stops and pulls out earbuds.

"Yes?" Again, that unmistakable voice. She stuffs her headphones in a fanny pack turned around like a tummy pack.

I stare at her. She doesn't look like the all-powerful tyrant of my memories. She's just a little old lady gardening. Kind of like Nana, except white, and not growing anything illegal that I can see. I almost abort my mission right then.

Until she recognizes me. "Ava Butler."

I curtsy, like we used to in school.

"I always figured you'd show up someday."

"Sorry it took so long."

"Come in. I brewed a pot of tea."

So far, so civilized. Maybe she doesn't know I'm holding a two-decade-old grudge. We enter her house. It's pleasantly cool. The walls are bright white with watercolors of island scenery displayed. I lean in, liking one of them, and see the signature: *M.C. Flaherty.*

She pours two cups of tea in proper teacups with saucers. "Sugar?"

"Yes, please."

"I have cubes of brown or white."

"Two, brown. And cream if you have it."

"Of course."

She offers me the flowery teacup by its saucer, a spoon balancing precariously.

I take it, steadying the spoon with my other hand.

"Let's sit out back."

She leads the way to an ornate white iron table with two chairs. It's under a pergola with creeping wisteria, looking out over mounds of bougainvillea in pink, orange, white, and yellow, and, beyond, an ocean view.

"Your place is very nice."

"It was my sister's. She went to be with the Lord three years ago. Her gardens were her earthly life. I keep them up as a tribute to her." She sits up very straight, and her eyes are bright. "We were twins."

"I'm sorry. And you retired completely from the sisterhood?"

"Yes. But you're not here to make idle conversation about that, are you?"

I don't waver from her blue eyes drilling into me. "No."

"You're here to get closure, to stand up for the poor little girl treated harshly by the Mother Superior."

I don't answer fast enough, and she keeps talking.

"Every few years a girl like you would come along. A local girl. Flaunting herself like a temptress, because the devil himself flourishes here in this heathen environment of pagans and half savages."

I grip my teacup tightly, then force myself to relax. I'm afraid I'll snap the handle off. "Excuse me?" Her words are so hateful and demeaning that I stall. I'm at a loss for how to reply.

"I told Father Jerome when he arrived. The people are heathens, and we have to protect ourselves from them and the demons among them. He didn't believe me at first."

Demons. She was literally comparing me—well, my people and thus me—to a demon. Okay. I know how to respond to that. "The ones that needed protecting were us. From him. And you." I want to rip into her and good. But I hold back. There are things I want to know, about the girls. "I'm not here about me."

"Aren't you?"

"I'm here about Heaven."

She licks her lips, her tongue bright pink like her house. "Doubtful."

"Heaven, the St. Mary's student. About Lailah. And Shayna. Do you remember them?"

Her eyes are rheumy, and they slip away somewhere, moving back and forth, like they're looking something up in a card catalogue. "They were much younger than you."

"Yes."

"That Heaven. She was a bad one. Not as much trouble as you, but bad enough."

"Something happened. To them. I need to know what it was."

"Don't be ridiculous. Nothing happened to them."

"Like nothing happened to me?"

"Oh, Ava, what did he ever do to you, really?"

I shudder, almost a convulsion. "He took pictures of me. He . . . he touched himself. Under his cassock."

She sets her tea down and stirs it, not meeting my eyes.

The panting breaths start, growing faster in a hurry, and I fight them off. She's bringing images to my mind that I don't want to remember. "*You* hurt me."

"It was for your own good."

Bloody hands, my tears. *Don't bother tattling to your parents. You don't want them to be even more ashamed of you.*

"He took me into the bathroom, washed the blood off my hands, from your ruler."

She takes a sip of tea, makes a face like something tastes bad. "He was martyred, in the end. A horrible way to die, but a holy man should expect no less than to be persecuted for his faith."

Her words are just jibber-jabber in my ears. My mind is busy fighting an epic battle against remembering. But it loses. The memory hurts so much that I drop my cup. It shatters on the stone pavers.

"Look what you've done to my sister's china!" she exclaims.

"What I've done? What about what you've done? What he's done?"

The memory won't be denied. His hand taking my hand. Him, saying to me, "When you do nice things for me like this, I can do nice things for you, too. It'll be our secret and no one will ever know. So, what things do you like, Ava? Nail polish, I'll bet." His hand putting mine under his cassock, curling his fingers around mine around him.

I had long nails, even as a girl, because my mom had conceded to my dad. "Pick your battles, Anita," my dad had advised. I'd painted them every night.

"He did touch me. He did."

But not for long, he hadn't.

My favorite color of nail polish was red. Red like the blood my nails drew from Father Jerome when I'd clawed and clawed, until he'd released my hand. I'd clapped my hands over my ears as he roared in pain and anger. "Look what you've done!" he'd shouted at me.

And I'd run. Like I do now.

EIGHTEEN

I'M SHAKEN up pretty badly after my visit to the Mother Superior. *I could really use more Minerva, One God.* Driving way too fast with sweaty palms, I somehow don't sail off a bluff into the ocean, landing safely in the doctor's parking lot instead. I anchor the Rover. The water rocks us gently.

But it's not a boat, it just feels like one. The air conditioner is on high and all the vents point at me. The stream of cold air lifts my hair, and it flutters above my forehead. I hang there with it, absent from time and space. My mind and its contents float like helium balloons loosed from the hand of a crying child.

I have so many questions no one can answer. I don't understand how I could have forgotten so much of those St. Mary's years. I'm scared there may be more I don't remember yet, or, maybe worse, that these memories aren't real and I'm losing my mind. I recall in bits and pieces my certainty as a young girl that I had seriously injured Father Jerome. Had I? Maybe I had just convinced myself of that, hoping he'd never feel the urge or have the ability to do to other girls what he had done to me. Because I remember the whole guardian angel period so much more vividly now, after meeting with the Mother Superior, and a conviction that I had discharged my duty vis-à-vis him. That it was only the Mother Superior that I needed to protect the girls from.

As an adult, I'm no longer sure of anything. I'm not sure I understood what was happening to Heaven and her friends. I don't know now what they went through, or whether it was related to all that was happening to them now. Yet I don't believe in coincidences. That three best friends, St. Mary's girls, all go so wrong, and do it together, to the same horrible end.

The Mother Superior with all her talk of demons is the closest thing to true evil I've ever encountered. Possibly evil enough to do horrible things to other human beings. But in her eighties, fragile and weak, it's unlikely she'd be able to kidnap young women, to murder them. Plus, she would have started with me.

My phone rings. I yelp, startled, but it brings me back. It's the doctor's office. I answer.

"Ava Butler?" The calypso cadence is strong even on just those four syllables.

"Yes."

"You have an appointment at ten thirty today?"

"Yes."

"You're late."

The clock on my dash reads ten thirty-two. "I'll be right in."

The receptionist and I are not off to a good start. I check in at ten thirty-three. Three minutes late. That's early on St. Marcos. She glares at me, and I glare back. *Uptight, jealous, of-a-generation St. Marcos women. Matriarch-divas, delighting in the misery of others.* She has no idea the day I've already had, how on-edge I am.

"The doctor have to work you in now." She points to a chair in the tiny, cramped entry area.

I'm the only person there, so I know what this means. She's going to make me wait for the second coming. I settle in. The cushion is lumpy and the chair back wobbles. The whole place has a moldy smell, which in the islands means drywall and insulation instead of masonry and concrete block. Desperate not to return to my earlier thoughts, I snatch up a January 2011 issue of *Cosmopolitan*. Some actress famous for the *Twilight* movies is on the cover, wearing an outfit like I had on last night. Like I have on today. Ava undercover. I flip the slick pages quickly, unseeing.

My wired pen is in the off mode, because this doctor visit and Wyclef Jean's voice punching out "Sweetest Girl" are none of the FBI's business. I'm only here to make sure I don't need stitches, and that none of my cuts get infected. I'll mention my bump, casually. Katie. Chen. The EMT. Everyone's so overcautious these days. Dr. Megahy checked it when I was pregnant with Ginger. It was fine then, it will be fine now.

My thoughts return to the night before, and Galindo, Annalise, the mystery woman following me, and Katie's revelations. That leads me back to the Mother Superior, which takes me on a circuit of the others and back to her. I'm making laps of hell, and my lungs and eyes burn like I've been running through smoke. I flip more pages in the magazine. I try to imagine how Kenny's gotten along on my demo. That makes me think of Harry, which makes me think of Galindo, and I crash into the fiery loop again, sprinting.

What seems like hours later, the receptionist calls to me. I'm exhausted. She points to the door to the exam rooms. I turn, and the door clicks. I walk over and pull it open.

"Down the hall, number three, second one 'pon de left."

I glance over, see her profile, but she's not bothering to look at me, so I don't bother thanking her. Room three has a chart on the door. AVA BUTLER is typed in all caps on the tab, with my birthdate. It's not insubstantial, but then, I've been coming to this practice since I was a girl. I have an urge to leaf through it, but I squelch it, go inside, and sit on the table. It's too uncomfortable, so I cop the rolling chair. I know it's for the physician. So what? I don't see anyone but me in the room. I fan one crossed leg and concentrate on looking bored instead of frantic. My toe swings, and I have to chop the movement off to keep from hitting the wall with each kick.

There's one knock on the door, then a pause.

"Good morning," I say.

A nurse straight out of AmeriCorps and college not long before that bustles in. She fans my folder in front of her neck, a brisk movement. "Ava Butler?"

"Present."

"Birthdate?"

I recite it to her.

She eyes me meaningfully, or the chair, rather. I pretend not to notice. She drags a lesser one over, its feet scraping the floor, and perches on it between the door and me. She opens my folder in her lap, balancing it on her pink scrubs. Her knobby knees poke out from underneath my life history. She reads, purses her lips, flips a page, then unclips a form for today's visit from the outside of the folder.

"Let's start with a medical history."

"It all in there."

She poises her pencil over the paper. "Not taken by me. I'm very thorough."

"But I'm only here because of some cuts and scrapes."

Her voice is prissy. "And I'm only concerned with providing you the high-quality healthcare you deserve."

I sigh. Harry will understand me being a few more minutes late. "Fine."

We make it through confirmation of my vitals, and I gird myself for the assault about to start.

"Race?"

"Mixed."

Her eyes rake over me. "You need to pick one."

I resist telling her to decide for herself. She has boxes to check. "Black."

She continues to lifestyle. "Exercise."

"Some."

She prods. "Half an hour a day? Walking?"

"Sure." It's easier than telling her my real habits.

"Drugs or alcohol?"

"Nah."

"None?"

"Social."

"Which?"

"Excuse me?"

"Drugs or alcohol? Or both?"

I laser a hole in her forehead with my eyes. "Alcohol."

"More than two drinks a day?"

"No." I win the fight with myself to keep my gaze up, off the floor, where I want to hide the truth. I know I drink too much, and I've been known to say yes to the occasional recreational drug when somebody offers to share after a gig, when he or she is trying to pick me up. And that if the nurse turns back in my file far enough, she'll know my parents sent me to rehab in high school (a huge overreaction on their part), but I don't owe her any of that.

"Anything else?"

"No."

"STDs, HIV, or AIDS?"

"No." Because it's true. Mostly due to luck, not good behavior. But I'm clean. Clean. A multifaceted concept best to avoid contemplating.

"Last period?"

"Last month."

That gets me a sharp look, and I smile sweetly.

"Are you sexually active?"

"Not this week."

"Birth control?"

"As a last resort." Since explaining that intercourse does nothing for me except result in a child is probably too much for her, I relent. "Condoms. As protection."

"Pregnancies?"

"A daughter, and she's about to make one."

"Any others?" Her question is sharp, and I realize she *has* read my file. Witch.

There's another knock on the door, delivering me from her intrusion, from questions having nothing to do with wineglass cuts or a lump on my breast.

She answers with weary patience, worn paper-thin by a difficult island woman. "Come in."

The doctor enters. He clicks a pen as he turns to us, and I automatically squeeze the purse I'm clutching in my lap, which holds my special pen. His face registers surprise at the role reversal inherent in the seating arrangement.

Mine probably registers mine, because I know this boy. Or man now, rather. He lived next to Heaven, and he was a mainstay during my babysitting days. Sometimes I wondered where his parents were, and why they didn't pay me, too, as much time as he spent with me. He's bookish and thin, his complexion a shade lighter than mine, his scalp close cropped, his lab coat hanging from the knobby points of his frame.

I speak first. "Ezekiel Willie. Easy."

He clicks the pen again, three quick ones in succession. "I wasn't sure if you'd remember me."

"Of course I do. I didn't see you at Heaven's memorial. Or Nevaeh, as she went by in recent years."

He slips the pen over his breast pocket, hanging it by its clip. "Full schedule of patients."

I picture the empty waiting room. "Too bad. It was nice."

He rubs his upper lip. The skin there is lighter in color. "Yes, yes."

The nurse, who'd never introduced herself to me in addition to neglecting to say good morning to me, says, "You knew that murdered girl?"

Easy doesn't answer, so I do. "The doctor and her were school chums. I babysat her."

"Dr. W, wow."

He stops rubbing his lip. He's left a discoloration. "I lost contact with her years ago."

"Me, too," I admit.

The nurse shoots me a look like she doesn't believe me. I realize she's made assumptions about me from her read through my pain. Because that's what you come to a doctor for, mainly, isn't it? Pain. The words I know are in my chart burn into mind. No, Ginger was not my first pregnancy. Or my second. But that was all a long, self-destructive time ago. The young nurse's eyes hold judgment that borders on slut-shaming, and I want to scream at her, *You know nothing about me or life here. You know NOTHING about what I went through. Words on a chart aren't a life sentence.*

Except that sometimes they are.

Easy cuts off this line of conversation, saving me. "You haven't been in since your daughter was born." I notice his voice is pure yank. Of course, I've been yanking with the nurse, too.

Speaking of her, she says, "We aren't done with her medical history, Dr. W."

He holds up a finger. "Just a moment. Ava?"

I gesture to my legs. My bandages are in plain sight below the hem of above-the-knee stretch pants. "Aches and pains. I cut myself on broken glass."

Nodding, he says, "May I?" and touches the bandage on my knee.

"Of course."

Gently, he removes the dressing, then repeats the process with all of my wounds, including the elbows, after I hold them out to him.

The nurse stands next to him, taking oozy, blood-speckled bandages and depositing them in the trash.

"This one could have used some stitches earlier." He palpates my knee. "I can still help it some, but you're going to scar no matter what."

"I understand."

After they clean my wounds and dress all of them except my knee, she injects a local anesthetic near the cut. Easy stitches it with tiny, measured movements. His forehead shines. It's stuffy in the closed room, and I want to fan myself, but I hold still for him. When he's done, she gives me a tetanus shot while he writes me a prescription for an antibiotic, in case I get an infection.

While she bandages me, Easy asks, "Anything else?"

The words are in my mouth, but they won't come out. It's like the Mother Superior's demon is holding my lips shut. I engage in a battle with the little bastard, willing my throat to push harder. It takes several seconds, during which Easy never glances away.

I like the man the boy became.

Finally, the demon gives up. "I have a lump."

NINETEEN

WALKING down the hall at M-Squared that afternoon, the carpet is like hot beach sand. My steps are uncertain on it. I don't know where to put my feet. I don't know what's real and what isn't. I don't know whether to laugh or cry or scream in fear.

Things with the lump are uncertain, and I won't have an answer about it for several days. Dr. Easy did something he called a core needle biopsy and sent the results off to a pathologist in Puerto Rico. He told me not to worry in the meantime.

The look on his face had told me a different story. And he'd still gone ahead and given me the name of an oncologist on the mainland. I decide to hold off calling my parents. No reason to worry them when they have the reality of Dad's condition, and with mine nothing more than a possibility.

It isn't just that, although that feels like plenty. It's Galindo and the Mother Superior and two funerals in a week. Or, two memorials. Samuel's funeral will be back in his South Carolina hometown. I wonder about Lailah's. I wonder where Shayna is, what has happened to her.

As I walk past the break room, people are talking about Samuel. They hush when they see me. Cora, Harry's assistant, calls a good day to me. Which reminds me that I have to tell someone here I mashed up the Rover's front bumper. But why do today what can be put off as long as possible?

Per Galindo's texted instruction, received after I finished with Dr. Easy, I have turned my wire on, so he's now eavesdropping on every sound I make. I set up my laptop quickly, keeping my eyes on my task, careful to avoid the stares from all directions. There's no reason for it. They don't know about Samuel and me, my relationship to the dead and missing girls, or the FBI and this damn wire. They don't have X-ray vision to see the sharpie circle on my breast covered with gauze. I have to be imagining the stares.

But when a voice interrupts me, it's not about any of those things.

Harry calls out, "Ava, when you have a second, come tell me about New York."

I lift my eyes, scanning the room. Yes, everyone *is* staring at me, but suddenly I have an inkling why. They know about my trip to New York. They sense glamour, celebrity, fame, and fortune. Some of the faces are eager and excited, a few sour, like they've bitten into an under-ripe guava.

"Okay."

He's the main person I want to avoid today. Betraying this good man by recording him is wrong. I'm a pawn in a hurtful game. I console myself that I'll be proving him innocent. I have to breathe. I have to do this, or I could lose everything. Ginger. My chance at a music career. My parents' peace and livelihood. I clench my teeth, feeling my nostrils flare and air rush in. No panting. No panic. I want to ditch the wire, but if I do, Galindo will know instantly and be on me like stink on a bug. Speaking of bugs, I wondered again about them. And whether any of my coworkers are undercover. This sudden suspicion of everyone and everything has stopped all my forward momentum, like the hem of my long-ago bell-bottom pants caught in my Huffy's chain. Then the worst thought yet occurs to me. Samuel could have backed out of working for the FBI. They could have killed him.

I could be risking more than a St. Marcos police murder charge.

With quivering hands, I arrange my pens in a Tar Heels coffee mug, straighten papers, log back out of my laptop. Finally, I walk the plank from my desk to Harry's office. I stand at the end, hand poised to knock and announce my presence.

"Ava," he says. A smile takes over his whole broad face.

I peer over the edge of the precipice. Sharks circle, but they're circling for Harry, not me, aren't they? I dangle a foot, and a hammerhead surfaces, jaws open. I don't want to do this. I could throw myself at the mercy of the local police, but I remind myself of the three really good reasons I have to cooperate, all blood related to me.

I have to trust that Harry will prove himself innocent. If he doesn't, well, then, he isn't worth putting my loved ones at risk.

I jump. Water shoots into my sinuses, down my throat, into my eyes. Around me is a violent thrashing. Blood reddens the water. Mine? I kick out, viciously, fighting the water and the sharks, wanting more than anything to get back to my daughter.

"You're in another world." Harry's concerned voice draws my head above water.

I gasp in a breath. "I am. I'm . . . rattled. Samuel."

He does a K-turn and moves to his doorway, to me. "Yes. What an ordeal for you. And I know you two had become close. It's a sad thing for all of us."

"Thank you."

"There's a get-together tonight at the Pirate's Cove Resort, nothing formal, just friends and coworkers, trying to make sense of this. Cora can get you the details."

I nod, afraid to speak. I will not cry, because I don't cry. After a moment, I say, "Were you friends long?"

Harry adjusts his body in his chair, planting his fists and lifting himself with his shoulders, swinging just slightly back and to the right. His shoulders bunch under his shirt, and I realize how strong he is, the parts of his body he can control. My eyes stray down to khaki trousers covering stick-like legs. Crap, I realize I'm evaluating him as Samuel's potential killer. My brain won't stop its morbid analyses. I decide he couldn't have pulled it off in the shower, that it had to be someone more mobile. But that doesn't mean he didn't hire someone to do it, if he found out Samuel was betraying him.

Stop. Harry is Mr. Clean, not a killer!

"Not really. But I enjoyed working with him. Such a tragedy."

I push on, navigating the sharks, self-loathing welling in me. "If you weren't friends, what brought him to Mahogany?"

Harry wheels to his desk, putting it between us. "Referred by another partner."

I start to speak again, but he holds a hand up.

"My turn. I want to hear about your trip."

Galindo's instructions hang in my head. But I don't have an agenda or a script of questions. I want to push it, to get it over with yesterday, so I can crush the pen under a heel and walk away.

I try to force life into my wooden face and voice. "The experience of a lifetime. Thank you so much."

"I called Kenny this morning."

"Oh?" Funny the difference a day makes. I'm interested, but it no longer rules my thoughts.

"I can't repeat what he said." My face must have registered dismay, because he shakes his head. "Too many expletives. I don't even know what he means half the time. But he loves you. He's especially keen on one song. And he said your photo shoot was a home run. In so many words."

I regain a weak smile. "That's great."

"He thinks he'll have you offers in a few days."

"Really? That fast?"

"Technology. No more walking around delivering cassette tapes and headshots."

Zach had texted that morning, telling me I need an agent. And a manager. He sent me names and numbers. I didn't bother to reply that it seems I already have an agent here on St. Marcos. Special Agent John Galindo of the FBI.

"Is it normally this fast?"

"No. I don't usually get involved, but even I know that much."

I sink into the chair in front of his desk, feeling weak for many reasons. "Wow."

"Yes, wow." He clears his throat. "A change of subject. I need you to set up a few leases and post office boxes. Cora has the details. And the governor is throwing some big shindig Friday. I'll be going, and I need you there."

Not only is tomorrow Friday—a nonworking day for M-Squared—but it's an official Virgin Islands holiday, July third. I thought about my plans for the three-day weekend, or lack of them. Beach time with Ginger. Limin' with friends and family.

And I think about Galindo listening in on the wire. His expectations, his *demands*.

"No problem."

TWENTY

I BLAZE around the island the rest of the afternoon doing the tasks Harry assigned me. He has no idea how fast I can finish them, his only frame of reference being how long it takes a nonnative. I have plenty of time left for dinner with Ginger on the way home from my parents' place—a McDonald's Happy Meal with chicken nuggets—before Nana is due to come watch her while I'm at the week's second wake or death party or memorial or whatever you want to call it.

Ginger babbles nonsense in the bath. Elvis sits on the toilet tank, tail swishing. He hates baths, and it appears he's not happy with me for subjecting Ginger to one.

"Anybody here?" Nana's voice calls.

"We in the bathroom getting Ginger girl clean." I wipe hair out of my eyes, leaving bubbles on my forehead.

Ginger laughs, splashing water at my face.

"I relaxin' on the porch."

"See you in a second."

After I give my daughter a good rinsing, I bundle her in a fluffy white towel big enough for Elvis, her, and me. I use a corner to dab the bubbles and water off my face. We snatch Ginger's diaper and a onesie from her room and take them out to the porch. It's a hot eighty-five degrees with the sun still an hour or two from setting.

Nana is in a white wooden rocker, eyes closed. I sit in the matching one beside her. She opens her eyes, resumes rocking.

"You look a fright."

"Well, thanks." I open the towel and tip Ginger back, holding her feet in the air with one hand. I tickle her tummy, and she chortles.

Nana gazes into the distance. There's a three-masted schooner entering the harbor. It's from another era, like her, and her eyes take on a glow as she watches it. I slip a diaper under Ginger and fasten the Velcro. The white velour onesie I tug over her head is one Nana gave her. With her wet curls, pink lips, latte skin, and Bambi eyes, Ginger is perfection. I set her on the ground, and she bear-crawls at her top speed into the house.

Nana says, "Secrets dem eatin' you up."

The woman is a witch or a seer or whatever you want to call someone with the uncanny ability to read someone else's life and business like it's displayed on a billboard. "What makes you say that?"

"You never one to run you mouth, but the less'n you do, the more going on."

Collin used to say something like that, too. Collin. I haven't heard from him today. I wonder if he's giving up, and a stabbing pain in my heart tells me I'm doing the right thing. I care too much. I can't stop the memory, though. His breath warm on my forehead. The back of his fingers stroking my collarbone.

"You're scaring me. There's too much going on in there when you're quiet."

I smile at her, banishing Collin and hoping she buys my grin. "Okay."

Ginger laughs from the other room. Elvis yowls. Poor, long-suffering Elvis. I stand. She's going to get into mischief if I leave her out of sight any longer.

"Look at you. Gonna bust if you hold it inside any longer."

I study her in profile. She's the polar opposite of the Mother Superior, her contemporary only in age. She is my confessional, I realize, and I consider what I can share. I grip the chair back. "Samuel was murdered."

"I sorry to hear." She nods once.

"A girl was killed, along with one of her friends, and another is missing. I used to babysit the girl, in their St. Mary's days. I was supposed to protect them, back then. I don't think I did a very good job."

"A baby ain't got no call to be protectin' other babies."

"I thought I had. I thought that I'd stopped a bad man who'd hurt me. I don't think I did."

"When a bad man hurt you?"

"When I was a girl."

She turns to me, holds a hand out to me, and I take it. She pulls me in like a tractor beam, so intense I can feel the heat transferring from her to me. "Listen to me. You listenin'?"

"I'm listenin'."

"It not you fault."

"But, I—"

Her voice gets louder. "It not you fault."

"You can't know—"

She's practically shouting now, in her thin old lady's voice, and she shakes my hand in rhythm with her words. "It not you fault. What a bad man do not you fault. You hear me?"

My mouth is so dry I can't get the words out, so I nod. My eyes burn, and I focus all my energy on keeping them dry.

She squeezes my hand, turns back to the view. She rocks in silence. I'm struggling with emotions, Nana's just rocking.

She says, "I ever tell you my father work on one of those ships?"

Ginger barrels back onto the porch. Ginger. I forgot about Ginger. She's managed to drag Elvis along under one arm. She's red, head to toe, and I jump up, afraid she's cut herself, then realize she's found my last remaining Ruby Woo lipstick. She even managed to smear some of it on her mouth. Elvis's, too, which I imagine elicited the yowl.

"Oh my," I say.

Nana smiles with her lips pressed together like she's holding in a laugh.

I clean up baby and cat, then return to the porch with her in a new onesie.

"Nana, she's all yours."

"Come to Nana, sweet thing. I like red lipstick kisses."

My mouth drops as Ginger stands up and walks to her, like she's been doing it all her life.

PIRATE'S COVE RESORT, the site for Samuel's get-together, is half an hour down a long and windy beach road from my place, almost to Estate Annalise, but below the big house on the rocky coast of the island's north shore. The beach there is short, bordered on both ends by a violent assault of water, and it's there, under a pavilion, that people are already gathering. My heels sink as I traipse across the white sand to join them. There's an off-road vehicle backed up to the structure, doing duty as a rolling bar. A green cloth flaps on a long folding table, weighted down with trays of shrimp, veggies, fruit, and tarts. Shrimp aren't local. They're shipped in, like Samuel and most of the people attending, which is clear when I enter and not a soul wishes me a good afternoon or good evening.

"Good evening, good evening." I get a few curious looks, but it's my island, and good manners count, even when no one else understands them.

The whispers and stares of earlier today are intensifying. Most of them are from M-Squared. No one speaks to me, but I know they're speaking about me. At least some of them have the good grace to smile and lift a hand in greeting. Jarod. Hanif, his buddy from the Odd Pod. Cora. But that's about it. My skin crawls, each meaningful glance like a no-see-um bite on my skin. Soon I'm covered in them. I lift my shoulders up and back and make my way to the libations.

The bartender is Ordy Jones. "Good evening, Ava," he says.

"Good evening, Ordy. Painkiller, please."

His work space is limited, but he gets the job done, his eyes sneaking over to me as he works. "Smile, miss. A woman beautiful as you deserve to be happy."

"It a wake, meh son."

"I sorry about your friend."

"Yah mon."

"The Kingdom welcome our brother with open arms today. That something to smile about."

I lift my sunglasses to get a better look at Ordy. He shines with sincerity. I set the shades back on my nose. I put a dollar in his tip cup. "True dat."

"Thank you. Have a bless day."

I nod. "You, too, Ordy."

When I turn, I am face-to-face with Katie. Only one of us is surprised.

"Drink for you, miss?"

Katie waves a hand. "Water with bubbles."

We stare at each other without speaking. He hands Katie the drink and she sips, daintily. She puts a five in his tip jar, making me the chump.

Katie squeezes my elbow. "Wanna go down to the beach, get away from this for a few minutes?"

I start to say no, and she sees it.

"We can stay close." She points to the water's edge. "Just over there?"

I don't answer, just slip my shoes off and start walking barefoot. She catches up quick.

"Rough few days."

I nod.

"You and I, we've had our ups and downs."

I chuptz, and she laughs.

"Well, you did hurt my brother."

"I not right for him."

"You are rubbing his nose in this thing with Zach, and it's so public."

"I not with Zach. That all paparazzi bullshiz."

"Really?"

Mostly. "Really."

"Luckily he didn't know about Samuel."

"Katie . . ." My voice goes up an octave on the second syllable.

"I love you, Ava."

I do what I do best. Ignore and deflect. "Don't go succumbing to my charms after all this time. You a married woman."

"I love you, and you've been lying to me. Hiding things from me. I need us to clear the air."

Air-clearing is way overrated. I step closer to her. "Who do your hair, your granny?" I reach for it and she ducks.

She looks out over the water. Her green eyes blend with the color of the sea today, and it's like the water is reclaiming her. A mermaid. A sea nymph. "Remember how Nick and I have been working on some stuff with Harry?"

"Yeah?"

"He asked us to look into the deaths of those three young women from the triple X Club."

"Wait, I thought—"

"One of Harry's colleagues has an interest in the club."

Her answer feels cagey. The sky clouds. As much as I am grateful for our conversation and need someone I can open up to, I remind myself that Katie is not that person. Nick either, more's the pity, because he knows more about the virtual currency system than anyone on-island outside M-Squared. As much as I'm holding back, I feel she's keeping the same or more to herself.

And another thought hits me. Galindo would flip out if he knew I'd forgotten to click the pen to activate the wire, but I'm so glad I did.

"Okay. What else haven't you told me?" Even as I utter the words I wish I could retract them, hope she doesn't ask me the same question in return. But she doesn't.

"They found the redheaded dancer. Shayna."

"Is she okay?"

"No. She's dead."

"Where, how, what?" My words tumble over each other. The last of the little girls. I wonder how many more blows I can take without going down for the count.

"She was strangled, with a garrote. Like the others. Tourists found her at Grapetree Bay."

"Assaulted. Sexually, I mean?"

"Yes. But no semen or spermicide. No evidence of a condom. Violated with something, though."

"Wait, is that the same as Lailah and Heaven?"

She nods. "All three."

I back into a chaise lounge and sit on the metal edge. I stare at the beach. A hermit crab in a shell the size of my pinky nail hustles by. The grains of sand are a palette of white to black, with every brown, tan, and gray in between, and a few corals, reds, and oranges. So much more than the eye can see from a distance or when moving by too fast.

There are things I hadn't seen. Maybe things Katie hasn't either. I had equated sexual assault to forced intercourse. But there were many ways to penetrate, and somehow knowing that was even worse than what I'd imagined before.

I say, "If we were in the States, they'd link the trace fibers in the neck wounds, find fingerprints and transferred evidence on the bodies that shed light on the perpetrator, review footage from photo and video you can't ever get away from. But here? We're like the Wild West. The Wild Caribbean."

Collin would be pulling out his short hair if he were here. Mr. Law and Order. As much as he hated bureaucracy, he'd make a fine police chief someday, because he was passionate about law enforcement.

Damn, I had to stop inviting him into my head.

Katie puts a hand on my shoulder. It's cool on my skin, and even that feels wrong. "Just stay safe, Ava."

The real irony is that if she knew the half of it, she'd fling herself on me and call for restraints. It's like I'd auditioned for a romantic comedy and showed up for rehearsal and learned I'd been cast as the terrorized victim in a psychological thriller. The scenes ran through my mind. A person fleeing Samuel's room the night Katie and I were there. Someone hitting Samuel in the heat of our moment. The XXX Club coaster on his bedside table. Galindo, Samuel's undercover work, mine. The Feds' suspicion of Harry. Samuel's murder in addition to the three St. Mary's girls. If she knew all of that, she'd be really worried.

Like I am.

Gunfire erupts on the beach, and we both hit the sand facedown.

TWENTY-ONE

THE NEXT AFTERNOON, Rashidi meets me in Taino to plus-one me to the governor's soiree, where we're to meet Harry. He's free and easy because he doesn't have any summer classes this year, which he'd sold as time for lab work and writing papers and used to interview for and accept a new job.

"And then what happen?" Rashidi hangs on every word as I tell him about the gunshots on the beach the night before.

"People dem scream and carry on. No witnesses. Nobody hurt. So I go back for shrimp while there no line. Police hustle everyone off, and there end up no memorial. Ordy pack me extra shrimp in a to-go box."

I leave out the part about how I lay on the ground paralyzed. I also omitted that Katie had the same look on her face. It was like each of us was convinced that the shots were meant for us, but neither of us admitted it. No, the air was most definitely not cleared. And I hadn't drawn an easy breath since. Samuel's death, the woman who followed me to Annalise, the shooter on the beach. Even now, my eyes are darting around, searching for threats I'd never in my life considered. Used to be, I knew exactly what threatened me. Now, it could be anyone.

I also trimmed an interlude from the story where Porky and

Babyface waylaid me in the parking lot. I demanded to know why they had never texted or called me back when I offered help on the girls. They launched into questions about Samuel. I clicked my wire on and loudly told them to stop harassing me. Porky's phone rang ten seconds later. I slunk into the Rover and drove away without looking back.

But Rashidi doesn't know I edited the tale, and he laughs at my shrimp story. He places a balancing hand under my elbow as we cross the uneven bricks in front of the Government House. The yellow masonry structure is several hundred years old, the survivor of countless tropical storms and hurricanes, which are the reason for the dark green shutters by every window. It's only July third, barely into hurricane season, but still I can see they're all mint. By the end of September, they may get a workout. But not in the summer. Now, as always in July, it's hot and sticky, and the sea behind us is flat calm.

We continue to chat like the old friends and lovers we are, easy, familiar. But on my part, it's an act. My special pen is on in my purse. Galindo made it crystal clear that I record every word from the minute I arrived. So Rashidi and I are performing for posterity, Galindo, and his pals. Rashidi grips my elbow tighter as we ascend the steps.

"I don't know why you wear such impractical shoes."

"You use to say they sexy."

"You kick me out of your bed. Now I worry you break an ankle and I have to carry you."

If he notices I'm not laughing at his jokes, he doesn't mention it.

I'm carrying a shawl because the Government House is a meat locker. Rashidi is in island summer formal attire. For him that's a slim-fitting white suit with a pale blue shirt of thin cotton. No tie. Chest hair above his top button. His long, well-kempt dreadlocks are securely bound at the base of his neck with a silver-plated leather thong. It says ONE LOVE on it. I know because I gave it to him a couple of birthdays ago. His dark skin glistens with moisture, but somehow he's not sweating noticeably yet. He's a gorgeous man, and it makes me sad he is such a nice guy. If only he had a little danger, a little bad boy in him, we might have had a chance.

"Ava." Harry calls to me from his chair at the top of the stairs. The island is a trial for someone who isn't ambulatory, but Government House has an elevator.

I introduce the two men, and they talk easily. Hosts of voices jump and bounce off walls, ricochet off floors and ceilings, even bodies. All aimed for my pen.

"What do you say, Ava?" Harry asks.

"Sorry?" I usually yank with my boss, but in this environment it feels unnatural, and I speak in our island patois.

"Ready to help me converse with the governor?"

"Sure. Maybe it help me help you if you give me the background. And what you aim to get from him."

"Or him from me."

I laugh, hollow. "True dat. More likely."

Harry pulls at a bow tie. He looks dapper, but it can't be comfortable. "The governor wants money. Cut and dried."

"The government take virtual currency?"

Beside me, I feel Rashidi shift and his body lift. I don't have to look to know he's raising his eyebrows.

Harry says, "They'll take anything. My goal is to channel our resources in a way that is best for Mahogany Management, helps us meet our EDC obligations for local investment and hiring, and helps with the governor's goal of making him reelectable."

Rashidi laughs. "That what most important to he."

"I know him." He'd been a crony of the murdered senator. "He not shy 'bout asking for what he want." And then some. "So what you want?"

"I hear horror stories about interference and sabotage. I just want them to leave us alone."

I nod, not feeling optimistic. It's not much to ask but the hardest thing to get.

Harry takes point on our way into the Governor's Ballroom. The doors open as if by magic, thanks to the young woman whose sole job it is to open and close them. Air conditioning hits us like a cold front, and I wrap a silver shawl over my sleeveless red sheath. A short queue has formed at the other end of the room where Governor Milton holds court. Buffet tables line one wall, and the succulent aroma of island le chon—pig roasted on a spit—coaxes a growl from my stomach. Waiters circulate in tuxedos, white linens draped over their arms, pouring champagne into flutes.

"Madam," an attendant says to me, indicating a table of empty stemware just inside the door.

We each take one. A waiter fills them immediately. I love champagne, and as always, I inhale the bubbles, then let the liquid glide across my tongue. Then I sip faster, trying to calm my nerves as we join the end of the line. I feel exposed, like a third understudy forced into a leading role, like everyone here can see I'm the pretender who didn't get the part. And it's not just because I'm spying on Harry while pretending to be a loyal employee, which is bad enough. I'm recording the governor, too, and if he asks for a bribe, I'll be catching it on my streaming audio. He isn't part of my assignment. Whether I like the guy or not (I don't), I hate tricking him. I want to bolt.

But it's too late. We've reached the front of the line.

"Good evening, Ava Butler, you more beautiful every year." The governor holds his hand out, like a potentate whose ring we're to kiss.

"Good evening." I put my fingers under his, bobbing my head and bending my knees, almost a curtsy. He stares at me until I lean in and kiss his cheek. His hot breath fans my ear, and he clasps my hand to hold me close.

"So, so beautiful."

I pull away and bat my eyes. "Look at you, Governor. Office agree with you." My stomach roils with acid as I throw him a line that always works. "How you find time to keep these muscles so big and strong?"

He throws his head back and laughs, slapping his knee. "Most say my strength in my back."

Thank goodness Harry doesn't know the governor just bragged to me about the strength and longevity of his erection. It's bad enough that I do.

"Good evening, Governor," Rashidi says.

In a deeper, man-to-man voice, the governor says, "Rashidi John, good evening, nice to see you."

"Governor Milton," Harry says, before the governor has turned to him. "I'm Harry Darnell. We met at—"

"Yah, yah, Mahogany Management."

The governor holds his hand out for Harry to shake, but makes him lean to the absolute limit of his range from his chair. I seethe on his behalf, but Harry doesn't blink.

"Thanks for the invite. I want to take this opportunity to tell you how excited we are about the initiatives we have going on with local employees, contractors, charities, and projects with the schools. It's a very exciting time for Mahogany Management."

Governor Milton's face is like stone. "So many times, rich folk from the States—rich white folk, like yourself—treat our island like a playground. They come and throw they money at everyone, act the big shots, leave garbage lying round"—this he says in a significant voice —"without giving thought to people dem, those whose backs they standing on to add to they wealth."

Rashidi and I look at each other. I don't completely disagree with the governor, but he's being a jerk. Without the EDC program, I, for one, wouldn't have a good job, a company car, and a boss who sends me to New York to cut a demo. And the Virgin Islands government, including his salary and expense budget, would be seriously underfunded.

The governor's still speechifying in Harry's face. "And on the back of the government which provide for people dem."

Harry acts like he wants to speak, but I kick his chair with my foot hard enough to jar him. He stops.

The governor gets bored looking at Harry and switches his attention to ogling my cleavage. "Even EDCs who say they livin' up to the letter of the law miss the fine print, that which between the lines. I hope you not one of them, Mr. Harry Darnell. I hope you support people dem, through their duly elected representatives. It not like I asking for much, since I hear Mahogany Management already slipping something-something to certain folks in government."

Is he saying Harry's already paying bribes? I have to stop this conversation. Ugh. I'm usually proud of my Virgin Islands heritage, but I'm not proud of how prevalent hand out, palm up is. Milton embarrasses me.

I wiggle closer to keep his attention on me. "I the official Island Liaison for Mahogany Management, Governor. It my responsibility to liaise with government officials dem. I sit with someone from your office and go over ways we improve our relationship with the government. And support the Virgin Islands economy."

He grunts. "That nice, but what say the fine Mr. Harry Darnell now?"

"I—"

"Oh, no you don't." I buss the other side of the governor's cheek. "Now you just toying with Harry. I call you office Monday. We talk."

I know I've overstepped my position. Worse, I know Galindo is screaming as he listens in. But I can't let Harry do it. I can't let him fall into the governor's trap. This is normal modus operandi in the Virgin Islands. But when you catch it on tape, it sounds incriminating, and I'm not going to facilitate Galindo gaining leverage on Harry or taking him down over something as natural to our governor as breathing. That is, if Galindo didn't already get what he needed from Milton's hint.

I give Harry's chair a push. He takes over and rolls away. Rashidi and I follow. When we reach the buffet table, Harry wheels, and I stiffen, ready for his wrath.

He's smiling ear to ear. "Ava, you were great. Let's eat."

RASHIDI ESCORTS me to my car through the long shadows cast in the streetlights. Ours walk beside us, Stretch Armstrong versions. "What that in there?"

I clutch his arm. He's right about my shoes. "My job." Waves crash against the boardwalk. The dark heightens smells, like salt water. Like dead fish.

"You shut the governor down. He not happy. He gonna take it out on you boss."

"I did the right thing. He demanding graft."

"That what he do. Just take care. Milton liable to be plenty angry at you now."

He can get in line. I click the key fob and the Rover blinks and beeps hello. "I deal with it Monday."

Rashidi pulls at his chin then gives me a push under the elbow to help me in the seat. "Something off with you I can't put my finger on. You born here. You go along to get along. But not tonight."

I wiggle my fingers at him. "Thanks for coming."

"And you blow me off." He scowls. "You're welcome." He walks away, still shaking his head and muttering.

I click my pen. *Eff you, Galindo.* I pick up my phone and scroll through messages in the dark, hoping to hear nothing from no one, then I'm disappointed when I don't. Collin's really giving up on me. I don't know why I'm surprised. He's a smart guy and not a doormat. The phone rings in my hand. The screen says Galindo. I don't feel like listening to him run me down, so I press DECLINE.

A loud crash sounds in my ear, and glass sprays across my lap. A brick lands with a thud in the passenger seat. I scream, but I keep my wits somehow, jamming the start button and throwing the Rover into reverse. I accelerate the back end of the car into the street.

Crack. Something hits the back of the Rover. Another brick? I don't wait to find out, just shift and burn rubber up King Street.

"Shit, shit, shit." I look for a person or vehicle in the rearview mirror. Nothing. No one. Just like at the Pirate's Cove Resort. I wish I knew if this was random or meant to terrorize me. It's working, either way. If I could tell him why, I could ask Rashidi to stay with me. But I can't, so I don't.

I race home along the dark streets. Alone. Incredibly, dangerously alone.

TWENTY-TWO

SUNDAY MORNINGS ARE churchizzle time on St. Marcos, which makes them a perfect time to snoop the M-Squared offices. So that's what I do, partly because Galindo is furious with me about how I handled things with Harry and the governor Friday night—saying I reneged on our agreement by rescuing Harry. Partly because I spent an idyllic Saturday with my daughter and parents, and that shit is hard work.

I leave Ginger with Nana. They're eating mango and watching a movie. Their favorite: *The Lion King*.

When I arrive at the blue building overlooking the West End pier, Cora is leaving the building. I check the time. It's nine a.m. She's wearing a linen dress, so she's probably going straight to church. I circle the block, not wanting her to see me. When I return, she's nowhere to be seen. I sit in the Rover for five minutes anyway, just to be sure she's gone.

I let myself in M-Squared through both sets of doors, then click my special pen. The offices are silent except for the sound of the split-unit air conditioners every fifty feet.

"Hello?" I call louder. "Hello? This is Ava. Hello?" No answer. I try a few more times, even down by the door to the Odd Pod, but don't raise anyone. Cora must have been the only one here.

I'm giving my eyes a contact break today, and I adjust my glasses upward on my nose. I take a seat and open my laptop, without even the slightest urge to check for bad news or bad horoscopes. I decide to explore the network first, to see what I can find to copy to my pocketful of thumb drives for Galindo. He's most interested in who is transferring virtual currency in and out, when, how much, and for what reason, plus now he wants me looking for records of bribes. I have complete confidence those files won't be available to me, but, whatever. I'll look through all the directories, take some screen shots to show him I tried. It will push me to the upper limits of my tech savvy, but I've got all morning, and, while I usually rotate every day, I'm channeling Minerva again, so I'm hopeful.

After an hour of hunting and pecking, I roll my neck. It cracks satisfyingly. I run through a few facial stretches and then some vocal exercises for shits and giggles. It helps me reset my brain. I decide I've done all I can do on the network, and it's a huge relief because I haven't found anything that looks shady to me, in the things I can access, anyway. I grab a coffee and call out a few more hellos before I head into Harry's office.

"Forgive me, Harry," I whisper.

I shut his door behind me and slip my phone from my purse. I lift the fronds of the fern. It's dry and lifeless. Noni must be slacking. I make a circuit of his office, taking photos of all his knickknacks. Between my trip to New York and running all over the island for my job, I haven't spent much time in here. There's a wedding photo of him with Mrs. Harry. They look young and happy. More pictures of them, but none of children, and then some of Harry without his Mrs., deep-sea fishing, skiing on a special chair, in a Jeep surrounded by giraffes. *Oh, Harry.* I force myself to keep going. None of the decorative items seem important. There are no filing cabinets or shelves of books or documents. This makes sense. Even M-Squared's money is digital.

Then I brace for the heavy lifting: his desk. There are three drawers: one for junk, one for office supplies, and one for files. I paw carefully through the first two, taking pictures of the contents and putting everything back like I found it. Nothing incriminating unless you count his hoarding of paper clips or a tendency to leave one Rolaids behind in a used roll. I count five of the wasted antacids, plus one full roll.

In the third drawer, I remove each file folder, take a shot of the outside and of each page of the contents, replacing the files in order as I go. Some of the files are standard stuff, like expenses, and a few are employees, like his secretary Cora, Jarod, and the heads of each division within the company. Again, though, I wonder if the meatier files are stored digitally. Half an hour passes, and I'm nearly done. My hand stops on the last file. It's labeled AVA BUTLER. I flip through, finding my resume, notes on checked references, one expense report, and a printed email.

To: Harry Darnell
From: 12345qwert@gmail.com
Re: Ava Butler

The anonymous sender replays my life from my teens, mistake by mistake in great detail, for three pages, finishing up with the dates and times I'd reportedly engaged in inappropriate shenanigans with Samuel.

A cry escapes my lips before I recall I have a listener. I recover. "Damn paper cuts." Then I rock back and forth, holding the folder. I can't decide whether to photograph it. Galindo might already know about it. The sender might even work for the FBI, for all I know. But the most likely scenario is that Harry asked someone to put together the information. And what if the "someone" was Nick and Katie? I think they do stuff like background checks for Harry. Of all the possibilities, this is the one I fear the most, because it would mean a betrayal of the worst kind. The best I can hope for is just a busybody.

One thing is clear. The "someone" does not think highly of me.

The entrance door to the office bangs open, then after a short delay I hear it shut.

"Lord Harry." The colloquialism rolls off my lips, and I only realize the irony after I say it aloud. I giggle, mostly from nerves, then stuff the folder back in Harry's drawer. I slide the drawer shut as softly as if Ginger's little fingers were wrapped around it. There's no time to escape Harry's office. Someone is going to open Harry's door, I know it, because M-Squared isn't a closed-door environment.

Improv, Ava. Time for improv. Wisdom and war. Wisdom and war.

I roll the visitor chair to the window, face the harbor, and sit, leaning my head back in repose, my cold coffee clutched in both hands. I am now the woman sneaking in to experience the power that comes with being a rich white guy from the States who owns this view. I breathe in, I breathe out. I summon soothing water to put out the fire inside as I hear the footfalls on the carpet in the corridor. *Visualize. Visualize.*

Behind me, the sound of the knob turning, the latch disengaging, and the door opening destroys my water imagery. I feign sleep, the coffee cup balanced between my thighs and cradled by my hands.

"Hello?"

I jump, swing around. It's Jarod from the Odd Pod in a long-sleeved black T-shirt that reads MT. BAKER BANKED SLALOM. "Oh!"

His brows furrow. "What are you doing in here?"

I don't have to fake being flustered. "I was, um, drinking coffee, there was nobody here, so I just . . . oh, this is so embarrassing . . . I just wanted to see what it felt like. You know." I lift a hand from my cup, gesture toward the glistening turquoise water. "The view. The office." I stand, letting my coffee spill on my skirt and drip down my legs. "Shit!"

Jarod's eyes drill into me, but they soften as they're drawn to my skin. He pulls tissues from a dispenser on Harry's desk. Instead of handing them to me, he bends at the waist and blots the cool liquid from my thighs. Then he moves the tissue to the bottom of the trickle, on the inside of my knee, and in a smooth upward stroke, wipes farther than he needs to until his hand is under my skirt. His back is rising and falling ever faster.

Suddenly, an imbalance of power between us is very clear. He's starting to think about how he can get me fired because he discovered me here. And that I might want to keep my job. He's aroused, and it's palpable. I can smell it, as real as the touch of his palm splayed on my inner thigh.

I stumble back, knocking into the chair, gouging the wall under the window. "Thank you, I'm good now." I turn toward the door.

Jarod—faster than I would have given most geeks credit for—blocks my exit. "Working on a Sunday. Industrious." His voice catches.

"Yeah, I was gone most the week. I have a lot to do."

"But you have time for coffee and a nap."

"Well, I—"

"Alone in here."

"It's quiet that way. I get more done."

"I've got some ideas on that."

It's time for me to steal this scene if I want out of here without having to do Jarod on Harry's desk. I rotate my ring, then I brighten my expression. "Me, too. Can I ask you a few questions? About some things that are way over my head?"

"Mm-hm." His pupils dilate. "I like the sexy librarian look with the glasses."

I push past him. "Come." As I walk and he follows, I press the app I use for dating emergencies. It makes my phone ring. Seems like a good idea in sexual harassment emergencies, too. "Hello? Hi, Mommy." I stop and turn to Jarod, holding up a finger. "Ginger sick? I leave right now. Be there in fifteen minutes."

Jarod is so close he's all but pressed against me.

"So sorry. Sick daughter. Give me a rain check on my questions?"

"What kind of questions?" He puts a hand around my wrist.

"Harry has me working on a project with the governor's office. I need to access a list of our clients and partners. Our charitable contributions. Our vendors. See where our"—I make air quotes—"virtual currency makes its mark. Where it can make a bigger mark with the Virgin Islands government."

His fingers tighten. "You sound like a reporter."

I laugh. "Nah."

"Or a cop."

I shake my head, twist my wrist, freeing it. "That hurts."

He grins, a wolf's hungry face. "You're sexy as hell. It's doing strange things to me. We can continue where we left off with your questions over dinner tomorrow night."

"Irie." I step back from him. "Now I have to go fetch my sick baby."

I don't have to act to make my retreat look hurried. I trot to my desk and run for the door, all the while thinking, *Like hell we'll continue where he left off.* But I can deal with tomorrow, *tomorrow.*

TWENTY-THREE

MY VERY HEALTHY baby giggles and splashes in the one-inch deep surf, topless in her swim diaper that afternoon. We're enjoying our second beach day in a row. I need the pulsing water, white sand, soft trade winds, and peace, and I need Ginger-time. I pull the brim of a floppy straw hat down farther, keeping the worst of the sun off my face.

We have North Star beach practically to ourselves. Tourists are sparse in the summer, and they tend to cluster nearer the resorts, anyway. A few other locals lounge on beach towels, and I see snorkels in the distance, where the water depth plunges from thirty to over three thousand feet. Diving the wall called to me when I was younger, like fast cars, swigging rum from a bottle, and wild boys. Now, I'm happier sipping rum and coconut water in the shade of a palm tree, with no fast cars or boys or men in sight. Though I wouldn't mind a man. The one surefire way I know to release tension and emotion is more fun with a partner, and I don't even have a prospect anymore. Nor could I indulge if I did, given the special pen I'm carrying around.

I reread for the hundredth time a message Galindo sent as I was leaving M-Squared: *Go on that date. Do whatever you have to do.*

I snarl, an ineffectual sound no one can hear. No one but me. But I count. I am not going to be prostituted by him or anyone. Sex is great, but only on my terms or not at all.

I finally decide what I want to say to him and text back: *FUCK YOU.*

That felt good. I add: *AND THE HORSE YOU RODE IN ON, COWBOY.*

A woman stoops to admire Ginger. I smile. Ginger is a beauty. The woman speaks to her, and Ginger keeps splashing, seemingly oblivious to her admirer.

I call out, "She not talking yet." Watching them, I wonder if Ginger even hears the woman. Maybe hearing problems is why she's late with words. I hadn't thought of that before. Another vexing thing, and I'm already vexed to the max.

Then Ginger plops over and bear-crawls toward me, her swim diaper soggy and legs sandy. She still won't walk for me, but at least now I know she can. Her lower lip juts out and she begins to wail halfway across the sand. It's hot on her sweet knees and hands. The woman follows her, and leans over to pick her up.

I drop my phone and run to my daughter. I hold out my arms for her.

The woman hesitates. She's short, making me feel tall, and my curves seem excessive compared to her spare body. Enormous Jackie O sunglasses cover her eyes and cheekbones. She squeezes Ginger, then hands her to me.

"There, there, Ginger Thomas flower. Mommy got you." I kiss her palms and knees.

She pouts but the crying stops.

"Thank you," I say to the woman, who is already walking away.

Then I see something in the sand. It's a phone. I look back at my towel. My phone is still safely on it. I lean over, keeping Ginger on the uphill side, and pick up the phone from the beach. The background photo on the screen is a picture of a familiar-looking woman kissing a gorgeous black man, one I know well.

Samuel.

It's obviously the woman that just picked up Ginger in the photo, but I've seen her before. Then it comes to me: Noni. The plant lady.

And finally my slow brain clicks. Seeing the two of them in the urgent conversation a week ago, in the deserted M-Squared offices. Bile rises in my throat. The woman on the private porch to his bedroom, the smell of lavender, lemon, and cigarettes. The person who beaned Samuel when we were going at it in his bathroom. She's violent, I realize.

"Stop!" I yell after her. Rational Ava has left the building. Emotional Ava has taken her place. "I've got your phone."

Noni doesn't break stride.

"Shit."

I stuff my towel, phone, and sandals into the beach bag, retrieving my keys at the same time. With Ginger heavy on one hip and the bag bouncing off my shoulder and into the crook of my other arm, I hobble after Noni, the hot pavement burning my feet. I don't stop to put on my shoes in the parking lot, just speed up. She's getting into a silver Saturn several cars down from the Range Rover.

A Saturn. Of course. Because she's the one that chased after me to Estate Annalise. Because she's crazy jealous. And she knew I was at Samuel's after he died. She could be the one who slit his throat and left him to bleed out in the shower.

"I said WAIT."

She pauses. I hit the clicker for the Rover, dump everything in the driver's seat, roll down the windows for the breeze, and clip my daughter into her seat in back, faster than I've ever done it. At the last second, I remember the wire. I click the pen on in my purse, and take it with me, strap over one shoulder. I squint. Even with sunglasses, the sun is blinding. I feel the mace and it's comforting. Noni waits, looking amused, like a cat disemboweling a lizard.

I close the distance between us in a few long strides, holding out her phone, panting and talking at the same time. "You forget something." I flash the screen at her. "Nice picture."

She takes it from me, clicks the button on the side to turn the LED display off. "You know you were just part of his cover story, don't you? Just like those two-bit whores at his client parties."

"What?"

"You, and those other girls. You all think you're so hot, that he's so into you, but you were nothing to him."

Crazy jealous.

"You killed them," I said.

And if she did, that means Samuel couldn't have, which would mean more to me than I'd realized, if the quivering in my chest is any indication. It's not a good feeling to wonder if you've been intimate with a kidnapper-murderer.

"I didn't do anything anyone didn't have coming."

Did she just confess? I pray the wire's working. "I'm turning you in to the police."

"How nice." She gets in the sedan, waggles her fingers at me, and backs out.

Rage courses through me. Rage at her, at Samuel, at Galindo, at this whole damn mess. Rage at the universe. I should have maced her.

The guardian angel in me rears up, to fight for vengeance.

"Maybe you're the one who was just his cover story, did you ever think of that?" I shout at her, shaking my fist, but her windows are up and she's already pulling away down the road back toward Taino. I'm not even sure what I meant, but it felt good to yell something at her.

I stomp and curse my way back to the Rover, going over it all aloud and in my head. I may have just solved the mystery of Heaven, Lailah, Shayna, and Samuel to boot. I'm dazed but mad like a caged crocodile at what happened to the three young women. I want to snap, roar, lunge, and instead I feel toothless and trapped as she drives away.

What a senseless, senseless waste. I get Ginger out of the car seat and take my time dressing her, then buckle her back in. I put on my cover-up and shoes, sticking my phone on the charger, and reassembling the beach bag, trying to calm myself. I need to be a mother first. Then I can figure out how to report a killer and see that she ends up in prison for the rest of her sorry life. I'll shower, change clothes, talk to Galindo, and get the ball moving for Noni's arrest after we're home.

"Let we blow this joint, Ginger."

Ginger gurgles.

"And why you not talk?" I turn in my seat. "Mommy? Can Ginger say 'Mommy'?"

She kicks her legs and holds out her hands to me.

I sigh and reach to press the ignition button. A horn blares as a truck pulls up beside me. I freeze. It's Nick.

He leaps out of the truck and runs to my still-open window. "You and Ginger. Out of the car. Hurry."

TWENTY-FOUR

I ROCK BACK and forth in the passenger seat of Nick's truck, cradling Ginger's head to my chest. She's sleeping, her thumb suctioned into her mouth. Porky and Babyface stand outside the window, harassing me with questions, asking about Noni, but also pressing me on the things they agreed not to. Nick is beside them, arms crossed, so I don't mention Galindo or the agreement.

I answer some, then clam up. "I told you what I know. Now let me tend to my daughter. You upsetting her."

A bomb. Someone—that bitch, Noni?—planted a bomb on the Rover while Ginger and I played on the beach. Two more seconds, hell, one more second, and it would have blown my baby girl and me to kingdom come.

Horns are blaring. The road is closed in both directions, and the motorists behind the ROAD CLOSED signs that the police erected on sawhorse barricades are angry.

Porky turns to Nick. "One more time, from the beginning."

"You didn't believe it the first time, what's going to change now?" Nick's scowl deepens.

"A woman name Annalise tell you son a bomb in she car?" he jerks his head at me.

Nick rolls his eyes. "Our home, Estate Annalise, has a jumbie spirit. Our son claims she talks to him. We haven't been sure whether to believe him. Until today, when he said, 'Annalise says to tell you that Aunt Ava is at North Star beach and there's a bomb about to go off in her carp.'"

I've heard him say all this five times now, and I still can't believe it. I whisper another prayer of thanks to Annalise and all the female saints, demigods, deities, and goddesses in every religion.

"In her carp."

"That's what he said, but he's only five. I knew what he meant."

"Which is?"

"Car, obviously." He said obviously in the same tone as he would have *dumbass*.

"So you knew Ms. Butler here and you drive here."

"No. I knew that my son said that a jumbie spirit said Ava would be here. I took it on faith. And here she is."

Porky isn't writing. "Mm-hm."

Nick drags his fingers back through his hair, leaving it like he's been electrocuted. "I arrive, Ava's about to start her car. I tell her to get Ginger out and stand back. I look under the car, and there's a bomb. I call you guys. You come here. You find it."

"With your fingerprints on it, I imagine."

"Oh Jesus H. Christ, probably, because I wasn't wearing gloves when I came to try to save the life of one of my wife's and my best friends and our goddaughter."

My purse is beside me on the bench seat, my wire inside. I need to get a copy of my recording to the St. Marcos police. So they'll arrest Noni. So they'll leave Nick and me alone. But I'm not giving it to them until I get an okay from Galindo, who is probably listening right this second, like a professional voyeur.

At the thought, I realize something that I should have long ago. Samuel worked with the FBI. Samuel was wired, too. My encounters with him, what we said, what we did: Galindo heard it all. Bile rises in my throat.

I slip one hand down from my daughter's back and check my phone for texts.

Galindo, from half an hour ago: *I'll pretend you didn't just tell me to fuck off & assume we're good to go.*

Katie: *Ava, don't get in your car. Don't turn on your car. Wait for Nick. He'll explain.*

Galindo: *Holy Christ, that fucking Noni is a fruitcake.*

Katie: *Is everything okay? Please let me know you're all right.*

Galindo: *This is a clusterfuck. A bomb. Really? She's insane.*

Katie: *Nick texted. Thank God. I'm the worst mother ever for not believing my son.*

I respond to Galindo's last text: *I need to give the cops the recording of Noni. They're hassling Nick and me.*

Galindo: *Give me five minutes.*

Babyface leaves Porky questioning Nick and sidles over to my window, addressing me softly.

"Can you repeat that?" I ask, sliding my phone under my thigh.

"I ask you, is that Rover registered to Mahogany Management?"

"Yes."

"So it not yours?"

"Isn't that what I just said?"

"Why you driving it then?"

"Because it's my work vehicle."

He chuptzes. "I hear about your work."

"What? From whom?"

"So let me get this straight. You find that dead ho?"

"I found a dead woman named Lailah."

"Samuel Lewis dead, after you sex it up with him?"

I grit my teeth. "I found Samuel dead."

Babyface shakes his head. "Something here shady. Something with you, I can't put my finger on."

Porky's radio crackles. He turns his back on us and strides off, speaking to someone on the other end. When he returns, he says, "You're free to go."

Nick and I share a look. His is perplexed. I think, *Galindo.*

"What about my vehicle?" I ask.

Porky doesn't answer me.

"Mahogany Management's vehicle. Impounded." Babyface starts typing on his phone.

"What are you doing?" I ask him, sure he's typing something about me.

He smirks. "Updating boss man." Then he walks away without a backward glance.

Nick rounds his truck to the driver's side, and I sneak a peek at my own phone.

Galindo: *I sent excerpt of recording to police, ordered them to stand down. Confirm you and Kovacs are released.*

I respond in the affirmative and add: *Confirm they've arrested Noni.*

There is no reply.

TWENTY-FIVE

MOM DROPS me at work Monday morning. She believes the Rover is in the shop, and I hate lying to her. Dad rides in the passenger seat. They're headed to see Dr. Easy straight from here, Ginger in tow. I kiss my daughter's sleep-warmed forehead, and her curls tickle my lips. Her baby powder scent makes me think of Zach and of New York. It's more a dream than a memory now.

I get out and stop to kiss Dad on the cheek through the window. The rush of emotion is intense. "I love you, Daddy."

He gives me a thumbs-up on the right, and a right-sided smile.

I go to Mom next. "I love you, Mommy." I kiss her high, round cheekbone, the skin thin and papery against my lips.

She grabs my face. "My baby girl." I am transfixed by her gaze. "I believe in you. Do what right today."

It feels like she sees into my soul, even though it's no different from the kind of thing she says to me most days. I nod, a lump in my throat. "Be careful." I wave goodbye as she pulls away.

At my desk, I answer a few emails. Jarod, reminding me about tonight, which makes me need those extra Rolaids in Harry's drawer. Hanif, asking if I'm okay and offering to take me to lunch. That one's a surprise. I don't know what to make of it. Cora, needing my benefits choices turned in. Which reminds me I saw her here yesterday when the office was closed. Something else I don't know what to make of. I stay away from the *St. Marcos Source* and horoscopes and anything else that could derail me, and congratulate myself on a four-day streak without them. I make a note to call the governor's office. I keep my head down, hoping no one even notices my presence. Harry is in his office, quiet. I wonder if the police called him about the Rover. If anyone here knows about Noni trying to kill Ginger and me with a bomb yesterday. If Harry knows of his plant lady's involvement with Samuel. I wonder where Noni is, if she'll make another attempt on my life. If my daughter and parents will be safe, as Galindo promised me.

So many worries, so many secrets.

I've received no word Noni is in custody. Which makes me wonder if Galindo's just shining me on. He could have facilitated her getaway yesterday. She might be working with the Feds, like Samuel did. Like I am. Noni's crazy, but you don't have to be sane to work for the Feds. In my experience, it's a good indicator of the opposite.

But Galindo did promise me he'd keep my family safe, and I will kill the bastard with my bare hands if he doesn't make good on that one. I stare at my nails, remember what they're capable of.

My cell phone vibrates. I've got the ringer on silent. I flip the phone over, praying it's not Galindo.

It's not. It's a New York number. Kenny's New York number.

"Hello?"

"Yo, sexy mama, you sitting?" He coughs, loud and liquid, just to prove it's him.

"Hi, Kenny." I cup my hand around the mouthpiece and cast furtive glances. No one seems to be listening. "Yes. What is it?" I close my eyes. This is good news. It has to be good news. Because I can't take any more bad.

"I've got a record deal in my hand for you, right this second." He pauses, then says, "What?" in a funny, multi-tonal voice that's supposed to make him sound cool.

"Really?" I hear my voice go up in pitch, louder, and I sink in my chair.

"No, I just pranking ya." His voice booms in my ear, "Like I don't have better things to do with my time? Of course *really*."

"Wow, I mean, thank you. Oh my God." My vision is suddenly spotty at the edges, and I feel like I'm in a sauna. I jump to my feet, fan my shirt. I'm still on my Katie-Kovacs-leggings-and-tunics kick.

"So you gonna jerk me around while you find an agent, or are we gonna do this? It's a package deal. I produce, you sign, Aphrodite Records foots the bill." He rattles off a few terms, money with zeroes that are life-changing, legalese I don't understand but don't care.

"Can you hold on a second?"

"What the f—"

I ignore him, typing frantically to Zach: *Aphrodite Records making me a BIG offer. Haven't called agent/manager. Need me to make up my mind.*

His response is quick: *AWESOM. Does this mean you'll move to New York? Could be your big brake. Probably should go fore it.*

I put the phone back to my ear.

I hear Kenny say, "Goddammit. She hung up on me."

"Wait, no, I'm here. And the answer is yes. Yes, let's do this."

"Good. I'm emailing you the contract. Call me if you have questions. Gotta jet."

The line goes dead.

I hold the phone against my chest. I twist the ruby courage ring. My first coherent thought is that now I can take Dad home to New Brunswick to see his family, something I know both my parents secretly want but can't afford. I can finally do something for somebody else. I put a fist to my mouth. This can't be real.

The phone rings again, but it's my doctor's office. I let it go to voicemail, the record deal consuming every cell of my being, all my thoughts, my energy, my emotions. The trembling in my hands works its way through my whole body like I'm a tuning fork. The phone falls to the floor.

I look up, and people are clustered at my door, staring at me.

"Well?" It's Harry's voice. My coworkers part to let him wheel through my door. The grin on his face is so big, I know he heard the news before I did.

"Aphrodite Records. I said yes."

The office erupts in cheers and applause. It's a mob scene. Hanif is pounding me on the back, people are laughing, Cora asks for my autograph, and everyone is telling me to remember them when I'm famous.

Harry finally holds up a hand for silence. "I've been sent an advance track." More cheering. "Anyone want to hear the song that just landed Ava a record deal?"

My coworkers get rowdy again. Harry grins. He presses some buttons on his phone. I expect reedy audio from the speakers on his iPhone. Instead, the kick drum sounds on a surround system wired into the office, and it shakes the room like an earthquake. I hadn't heard the final version of the song before, and, honestly, it sounds so effing awesome, I want to grab it in both hands and rub it all over my body. I don't, though. I stand, frozen, my mouth hanging in an O. More thoughts have come crashing into my brain, and I'm in limbo between excitement and confusion and fear. Because I'm not sure whether a recording contract will change anything for me. It doesn't make Noni disappear. It probably won't get Galindo off my back. It can't heal my dad. And it sure won't bring back Samuel, Heaven, Lailah, and Shayna.

Maybe it won't change any of those things.

My voice sizzles with electricity through the sound system, and I unfreeze. I've never missed a cue in my stage career. I throw my head back and sing, beating my chest like I did for Chen to the power of the three beats in four short syllables: BOMB-SHELL-BABY.

It's an instant dance party, with me at the center. I look out of the circle, find Harry watching, his fist pumping to the beat. He ducks his head and does a wheelie and three-sixty in his chair.

My heart cracks knowing what he's done for me, and what I'm doing in return to him.

TWENTY-SIX

JAROD KNOCKS on the duplex doorframe. "Ava? Anyone?" His voice through the screen door is loud, and close. I'm only fifteen feet away behind the bathroom door.

The duplex sits in a clearing hacked out of thick bush on the side of a hill. There's room to park a few cars, and that's it. No yard, no landscaping. Just a white masonry block dropped down in the trees and invisible from the road below. The Rover is still in police custody, and Nana and Ginger are having dinner at my parents'. With no cars outside, the place is a wasteland. An isolated wasteland. I usually like the privacy.

"In here." I'm just out of the shower, hair in one towel to keep it dry, body in another. I reach into my purse on the counter and press the button to turn on the wire in the pen.

I'm running late, and I'd hoped he would be, too. Dad had a tough afternoon, so Mom ran behind schedule, which backed me up. When I asked her to drop me but keep Ginger, her eyes were sad, her mouth tight.

All she'd said was, "And when you leave for New York? What about Ginger then?"

I bit my tongue, but I'd already handled that, having spent most of the day on arrangements. Zach's coming through for me. His buddy will sublet me a completely furnished rent-controlled apartment. It has a bedroom decorated in dragonflies and glitter, perfect for a little girl. Plus, Zach gave me the number of an extra on the show who babysits for the cast and crew. Kenny emailed me a plane ticket. Ginger and I will leave next week.

I have a feeling it's not going down easy when I take Mom's grandgirl to New York. For that matter, I'm worried about Nana with us gone. That's why I suggested Mom take Nana along for dinner, too. Mom surprised me with a yes, and it gave me a chuckle to see the two of them drive off together with Ginger. Nana could barely see over the dash.

And then I had to rush to get ready.

"I'll be out in a minute," I say. "Make yourself at home. There's beer in the refrigerator."

I'm glad I'm not ready. I want to stall this as long as I can. I feel like Galindo's pimping me out, and that wasn't part of our deal. He can't make me have sex with Jarod—I can shut off the wire and cut Galindo out if I have to, blame it on a technical glitch or my own ineptitude. I'll go through with a dinner. I'll flirt and ask questions. But I didn't kill Samuel, I'm not trained for this, and I'm not risking the lives of my family.

When I get to New York, I'll find someone to help me out of this mess. Someone with the label or through Zach and his endless network of contacts. Galindo's already been squawking about the record deal, but I sweetly explained it would blow my cover if I don't jump at it, and he's standing down.

"Cool." I hear the refrigerator open and the slight pressure release of a beer tab being pulled back. "Nice place."

It's not that great, but good manners and all. "Thanks."

My bathroom door lock doesn't work, so I rush. Elvis monitors me from his perch on the toilet lid as I swipe on deodorant and skip perfume. I'll be no siren tonight. I shimmy into my least sexy underwear and bra without removing my towel. I pull on a knee-length jean skirt, losing my balance when I have one leg in the waistband. I teeter but catch myself on the counter. The skirt has never touched my body before today. It's a gift from Mom, and it's so loose I can turn it all the way around without unbuttoning it, and it never touches my body. I've decided to wear Katie's top with it, the one that I borrowed after the wreck in Dad's truck, but without the safety pins to anchor it at cleavage-baring level. Just as I pull it over my towel turban and shrug it down, the door opens.

Jarod waves steam away and invites himself in. "Need any help?"

My laugh is brittle. I've got to find my motivation for this role tonight, and it's clear I haven't yet. I add a smile. "I got it, big boy."

He brushes against me holding two beers—Elvis dashing in the opposite direction, making the escape I wish I could—to get to the toilet seat, where he cops a squat. He's wearing a Beastie Boys concert T-shirt, *Licensed to Ill* era. I've never seen him in anything but loose-cut shirts with long sleeves before, and he's muscled up like Samuel was. Tattoos cover his arms. Not sleeves. Old school. A red Corvette with HOT ROD on a banner across it. MOM in a heart. And Poseidon, with coins at his feet that have SC stamped on them. I recognize Poseidon from his trident, but other than that, he looks more like a thug.

Jarod tips his beer back. "Mind if I watch?"

More than he'll ever know. "Suit yourself." I remove the turban and shake out my hair, a difficult thing in tight quarters.

Jarod shifts in his seat, slugs half his beer down. His phone rings. He slugs the other half, crushes the can and holds his phone up to his ear with his shoulder. As he speaks, he pops the top on another Heineken, exits the bathroom, brushing against me again, this time letting his fingers rub across my denim–clad bana.

Into his phone, he says, "Talk to me."

His touch reminds me of when one of our island's famous six-inch centipedes scuttled across my face while I was in bed, and I shudder, creeped-out. This isn't the Jarod I know from the office. When I met him, I just thought he was a pervy tech guy. A geek with a crush. A loser with women who'd developed a minor God-complex working with the imaginary money system he'd developed for Harry. The guy tonight is much surer of himself. I search for the right word. He's . . . scary.

I rack my brain for ways to make myself repulsive without being obvious. I skipped the perfume. Didn't do my hair. Dressed down, and then some. I decide not to wear makeup or jewelry. Out of habit, though, I slip on my spike-heeled first-date shoes. I'm about to take them back off—wrong message, Ava—when Jarod's voice rises in the other room.

"You forget who you're talking to. I'm the Hot Rod." He laughs, and it's not a pleasant sound. "That's why I pay you. To prevent problems, or take care of them. You fucked up the thing with Samuel so bad, now I gotta do this one myself. It's gonna cost you."

I'd heard the name Hot Rod before, from someone recently. *Think, Ava, think.* My phone buzzes with a text, and I remember. A text. Babyface sent me a text from Porky's phone, then accidentally texted again to someone he called Hot Rod. Someone he was demanding a package from.

That triggers another memory. Governor Milton prodded Harry for payola, telling him that someone in M-Squared was paying off a government employee already.

Bribes can come in packages.

Cops are government employees.

Babyface was a cop demanding a package from "Hot Rod."

And why do people bribe cops? To buy cover for something illegal. Because they're criminals.

Shit.

Jarod *is* Hot Rod. A criminal. Paying off a dirty cop. Sneaking around Harry's office on a Sunday morning. Suspicious of my interest in Amphy and the SeaCoin transactions. The guy who *created* Amphy, the whole system. Harry's brainiac, the one he trusts to make everything work. The guys with one hundred percent access to everything. The keys to the virtual kingdom.

And he said Babyface had messed up on Samuel. If that meant what I thought it did, then when Hot Rod said he'd take care of this problem himself, what did he mean? Was I the problem?

It comes to me, and I squeak like a mouse in a trap. The wire. Galindo sent a portion of my audio to Porky and Babyface. Porky let me go. Then Babyface told me when he was texting that he was "updating boss man."

He was telling someone I was wired. And the call Jarod just got? Was someone telling him the same thing?

I kick the bathroom door shut and lean against it, eyes closed, suddenly breathless. There's no way out of this room.

In the end, it's just like Galindo and his federal friends suspected: follow the digital currency and you'll find it tied to criminal activity. Jarod's the one Galindo is looking for. I reach for my purse to get my mace. Why did it take me so long to figure it out? He's—

The door crashes open, throwing me across the small room. I land sprawled on the toilet, catching myself on the tank, too surprised to scream. Jarod is on me in a second. He puts one arm around my rib cage, clamping both arms to my sides, and slides the other hand into my hair, gripping it near the base. He yanks me up, using my torso to turn me, and my hair to balance me. His legs pin mine against the cabinets. I see us in the mirror. There's blood on my lip.

I search for a weapon, but he's got my arms and legs immobilized, and my mace is still in my purse on the counter. Sex, I think. That's all I've got to use against him. No, sex is only part of it. I have my brain. And it's time to use it. Samuel had called me Venus. Gods and men of all types found her irresistible. Venus can distract Jarod just long enough, and make time for Galindo to get here. I don't want to be Venus, but I can do it. I'm a trained actress. We don't always like the roles we're given, but I promise I can find the motivation to play this character.

I lick the blood off my lips. Lower my lashes, get into my part, willing my eyes moist and inviting.

"You like it rough? Then hurt me, big daddy," I say, my voice childlike, my insides churning, my brain telling my heart to shut down this one last time, and turn it around on him. Because I can see in his eyes and feel in the bulge thrust against me that whatever else he plans to do to me, that he wants me alive for the next few minutes.

He sneers. Still holding my hair, he shoves his hand up my shirt, under my bra, down my stomach and back, between my legs. Then he starts over at my feet, jerking me down by my hair so he can reach, then working his way up.

He's frisking me.

"Oh, I think you know where to find it." I push my crotch against his, fighting to keep my face doll-like and purse my lips when they're curdling inside, like my mouth is full of spoiled milk.

He shakes his head. He shakes my purse out, dumping the mace, lipstick, pen, and little wallet on the counter. I have to stop him.

I can't raise my hands, but I can move my fingers. With one finger I tap the one thing I least want to touch. "What you got here?" I think about my long nails, what they can do, but I don't have enough range of motion.

I'm trapped.

My breaths instantly grow shorter. *You cannot afford this now.* This paralyzing panic. To be weak. But I have failed. I got myself into this situation, and now look what is happening.

A voice in my head says sternly, "It not you fault. What a bad man do not you fault. You hear me?"

"Yes, Nana," I whisper.

"What?" Jarod says. "You say something?"

My breathing normalizes. My mind clears. I angle my face up to his, the temptress face. The heathen the Mother Superior punished. "Yeah, I said haven't you heard about me, Jarod?"

He picks up the mace then discards it. He looks through my wallet then sets it down. He opens my lipstick then drops it on the floor.

I increase the pressure on his crotch, trying to draw his attention, use up his brain cells. "You nosy."

He smiles as he grabs the pen and clicks the push button. The fake writing tip retracts.

His gaze returns to mine. "You think I haven't seen one of these before, don't know how it works?"

My heart arrests at his words. It takes a few moments before it resumes and I can think. If I can keep Jarod occupied and myself alive, help will come. My cover is blown. Jarod is threatening me. Surely Galindo heard the assault on the wire before Jarod turned it off. If not, he'll figure it out soon enough with no audio streaming. Either way, he's coming. He's said he's always close. He has to be. Surely the FBI won't just hang me out to dry. But that's what they'd done to Samuel. Maybe what they'd done to Samuel, anyway.

Jarod's pupils dilate until I can't see where they end and his irises begin. His breath is heavy in my face, his grip on my hair tightens and he pulls my head further back. "But we can play first and talk about your little recording device later."

I throw myself into my role. "That better. Show me rude, boy. Give it to me raw."

Please let Galindo be close by, on his way.

Jarod turns me to face the mirror, pressing up on me from behind, then looks me in the eye in our reflection. "You're a whore. I knew it the second I met you." He pushes my head down with the hand holding my hair. The tile is cold and hard under my cheek. He grasps both my wrists in one hand, then transfers them to the other, sliding his elbow to my neck. The upward pressure on my arms is awful, but I don't cry out. I see my mace on the counter, useless to me, out of my reach.

Use the time you're buying to think. Not about him, about living. About winning.

"You like whores, Jarod?" It's hard to speak with my mouth against the tile, but I need to keep playing the role. I flashback to NYU theater school. The professor assigned me a rape-victim scene. It triggered memories and feelings that I couldn't face. I lost it and ran from the theater. A handsome blond boy chased after me, held me as I cried. I didn't speak, refusing to make my story true with words, and Zach made my tears and silence okay.

Nana's voice speaks in my head again, softer this time. "It not you fault. What a bad man do not you fault."

I'm not running this time. I'm staying here. I'm seeing it through. I'm playing the part until I win, because it's not my fault what a bad man does to me.

Jarod yanks my skirt up to my waist. "I like this," he says, cupping me with his hand. Then he tears the granny panties off me. "I like this better."

"It all for you and that hot rod of yours," I growl. This *is* my Tony Award performance, I know, but my mind floats far away again. This time with Collin. Collin, and the ridonkulous shoes. Yes. Oh yes, yes, yes.

"Oh, Collin," I whisper. "I love you, too."

Jarod ignores my words this time. He grunts, unzips his pants, pulls aside his underwear, and just as he gets ready to violate me, I catapult both my sharp spiked heels up, using my torso as a lever. I drive them as hard and high as I can go, pushing with all my strength.

Jarod screams like I've never heard anyone scream in my life. His body falls backward, away from me, and something large and hard clatters to the tile floor. I'm barefoot now and free, but I can't waste a single second. I grab my straight iron and wrap the cord around his wrists, tight, and then around his ankles, trussing him. I drag him— still howling with pain, my shoes still in his lap—out of the bathroom. He starts to thrash. I've got to restrain him, just in case. But I've also got to call for help, and do it somehow over Jarod's enraged rant about the hole in his wood.

Ugh, I'm wigged out, and I can see it, but there's nothing I can do about it now except ignore it and Minerva his ass. I grab the pen and click it on.

I shout, "You son of a bitch, Galindo, you better be here in the next thirty seconds, or I'll be the jumbie haunting you for the rest of your days."

I glance down at myself. Sweat and blood drip down my chest onto my blouse, and if it weren't for the modest skirt mom gave me that covers where Jarod ripped away my panties, I'd be exposed.

I hear gravel outside as a car comes to a sliding stop on the far end of my house, over where I park. If it's not Galindo, I'm in big trouble. It could be Noni, who also wants me dead. Babyface, who probably does, too. I look into the sea of my blue bathroom and see something on the floor halfway behind the toilet. The barrel of a gun. The loud crash. Jarod the gangster. He was carrying. I scramble back into the bathroom. I hate guns. I grab it anyway.

Jarod is rolling around, trying to get to a seated position, and I yank the cord as hard as I can. He topples back over. "Crazy bitch," Jarod snarls.

And in an instant, it doesn't matter what happens next. I'm a bombshell, baby. What bad men do to me isn't my fault, and they deserve every bit I blow up on them.

I walk halfway to Jarod, turn my face upward and spread my hands. "You lose again, Father Jerome."

Jarod spits at me. "Who the fuck's Father Jerome?"

I hold the grip of the gun in both hands, raise it over my head, and bring the barrel down on Jarod's skull. The thunk is satisfyingly loud. He falls over with another thunk as his head lands on the floor. He groans. He hasn't lost consciousness, but he's not fighting me anymore.

"You lose, too, Jarod."

Galindo steps through the door in his usual Hawaiian shirt with his shiny black handgun trained on Jarod's head. I release the straight-iron cord and return to the bathroom, where I grab the pen. Galindo is cuffing Jarod, who's moaning about the hole in his dick. Actually, I think I got a little more than just his hot rod, but I'll let the EMTs break that to him gently. He's lucky I didn't have a knife, or there'd be less of it left than there is.

The sound of another vehicle pulling up outside gets Galindo's attention.

"You expecting company?" he asks me.

"No. You?"

"Get back," he says in a soft voice. He retreats to the bathroom, motioning me away.

"What about me?" Jarod whines.

I don't have to be told twice. I'm making tracks for my bedroom, when I glance back and see Babyface sneak in. He hasn't seen me. His eyes are locked on Jarod.

"Stop. Don't. There's a man with a—" Jarod says.

Babyface pulls a gun from his holster and points it at Jarod, but not fast enough. Galindo pulls the trigger and Babyface goes down clutching his thigh.

Galindo says to me over Babyface's howls, "Grab me a second set of handcuffs from my car. They're in a bag."

I bring a pair to him, and he snaps them over Babyface's wrists. For all the times I've worried about cops being shot and, more specifically, about Collin being killed, I realize that I don't mind at all that Galindo plugged some lead in Babyface. In fact, I'm pretty giddy about it.

"Two for the price of one," Galindo says.

"Stupid fuck," Jarod shouts, this time at Babyface.

While giddy with relief, I find that as my adrenaline wears off, I'm pissed. I'd done nothing wrong, yet this man with our own government had blackmailed me into demeaning myself, betraying friends, and risking my life. Gives a whole new meaning to "We're with the government, and we're here to help." Count me not a fan.

"Galindo?"

He glances up at me.

"Thanks for letting that asshole almost rape and murder me."

He grunts. "Good work."

I snap the pen in two and throw it at him. I walk out my front door and head down my driveway, bloody and shoeless, and I don't care where I end up. It's not much as far as dramatic exits go, but it's all I've got. This show is over.

TWENTY-SEVEN

INTERVIEWS WITH A PHALANX of federal agents from A-Z agencies last all through the night. They've got me holed up in a conference room in the federal building. I'm surrounded by framed portraits of Virgin Islands Delegates to the US House of Representatives. The room isn't opulent, but the leather swivel armchairs are comfortable, with good back support and nice tush cushions. There's enough of them for an army, too. My guess is thirty chairs. The Feds never use more than a handful of them all night, preferring to do their interviews one after another, so that I get to repeat everything five times and wreck my voice. I won't be able to sing for days.

It's like a prison, really. I can't even go to the bathroom without an escort. So many things about this marathon interrogation are wrong. Depriving me of sleep, leaving my daughter without her mom, and forcing me to continue conversations in close quarters even after my breath grows stank and my pits rank. It's demeaning. I'd done them huge favors, and they treat me like a criminal.

The contrast between the good cops I've known—with Collin and the Jacobys at the top of that list—and these Feds is stark. Oh, and one of the Feds lets it slip that Noni is a former FBI agent herself. Nice. So excuse me if I am a less-than-cooperative witness. Seems to me they have all they need from my wire, but their opinion differs. I can't answer most of their questions, but I glean from them that Jarod and his cronies had quite a profitable sideline going, assisting crooked buyers and sellers with off-the-books transactions in everything from gun running to drugs to human trafficking. The big boss of it all may slip through the cracks. The Feds suspect he's some New York wiseguy, but no one's given him up yet. I told them Babyface texted him in front of me on a phone, but it appears to be a burner, and missing. Of course. Galindo hopes to catch the guy using computer records and stuff, and I get the impression that hell is raining down on a lot of people tonight.

I hope not on Harry.

When I think about Galindo trapping me, an innocent civilian, with those kinds of people, it brings out my crazy mad. Especially when the truth hits me: he victimized me and took, took, took, just like all the other bad men in my life, and some of the not-bad-but-less-than-good ones, too. Something is building in me, something I don't understand yet, but one thing's for sure: this will never happen to me again. Meanwhile, I do my best to ruin his career as I tell my story. He'll probably get a promotion and a medal or something out of all this, though.

Galindo finally announces the Feds are done with me. I expect to be released. Hallelujah. But when he opens the door, it's to let Porky in. Galindo shakes Porky's hand, then tries to shake mine. I refuse and stay seated. Porky wisely doesn't force the issue with me. Galindo gives up, muttering, "What's with her?" and leaves me alone in my prison with my former classmate.

Porky and I don't say anything for a long time. He looks as tired as me. I'm about to let my eyes close when Porky final speaks. I jerk awake. I'd forgotten he was there.

"I trust Babyface too long. I push you on the Samuel case. I sorry," he says, his voice low.

"Thank you. And I not upset about those things." I've had hours to think about this, and the tragedy of the whole situation is Heaven, Lailah, and Shayna. They were the victims. Back when we were kids, and now. "I upset that it your job, those girls, and it takes someone like me almost getting blown up to find their killer. And they St. Mary's girls, too. We owe them better."

Porky's face is stoic, but he bites his lip.

Because he doesn't acknowledge what I feel is pretty noncontroversial, my emotions rise. I lean at him. My hand comes down on the table—smack!—harder than I expected. "Do you know what they went through, back then? What I went through? It damage them."

His lips tremble. "It damage us all."

I didn't think anything else tonight would surprise me, but this does. I peer at him, and the lip doesn't stop, so he captures it with his teeth. "You, too?"

"It not just girls Father Jerome like, Ava."

I put my hand across the table. He reaches for mine and squeezes it.

I talk fast, in a whisper. "I couldn't save them."

"You help them, though."

"I only save myself."

"Stop that. There stuff you don't know. Stuff nobody know."

I put my other hand on top of his holding mine. "Tell me."

He closes his eyes. "My rookie year, somebody murder Father Jerome. It brutal. Worse than what you did to Jarod's . . . wood."

"I hear 'bout that."

Tears roll down his cheeks. "I find evidence, and I hide it."

"What?"

"Heaven, Lailah, Shayna. They do it. Together. They do everything together, like work at that club, like dance for Samuel and his friends. Like kill Father Jerome. I know it, and they know I know it." He wipes his eyes, a rough motion.

"No!"

"Yes. I regret it ever since, not arresting them."

"Why?"

"Because that what they never get over. That why they lives go a bad way. Because they never confess and atone. The guilt eat them up. It take their choices away." He's not crying anymore. Now he just looks sad, and a little lost. His cheeks droop. "Now I carry my own guilt."

"You confess to me."

"Now all I got to do is atone?"

I pull my hands back and stand up. So does he. I walk over and hug him up, tight, tight, tight. "Porky, you atone every day you put on your uniform and do your job."

"Maybe so."

We release each other.

I open the door.

"Ava?"

"Yes?"

"You grow up to be a fine woman."

I roll my eyes. "I get a lot of that."

"No, not like that. A fine *person*. I hope I can call you my friend now."

And I stick out my hand and grasp his, giving it the kind of shake you give to someone you respect.

I'M on fumes when I stumble out of the federal building, still wearing my torn, bloody clothes from the day before. The bright early morning sunlight makes the mustard-hued masonry less uninviting than normal. Mom and Dad are waiting in his truck, which is back from repairs.

I stumble alongside of giant coconut palms lining the sidewalk. I am sleep-deprived and slightly delirious.

Mom jumps out, smothering my cheeks and hands in kisses. "Baby girl."

We get in the car, and something is missing. "Where's Ginger?"

"With Kurt and Julie Kovacs. Nana too tired. We up the whole night."

"Where are Nick and Katie?"

"In there." Mom points back where I came from.

"What?"

Dad speaks, haltingly. "They were working on the same case as you."

Of course.

He keeps going, and I'm proud of him. "Harry suspected an employee was exploiting the currency system."

Mom added, "Katie and Nick are giving statements."

Relief courses through me. Harry is innocent. Jarod was double-crossing him. Katie was keeping secrets from me, but not bad ones. "Oh my goodness. Now everything makes more sense."

"Detective Bachoo call us, too. He say they catch that woman who tried to bomb your car. Tell you not to worry."

I nod. Porky and I hadn't talked about that, but it's great news. With any luck, that means the threat to my family and me is over.

"And he say she swear she never touch Samuel. She say it his job get he killed."

Yes, that I know. Killed by a crooked cop, by one of his local brothers in the thin blue line. Babyface.

My phone rings. The FBI took it from me before they started my night of interviews. I'd only just got it back on my way out. It's my doctor's office. I try to send the call to voicemail with fumbling, puffy fingers, but accidentally answer.

"Hello? Hello? Is anyone there?" a woman's voice asks.

I sigh and put the phone to my ear. "This Ava."

"I from Dr. Ezekiel Willie's. You listen to our message?"

"No, I haven't had a chance yet."

She chuptzes me.

I shake my head. No use explaining. "Sorry. What this about?"

"Your test results are positive. You need to schedule an appointment to discuss treatment options."

I double over. "Positive? What that mean?"

"Malignancy. Breast cancer. Dr. Willie have an opening tomorrow at eight a.m. That work?"

Malignancy. I put a hand over my lump. "I call you back."

A knock sounds at the window by my head. Katie's alabaster face smiles through the glass at me.

I open the door and throw myself into her arms.

WHEN I WAKE from the sleep of the dead, Ginger is staring into my eyes. She's surfing the edge of my bed, holding on as she walks.

"Ma-ma." Her breath is sweet, the tone of her Minnie Mouse voice a caress to my ears.

I sit up, the sheet falling away from me. I'm still in the clothes I was wearing when I left the federal building after a night of interrogation. "Ma-ma," Ginger had said. Is it real? Or is she just babbling nonsense?

"Ma-ma," she repeats, insistent. She holds one arm out to me, the other fisting the sheets as she wobbles.

I pull her onto the bed and wrap my arms around her so tight she grunts and squirms, but I just laugh and hold on tight. Baby powder and little-girl smell flood my sense. "Mama," I say back to her.

She thrashes.

I relent, reluctant and a little bit empty as I let her go. "I heard you say Mama, Ginger Thomas flower."

She scoots back off the bed, feet first, and resumes her surfing, not even making eye contact.

"You're talking."

She emits a series of random noises, ending with a chirp.

Or maybe not. I stand, letting the sheet pool on the ground. My daughter keeps talking to herself. She's oblivious to me. Like a tsunami, I'm bowled over by the memory of my breast cancer diagnosis. It's real. I remember it clearly. But it seems impossible in the light of day, with a daughter depending on me.

I try saying it aloud. "I have breast cancer." My voice breaks. The girl in front of me, only one year old, doesn't have the slightest clue what I'm saying. But I do.

I lift my shirt and close my eyes as it reveals my chest. I don't want to look at it. I force my eyes open, and I pull my bra away. There's the lump. The tumor. The cancer. I press my fingertips into it, gently, hoping it's not really there. But what the eyes see, the fingers confirm. I have a solid lump, a lump my doctor is calling a malignancy. A cancer.

Ginger is no longer surfing. She's sitting with her legs in front of her, knees bent, and she has my sandals in her hands. First she claps them together like tambourines. Then she puts one up to her ear and mouth, like a cell phone, and she makes her funny noises into the heel.

I muffle my laugh with a fist. Finally, she puts the shoes one at a time in front of her feet, struggling mightily to slide her chubby little feet and piggies into the grown-woman sandals. It hits me. She wants to be like her mother. Like I wanted to be like mine.

Tears roll down my cheeks. There's still so much left I want to do. Raise my daughter. Shout at her when she won't listen as I teach her how to parallel park. Kiss her cheek and pretend I don't know how she'll spend her prom night. Give her away at her wedding, in place of the father who doesn't have the heart to appreciate what he's missing. Rock her own daughter in my arms while she grabs a few hours of much-needed sleep.

My dear mother's face fills my mind. Next, Daddy's. There's so much I want to do for them. How much time will I have left? Will Kenny and Aphrodite Records honor my contract? Is there enough money to secure Ginger's future and take care of my parents as they age, with my dad's expensive, incurable condition?

I wipe the tears away.

Ginger gives up on fitting her feet into my sandals. She rocks forward onto her hands and knees and slides her hands into the shoes. Now she marches around the room in her familiar bear-crawl, the shoes clomping. She struggles not to go face-first into the tile. I want to swoop in to prevent it, but I don't dare. My job is to raise her, for as long as I have left. As long as this lump will allow me.

My job is to fight the lump, to give her as long with me as I can. Ginger needs a mother. Which means I need to take a shower and get to work finding answers to some of my questions. My own mother didn't raise me to give in without a fight.

TWENTY-EIGHT

I TAKE A DEEP BREATH. I'm in a familiar place for a Saturday night, on the small Boardwalk stage. I'm better than I was a few days ago, but still not quite at the top of my game. The packed house doesn't seem to notice. Of course, they don't know. The cancer is a big secret, except from Harry (who was super chill about the damage to the Rover when I finally told him), Kenny, and my family and best friends. Luckily, the record label, the studio, and Kenny are being supportive, Kenny in his own way: "It's not like they're removing your voice box. If they have to take a boob, you can get fake ones. They film better anyway." Meanwhile, the label leaked "Bombshell," and it went nuts. Kenny says that's a good thing. People will pay for the final studio version, but it's becoming a viral sensation now, along with video and a montage from my photo shoot.

So now everyone here thinks I'm some kind of hotshot. So I sing to them, pounding my chest, channeling my goddess of the morning-after power. When I finish "Bombshell," the little island crowd goes mad. All this "Bombshell" hysteria feels ironic to me, in light of real bombshells. Coworkers who are killers. Lovers who are FBI agents. The time bomb inside my breast.

Dr. Willie has transferred my care to an oncology surgeon in New

York, and we've all Skyped together. They've seen my results and everyone keeps telling me how lucky I am. How of all the breast cancers you can have, this one is the least likely to kill me. Still, I'm scheduled for surgery and radiation. It's terrifying. Mom and Katie insist they're going with me. I can't let Mom leave Dad, but I'm not going to tell Katie no if she wants to stay with me afterward, for a little while. Now, how evolved and un-Ava-like is *that*? I'll admit, it's been hard not caving in and contacting Collin. But the reasons not to are bigger now than ever, because I've finally found the man I care enough about to protect him from me.

I work my way to the bar, accepting congratulations and laughing at jokes. It's like a receiving line at a wedding, and me with no groom. I hug and kiss and promise to keep in touch and that my couch is always open for visitors. My parents are waiting with Rashidi, Harry, Nana, and the Kovacs at a reserved table, sans kids, who are having a fun night with Kurt and Julie. I join them, but before I can relax, I hear someone using my sound equipment, which is a big no-no. I'd hoped to enjoy myself for a moment before packing up, but I can't risk it. I jump up.

To my group, I say, "Excuse me. Some drunk's about to ruin a few thousand dollar's worth of electronics."

Katie reaches for my hand. "Hold up."

"What?"

"I want you to stop. That's what hold up means." She sticks her tongue out at me. "And then, if you'll turn around, stand with me, and watch. Please."

So I do. And I see a man onstage punching buttons on my board, his brow furrowed, his dark blond hair in a military-like cut. He was born to wear the 501s hugging his butt. And the blue Dallas Cowboys T-shirt he has on matches his eyes perfectly, something I don't have to see his eyes to know.

Once, as a girl, I held a baby mongoose in my hand. Its little heart had hammered as hard and fast as mine is now. I'd worried it would wear itself out and die. Dad told me, "No, it's made to do that." Watching the man I love, I hope that mine is made to do this, too, because it feels so good.

"Crap. She makes this look easy. Whoops, I'll be keeping it family-friendly, y'all." The sound system squelches. He jumps, covers the mike with his hand. "Sorry. Almost got it."

Music begins to play, the reggae version of "All of Me." Collin, my Collin, bites his lower lip like the white guy he is and begins to get into character. He dances like I've never seen him dance before, shoulders shimmying, hands fisted and making little circles at his hips as he rocks back and forth. He grabs the microphone again, and he's not the fumbling guy setting up equipment anymore. His voice sounds like velvet. "This one goes out to the pretty little lady in pink Lycra and not much else."

People titter, turning, looking for me. My hands are over my mouth, although I don't know when I put them there.

Katie puts a hand on my shoulder. "I hope this is okay."

I swallow, trying to answer, but I don't have the words. I lower my hands, uncovering a smile.

"Phew," Katie says.

Mom comes to stand on the other side of me, escorting Nana. "This him?"

Katie nods, smiling. "I'm so sorry, Anita."

Mom grabs my hand. "He cute." She bumps my hip with hers.

I bump back, and Katie takes my other hand.

Nana is using a walking stick tonight, something she does when she goes out. She leans on it heavily, watching Collin with hawk eyes, not ready to weigh in yet.

Collin croons the lyrics—he's not bad, even though he's playing this one for laughs, hamming and vamping, double-tap pounding on his chest, handing me the heart in his hands. The tittering in the crowd grows to full-blown laughs. By the end of the song, he has them shouting to him (a St. Marcos crowd talks back when they dig you), and he's made his way nearer to me, as close as his cord will let him go. He wraps up the number, hips pumping gently as he leans back, eyes closed, forearm across his forehead.

Nana shakes her cane at me, smacking it down by my foot. "Go on make baby with he and quit your fussin."

Katie and Mom laugh.

I wag my finger at Nana.

Mom says, "No more babies without a church wedding."

I think, *No weddings at all, ever.* But it's not because I'm ungrateful. So I add a quick prayer. *Dear one God of all things (even the Catholic ones) who understands my confusion and hurt: thank you.* I do a quick curtsy before I realize that God generally prefers "Amen" instead of a plié at the end of supplication.

Collin bows, gestures to me. People cheer.

I shake my head at him, but I know my heart is leaking out of my eyes, that I can't keep him at bay when he's here to see the truth. His smile warms me to my toes. He stretches his hand to me, and I release Katie's and Mom's, put mine in his, following his tug as he leads me away from the hooting crowd, out of the spotlight, where it's just the two of us on the boardwalk. It feels so good, so terrifyingly good.

"Well, shee-yut. I should have done 'You've Lost That Lovin' Feelin',''' he drawls, pulling me tight against him.

I hate how I've missed this man, and I love it. "Wouldn't fit."

His lips touch mine now. "Whyzzat?"

"Because you're not the type to get down on your knees."

His smile lifts the corners of my mouth. "We'll see, one of these days."

I lean my head back so I can look into his eyes. "Take me to bed or lose me forever, Maverick."

"Now, that can be arranged." He kisses me again, gentle, undemanding.

We stare at each other until I say, "Really, why are you here?"

He shakes his head. "You think I'm letting you go through this alone?"

"Katie told you."

"Yes, and you should have, but I forgive you."

"But I dumped you. I've ignored you. I've been with other men."

He sighs, like I'm slow. "Shut up, Ava." He pulls me in tight, rocking me to and fro.

My knees buckle, and he holds me up. I let him, just for a moment. But I feel tears fighting to unleash. That's where I draw the line, though. I don't cry, and certainly not in public.

So it's a good thing it's dark, and no one can see my face.

NEXT UP: More Ava and Collin in *Stunner*, the second Ava Butler Caribbean mystery in the *What Doesn't Kill You* series.

A nationwide tour. A popstar in the crosshairs. Touring with the band just got deadly.

Stunner is your backstage pass to scandals and edge-of-your-seat mystery. **Get it free in Kindle Unlimited** at https://www.amazon.com/gp/product/B07C83S7VK, along with *Knockout*, the third Ava Butler Caribbean mystery.

(Just need *Stunner*? Here it is standalone: https://www.amazon.com/gp/product/B079VJ42VS.)

Or **get the <u>complete</u> *What Doesn't Kill You* series** here: https://www.amazon.com/gp/product/B07QQVNSPN.

***

And don't forget to snag the **free** *What Doesn't Kill You* **ebook starter library** by joining Pamela's mailing list at https://www.subscribepage.com/PFHSuperstars.

To the rock star of my life.

OTHER BOOKS BY THE AUTHOR

Fiction from SkipJack Publishing

The *What Doesn't Kill You* Series
Act One (Prequel, Ensemble Novella)
Saving Grace (Katie #1)
Leaving Annalise (Katie #2)
Finding Harmony (Katie #3)
Heaven to Betsy (Emily #1)
Earth to Emily (Emily #2)
Hell to Pay (Emily #3)
Going for Kona (Michele #1)
Fighting for Anna (Michele #2)
Searching for Dime Box (Michele #3)
Buckle Bunny (Maggie Prequel Novella)
Shock Jock (Maggie Prequel Short Story)
Live Wire (Maggie #1)
Sick Puppy (Maggie #2)
Dead Pile (Maggie #3)
The Essential Guide to the What Doesn't Kill You Series

The *Ava Butler Trilogy*: A Sexy Spin-off From *What Doesn't Kill You*
Bombshell (Ava #1)
Stunner (Ava #2)
Knockout (Ava #3)

The *Patrick Flint Trilogy*: A Spin-off From *What Doesn't Kill You*
Switchback (Patrick Flint #1)

Snake Oil (Patrick Flint #2)

Sawbones (Patrick Flint #3)

Scapegoat (Patrick Flint #4)

Snaggle Tooth (Patrick Flint #5)

Stag Party (Patrick Flint #6): 2021

The What Doesn't Kill You Box Sets Series (50% off individual title retail)

The Complete Katie Connell Trilogy

The Complete Emily Bernal Trilogy

The Complete Michele Lopez Hanson Trilogy

The Complete Maggie Killian Trilogy

The Complete Ava Butler Trilogy

The Complete Patrick Flint Trilogy #1 (coming in late 2020)

Nonfiction from SkipJack Publishing

The Clark Kent Chronicles

Hot Flashes and Half Ironmans

How to Screw Up Your Kids

How to Screw Up Your Marriage

Puppalicious and Beyond

What Kind of Loser Indie Publishes,

and How Can I Be One, Too?

Audio, e-book, and paperback versions of most titles available.

ACKNOWLEDGMENTS

It's no accident that my husband Eric and one of the best friends of my life are both Crucians (that means "from the U.S. Virgin Island of St. Croix" for you landlubbers). The nearly ten years I spent on St. Croix blessed me with the best of relationships. Talk about life-changing; it was all that and a guava tart with cream on top. The island of St. Marcos is loosely based on St. Croix, and Ava is inspired by this dearest friend, Natalie. Assume Ava's best traits come from Natalie while her worst, and the actual events in *Bombshell*, are pure fiction. Ava appears in *Act One, Saving Grace, Leaving Annalise, Finding Harmony,* and *Earth to Emily*, so devoted readers know her from the perspective of other characters already—she's my most requested supporting character, by the way, as in, "Write one about Ava! Write one about Ava!"

I had so much fun figuring out Ava from inside Ava's head. I'm not going to lie. I was scared to write her. For starters, while I can with true humility only try for authenticity in the perspective of any character not one hundred percent like myself, Ava is quite different from me. She is black West Indian, with a black Jamaican mother and white Canadian father, and she is a native of the Caribbean. *Bombshell* and the upcoming *Stunner* and *Knockout* are love letters to Natalie, not blind cultural appropriation on my part. I know I am not Crucian, I know my mother is not Jamaican, just as I know I differ from my other protagonists in a myriad of ways—I try not to populate my novels with clones. I wrestled with this issue, but ultimately Ava is my character with an origin in my stories, which makes me the one to write her. Whether I do that respectfully and skillfully will be up to each reader to decide. Between the input of the real Ava, aka Natalie, and my Crucian husband, I pray I did Ava justice. She deserves it.

Also, Ava's a little more risqué than I've written before, but when I delved into her, I figured out her *why* is more important than *what* she does, and I grew to love her at an even deeper level. I hope you enjoy her, too. As for the plot line, let's just say that my family has some experience with USVI EDCs and with federal law enforcement that left us with a much deeper appreciation for "innocent until proven guilty."

Thanks to my husband, Eric, for brainstorming *Bombshell* with me despite his busy work, travel, and triathlon schedule. He always manages to fit me in first, and never leaves me hanging when it comes to the writing. I am a lucky woman, in so many ways. Eric gets an extra helping of thanks for plotting, critiquing, editing, listening, holding, encouraging, supporting, browbeating, and playing miscellaneous other roles, some of which aren't appropriate for publication.

Thanks to our five offspring. I love you guys more than anything, and each time I write a parent/child (birth, adopted, foster, or step), I channel you.

To each and every blessed one of you who have read, reviewed, rated, and emailed/Facebooked/Tweeted/commented about *the What Doesn't Kill* You books (so far, this includes Katie, Emily, Michele, and Ava, but watch for Laura and Maggie, in the next few years), I appreciate you more than I can say. It is the readers who move mountains for me, and for other authors, and I humbly ask for the honor of your honest reviews and recommendations.

Editing credits go to Rhonda Erb, Sara Kocek, and Whitney Cox. The beta and advance readers and critique partners who enthusiastically devote their time—gratis—to help us rid my books of flaws blow me away. The special love this time goes to Marcy, Susan,

Kim, Susie, Eric, Karen, Tara, Ginger, Ridgely, Michelle, KC, Rene'e, Pat, and Nandita. Thanks mucho to Bobbye and Candi for putting up with my eccentric and ever-changing needs.

Kisses to princess of the universe, Heidi Dorey, for fantastic cover art. Thanks for evolving with us as we evolve with the world of publishing.

SkipJack Publishing now includes fantastic books by a cherry-picked bushel basket of mystery/thriller/suspense writers. If you write in this genre, visit http://SkipJackPublishing.com for submission guidelines. To check out our other authors and snag a bargain at the same time, download *Murder, They Wrote: Four SkipJack Mysteries*.

ABOUT THE AUTHOR

Pamela Fagan Hutchins is a *USA Today* best seller. She writes award-winning romantic mysteries from deep in the heart of Nowheresville, Texas and way up in the frozen north of Snowheresville, Wyoming. She is passionate about long hikes with her hunky husband and pack of rescue dogs and riding her gigantic horses.

If you'd like Pamela to speak to your book club, women's club, class, or writers group, by Skype or in person, shoot her an email. She's very likely to say yes.

You can connect with Pamela via her website
(http://pamelafaganhutchins.com)
or email (pamela@pamelafaganhutchins.com).

PRAISE FOR PAMELA FAGAN HUTCHINS

2018 USA Today Best Seller
2017 Silver Falchion Award, Best Mystery
2016 USA Best Book Award, Cross-Genre Fiction
2015 USA Best Book Award, Cross-Genre Fiction
2014 Amazon Breakthrough Novel Award Quarter-finalist, Romance

What Doesn't Kill You: Katie Romantic Mysteries

"An exciting tale . . . twisting investigative and legal subplots . . . a character seeking redemption . . . an exhilarating mystery with a touch of voodoo." — *Midwest Book Review Bookwatch*
"A lively romantic mystery." — *Kirkus Reviews*
"A riveting drama . . . exciting read, highly recommended." — *Small Press Bookwatch*
"Katie is the first character I have absolutely fallen in love with since Stephanie Plum!" — *Stephanie Swindell, Bookstore Owner*
"Engaging storyline . . . taut suspense." — *MBR Bookwatch*

What Doesn't Kill You: Emily Romantic Mysteries

"Fair warning: clear your calendar before you pick it up because you won't be able to put it down." — *Ken Oder, author of* Old Wounds to the Heart
"Full of heart, humor, vivid characters, and suspense. Hutchins has done it again!" — *Gay Yellen, author of* The Body Business
"Hutchins is a master of tension." — *R.L. Nolen, author of* Deadly Thyme
"Intriguing mystery . . . captivating romance." — *Patricia Flaherty Pagan, author of* Trail Ways Pilgrims
"Everything about it shines: the plot, the characters and the writing.

Readers are in for a real treat with this story." — *Marcy McKay, author of* Pennies from Burger Heaven

What Doesn't Kill You: Michele Romantic Mysteries

"Immediately hooked." — *Terry Sykes-Bradshaw, author of* Sibling Revelry
"Spellbinding." — *Jo Bryan, Dry Creek Book Club*
"Fast-paced mystery." — *Deb Krenzer, Book Reviewer*
"Can't put it down." — *Cathy Bader, Reader*

What Doesn't Kill You: Ava Romantic Mysteries

"Just when I think I couldn't love another Pamela Fagan Hutchins novel more, along comes Ava." — *Marcy McKay, author of* Stars Among the Dead
"Ava personifies bombshell in every sense of word. — *Tara Scheyer, Grammy-nominated musician, Long-Distance Sisters Book Club*
"Entertaining, complex, and thought-provoking." — *Ginger Copeland, power reader*

What Doesn't Kill You: Maggie Romantic Mysteries

"Murder has never been so much fun!" — *Christie Craig,* New York Times *Best Seller*
"Maggie's gonna break your heart—one way or another." — *Tara Scheyer, Grammy-nominated musician, Long-Distance Sisters Book Club*
"Pamela Fagan Hutchins nails that Wyoming scenery and captures the atmosphere of the people there." — *Ken Oder, author of* Old Wounds to the Heart
"You're guaranteed to love the ride!" — *Kay Kendall, Silver Falchion Best Mystery Winner*

OTHER BOOKS FROM
SKIPJACK PUBLISHING

Murder, They Wrote: Four SkipJack Mysteries,
by Pamela Fagan Hutchins,
Ken Oder, R.L. Nolen, and Marcy Mason

The Closing, by Ken Oder
Old Wounds to the Heart, by Ken Oder
The Judas Murders, by Ken Oder
The Princess of Sugar Valley, by Ken Oder

Pennies from Burger Heaven, by Marcy McKay
Stars Among the Dead, by Marcy McKay
The Moon Rises at Dawn, by Marcy McKay
Bones and Lies Between Us, by Marcy McKay

Deadly Thyme, by R. L. Nolen
The Dry, by Rebecca Nolen

Tides of Possibility, edited by K.J. Russell
Tides of Impossibility, edited by K.J. Russell and C. Stuart Hardwick

My Dream of Freedom: From Holocaust to My Beloved America,
by Helen Colin

FOREWORD

Bombshell is a work of fiction. Period. Any resemblance to actual persons, places, things, or events is just a lucky coincidence.

www.ingramcontent.com/pod-product-compliance
Lightning Source LLC
Chambersburg PA
CBHW052031020726
47501CB00004B/1350